"Jeannie Moon always delivers a feel-good, warm-your-heart, can't-stop-turning-the-pages story!"

—*Carly Phillips, New York Times bestselling author*

"Jeannie Moon writes a sweet, sexy escape."

—*Jill Shalvis, New York Times bestselling author*

"Jeannie Moon immerses readers in an emotionally engaging and sexy story of lost love and new beginnings."

—*JoAnn Ross, New York Times bestselling author*

The Second Chance Hero

A Forever Love Story
Book 4

Jeannie Moon

Five Harbors Press

New York

Prologue
Role 3 Joint Forces Medical Facility

Kandahar, Afghanistan
Late June

SOMETIMES IT WAS THE QUIET THAT GOT TO HER. Kim knew that if people were screaming, at least they were still alive. But now, there was nothing. Nothing except the hum of the equipment, the glare of the harsh lighting and the beating of her own heart.

Looking down at her hands, her breath caught; her throat tightened. So much blood.

Tom's blood.

She snapped the gloves off her hands and threw them in with the other biohazards, then pressed her back against the wall. As she slid down, her arms folded over her middle. Holding in her heart, maybe? Her battered, breaking heart.

Her emotions started to close in, her eyes started to burn and she wondered if she would ever get the memories out of her head. If she would ever be able to see his face as it used to be. The boy next door. Her handsome Marine. Her love.

Usually, the team knew at least fifteen minutes before the inbound dustoff landed with wounded—especially when it was coming from that far out. Today, they didn't have near that. They had five. Five minutes to prepare for men who were so gravely injured they shouldn't have survived the flight.

The gurneys came crashing through the doors and they all had their jobs in the ER. Kim was ready for her patient—an alpha—the designation given to the patients with the most life threatening injuries. They knew he had a massive belly wound and burns on his neck and face. As bombs went, this one was a widowmaker.

Kim remembered descending on the patient with scissors, cutting off the bandages applied in the field so they could get to the bleeding in his abdomen. If they could get that under control he had a chance. A slim one, but a chance. She hadn't gotten far when the big man took a gasping breath and she heard the impossible.

Hoarse. Strained. "Kim."

No.

"Baby, look at me." It was barely a whisper, but the words were screaming in her head. Her eyes traveled away from the blood, hesitating for a moment over his chest where his name was displayed. *Albanese.* God. How had she missed it? Again she took in every inch of him and when she got to his face, and looked in his dark eyes, she saw the pain, the fear, he was facing. And Kim knew they would be saying goodbye. Even as the doctors worked on him, she knew.

He was dying. And there was nothing anyone could do.

It seemed unimaginable. She and Tom were part of each

other. Together since they were just kids, he went into the Marines after high school, she went into the Navy after nursing school. He gave her a ring.

The wedding was in six months.

His fingers found hers and he gripped them with desperation. He squeezed hard. Kim reached out and wiped away the tear tracking down his face. His breathing was more labored, shallower. And he was scared. So scared. She leaned in and kissed his temple.

"It's okay," she said softly. "I'm here."

"I'm sorry. I love you. I'm so sorry."

"I love you, too. It's okay. It's okay."

But there was no response. The end rushed up. She could see he was losing his fight, his body convulsed, his eyes rolled back--then he flatlined.

The tone from the cardiac monitor numbed her brain, told her a truth she wasn't ready to hear. Tom was gone.

There were no measures taken. No dramatic chest pounding. No paddles. The doctor called his time of death.

That's when Kim turned and walked into the corridor. That's where she was now and where she would likely stay, running over the last few minutes again and again.

MAJOR OWEN KENT eased his way out of the passenger seat of the MRAP, blasted by the oven-like temperatures that had baked the provinces for the past week. They'd been driving for an hour and a half and even with the windows closed and the air conditioning cranking, he still felt like he'd eaten a bag of dirt. As he turned toward the building, he saw his driver, Corporal Lynn, take off into the hospital at a dead run, almost forgetting to turn off the engine. Everyone knew about the rules regarding fraternization between the troops, but war being war, and humans being humans, sometimes the regulations were ignored. Owen wondered what she was going to find inside. The Marine she'd been involved with probably wasn't going to survive his injuries.

Carlson, the corpsman who'd traveled with them, checked the wound on Owen's left hand. It hurt like a bitch, but it wasn't serious, a single gash that might need a couple of stitches. "I just want to make sure this is completely cleaned out, sir."

"I understand." Owen glanced toward the door. They could have irrigated and dressed his wound back at their base, but like the corpsman Owen wanted to know what had happened to the two men who had been airlifted. "What do you think?"

It was a vague question, he knew that. But he was too superstitious to ask anything more specific. And it was likely the corpsman wouldn't answer.

Carlson shook his head. "I don't know. We did our best."

Owen's stomach lurched. He'd only been back in country for two weeks. It was his third tour and it was going to be a long one. Now for the duration, he'd think about the twisted, smoking metal. The bodies. The smell. The men were under his command and that made him responsible. They were checking out possible insurgent activity in a small village and had made a quick detour to drop off some toys for kids they knew didn't have anything. They were just trying to do a nice thing and now, more than likely, they were both dead.

He thought about the families...the parents and grandparents and siblings. All the people who would miss them. Neither one was married, but they'd both left people behind.

A picture of his mom popped in his head. It had been too long since he'd called her.

The hospital on the airbase provided the best care in the field to both soldiers and locals, but all Owen could think about was that it smelled like death. Holding the compress on his hand he saw people milling around at the end of the hall. He recognized Lynn, and as he closed in he saw there were three people in scrubs...two were talking to the MP, consoling her, and a slender dark-haired woman was standing against the wall, her back stiff, her lips pressed tightly together, her knuckles white. Something was up. Finally she looked at him and that's when he saw it. Something in the grey-green depths of her eyes revealed her pain.

She reached behind her and took a pair of rubber gloves from a dispenser on the wall, donned them and moved in his direction. She stopped in front of him and reached out cradling his hand gently in hers. *Torres. USNR. RN.* "You're hurt," she said.

So are you, he wanted to reply, but didn't. "It's a pretty deep cut."

Her lip quivered and she nodded, carefully pulling away the bandage. Blood oozed from the wound, but the bleeding had definitely slowed down. "You're going to need some stitches. I can..."

"Lieutenant Torres, why don't you take a break?" A tall man, an Air Force doctor according to the information embroidered on his scrubs, stepped forward and laid a compassionate hand on her shoulder. He knew what was wrong, what was eating at her.

"Thank you, sir, but I was going to take care of..."

He cut her off, looked at Owen. "Major, if you want to step

into the treatment room, I can stitch you up and get you and your people on your way." He nodded toward the corpsman and Lynn and then turned back to the nurse. "Kim, it's okay, I'll handle this. Go take care of yourself."

"I'm FINE." The pretty young woman was still holding onto his hand, but now Owen could feel her trembling. "I don't want to take care of myself. I want to take care of my patient." Her words were controlled, but strained. He'd seen this before. This was a person who was about to break. "I... need..." She drew a shaky breath. "I n-need to do...m-my...j-job."

No one said anything. No one moved, until finally the woman's knees buckled and she crumbled right in front of him. Owen's arm shot out and grabbed her around the waist, pressing her back into his chest as she started to go down. Unable to stop the momentum, he went with her to the floor.

Holding onto his good arm with both of hers, she clung with everything she had, her body shaking and her breathing coming in gasps. Her tears weren't dramatic, but soft, personal. Owen had no idea what had caused her to lose it like this, but listening to her broke his heart.

"Shhh," he whispered. "I've got you. Shhh." Her head was against his bicep and something inside him stirred. Something primal, protective. While he was there, no one would hurt Lieutenant Torres. *No one.*

He was still holding tight, trying to console her when another nurse crouched before them. "Sir, let me take her somewhere private. She needs to be away from here."

He nodded, because that was the right thing to do, and started to release her, but the lieutenant held on. "Go with your friend," he said, taking in the light flowery scent of her hair. "She'll take care of you."

Looking up at him, awareness flooded her eyes and pink stained her cheeks. Damn, she was beautiful. She was also embarrassed and he wished she wasn't.

"Oh, God. I apologize, sir." She rose and he did as well, each taking a step away from the other. "That was inappropriate. Excuse me."

"Don't apologize, please." He didn't know exactly what had happened, but he couldn't help feeling responsible and the last thing he wanted was her apology. "I hope…" *I hope I see you again.* "I hope everything is okay."

She nodded and went with her friend, looking back once and offering him a weak smile. He turned to the doctor in charge once she was out of eyeshot, grateful to focus on something else, even the fate of his two Marines. "Albanese and Scott?"

"Dead within minutes of arriving."

"Shit." Owen pinched the bridge of his nose to quell the emotion welling up. Two more dead. To call it senseless was an understatement. Then, he looked toward the door through which the nurse had gone. "Will she be okay?"

Shrugging the doctor let out a long breath and pulled Owen aside. "Staff Sergeant Albanese was her fiancé." He tilted his head toward Lynn. "It went from bad to worse when his girlfriend made an appearance. Obviously, the lieutenant didn't know about her."

"Oh, my God—" It was time for him to get Corporal Lynn out of there in case Lieutenant Torres came back. "We'll get out of your way. "

"Not so fast. You aren't making the drive back to camp

with your hand like that. Come back here, I'll stitch you up and get you out of here."

Glancing down, he remembered his hand. Great. The stitches were going to hurt like hell, but then he thought about today's casualties, and nothing compared. Nothing.

1

Memorial Day—the following year

KIM HATED THIS.

It was a beautiful day—the unofficial first day of summer—and she was standing with Tom's family around his grave at the Calverton National Cemetery on eastern Long Island. They came every month. Sometimes she was with them. Sometimes she wasn't. Lately, it was getting harder and harder to stand there and hear about their wonderful, honorable son. The man who could do no wrong. How she was so *lucky* to have had him in her life.

That it was a privilege to be loved by a man like him.

The problem was she didn't feel lucky or privileged. In fact, she doubted if he really loved her at all. How could he when he cheated on her?

Tom Albanese was a model Marine. Larger than life, even as a kid, he was strong and brave and loyal to his buddies. He was a good leader, and she wished he hadn't died. But he wasn't loyal to her and she couldn't let it go.

So, as she stood there, listening to his family take turns talking to his headstone, Kim was wondering what they would do if she made a run for it.

She was next. His youngest sister, only nineteen, was standing next to her and pouring out her heart. They missed him. She knew that, and she did too. But Kim lived in a silent world of hurt and betrayal that wouldn't allow her to grieve, wouldn't allow her to miss him the way they did.

How could she love and miss a man she obviously didn't know?

"Kim, honey," his mother said through her tears. "It's your turn to talk to Tommy."

"Not today, Mrs. Albanese."

"Come on, you'll feel better."

"No," she said quietly. "I don't want to talk."

"But Tommy would want you too."

That was it. Unwilling to keep up the charade, unable to keep faking it, Kim turned and walked away.

His sister, Jenna, one of her best friends, grabbed for her, but Kim brushed her off. She wasn't going to be disrespectful to his family, but she didn't give a shit about anything Tom may have wanted from the great beyond. Kim would have liked to have avoided the breakdown that forced her to leave the Navy, the nightmares that were keeping her from being a nurse anywhere because she didn't know if she could handle it. Hell, she wanted to trust people again.

She walked and walked. Past the rows of headstones adorned with small flags. Past other families paying respects, finally settling on a bench close to the main entrance. She had to stop running. From her grief. From her past. From everything.

"Kim! What the hell?"

She looked up and coming toward her was Tom's oldest sister, Christina. Tina was one of the good ones, but she was fiercely loyal to her family. She was a doctor and she'd been the only one not to press her too hard.

"You got the job of coming after me?"

Tall and leggy, she sat on the bench with a huff and smiled. "You are damn quick for someone so small."

"Am I?"

"Yeah, but the real question is why did you bolt? What's going on, Kimmy?"

Kim's eyelid started to twitch, a sure sign her nerves were getting the better of her. She needed to tell her. Needed to be honest, but how? "Tina, I can't do this with your family every month. I can't stand here and live this over and over again."

"I know it must be hard for you."

"Not for the reasons you think..." Shit. She didn't mean to say that out loud.

Of course, his sister didn't miss a beat. "I don't understand."

She had to cut ties with them. It wasn't fair to her and it wasn't fair to them to keep pretending that she was going through the same thing. She wasn't. They were mourning the loss of their son and brother. Kim was morning the loss of, well, everything. "I won't be coming around anymore."

"Kim, you're family. Take some time if you need it, but don't cut us off. I mean, you've already cut Jenna off and it's killing her, but Tom would have wanted us to be there for you."

She shook her head. How could she tell his sister that Tom didn't even want to be there for her? That after asking her to marry him and promising to love her forever, he cheated on her. "I know you might think this is selfish, but I have to deal with this my own way."

At first, Tina didn't say a word, and in truth, Kim didn't want her to. His sister rose, circled behind the bench several times, getting her bearings, no doubt, and figuring out what this all meant.

"He loved you. You wore his ring. His memory has to mean something." There was no sympathy in her voice now, just betrayal. Anger. "What the hell happened over there?"

"I know this seems cold, but every time I come here I relive that day. I need to back away from it for a while." That wasn't a lie. She did relive it. She relived every minute of seeing the MP from his base cry when they told her he was dead. "As far as what happened? I watched my fiancé die a violent death. Let's leave it at that."

And he took my heart with him.

Kim knew she'd probably just destroyed her relationship with Tina and everyone else in the family and that upset her, but she couldn't keep living the lie. "I'm not feeling the same things all of you are. I'm grieving, but it's different."

"You're not telling me something." Tina dropped her head in her hands. "Are you ready to move on? Is there someone else?"

"No. That's not it." It wasn't. She didn't know if she'd ever be able to trust anyone again, so she didn't know if moving on was in the cards for her. "I can't explain it."

"I don't understand and I don't think anyone else will either. I'll say it again...you are family, Kim. Family sticks together."

"*I'm not family*. He died." *He betrayed me.* "We all need to accept it."

She didn't know if the Albanese's would ever accept it. Tom was the only boy. He was worshiped. She and Tina sat in silence for several minutes, the only sounds were birds flying overhead and the breeze rustling the leaves.

"Are you doing okay?" Tina finally asked. "We're all worried about you."

"I'm getting there. It's slow going, but I am. I really just need to focus on myself for a while. I mean, my new job is great. Nothing gets you farther away from war than taking care of a baby."

"You like being a nanny?"

"I do. The change has been good for me." Her job as an au pair to a beautiful little girl had done the most to heal her broken spirit. Harper, her boss, had become a good friend and had welcomed Kim into all aspects of their lives.

His sister stood and nodded. "I'm not going to say I understand. I don't. But get back in touch when you're ready, okay?"

Kim didn't think she'd ever be ready. There was too much pain associated with the relationship, and it wouldn't be fair to destroy their memories of him.

Cutting ties with Tom's family, even if it did end up being temporary, was hard, but she couldn't help but feel relief as she got in her car and pulled out of the cemetery knowing she wouldn't have to go back there until she was ready. Everything she'd accomplished since she'd left the Navy had been a series of baby steps.

This time she'd taken a giant leap.

. . .

OWEN WAS STILL EXHAUSTED. He'd been back from his deployment for three weeks, but it had been an especially tough tour. Six men in his company had died. Six, starting with two just weeks after he arrived. It sucked, and it always would.

The smell of fresh coffee made him think about his need for caffeine even though he'd slept a ridiculous fourteen hours. But he had to get moving if he was going to be on time for the big barbeque at Jason and Meg's house. He was looking forward to seeing everyone, getting back into the groove with his friends, but his brain was all over the place. He still hadn't been to work, because he hadn't been able to focus and thinking about anything more than a sail and a beer made his head hurt. But he did find he was getting itchy to do more, to get back to his life.

That didn't mean he wasn't getting work to do. Jason Campbell and Nate Bayard, his partners at Reliance Software and his best friends, sent him plenty. He was just doing it from the deck of his boat. Also not like him.

He poured himself a cup of coffee, put in the milk and four sugars and looked out the back window across the harbor. It was going to be a gorgeous day, sunny and warm but not too hot. Which was good because he was done with the fucking heat. Nothing sucked worse than an Afghan summer.

He'd missed a lot being away from home this past year. His parents finally sold their old house and bought a great condo on the North Fork as well as a place in Florida for cold months. Meg and Jason had had a baby, and were expecting another, and Harper, their Director of Operations, who was pregnant when he left, had given birth to a little girl. She was marrying into that damn Rossi family, too. Sipping his coffee, he grinned wondering if there was a secret Rossi sister for him.

Great. He had to go and think about women. Now he'd have a raging hard on for not keeping his thoughts in check. Although, since he hadn't been laid in months, he could get hard thinking about a bag of potato chips. Beyond the sex, though, he was starting to hate the whole being alone thing. This last tour showed him family was everything and while a warm body in his bed was nice, he was starting to wonder about what his life would be like moving forward.

When his cell phone buzzed, he figured it was one of three people calling. Jason, Meg, or his mother. He was surprised when he saw Harper's name on the Caller ID. "Hey," he said, answering the phone. "You finally decided to call me."

"And your fingers are all broken?" Leave it to Harper not to cut him any slack at all. Which was good, he needed to get back to the real world and there was no one better to do that than Harper Poole.

"I'm glad you called. How's the baby?"

"She's the most amazing thing in my life, and you'll get to meet her later on, Uncle Owen."

"Awesome. And when is the wedding?"

"November. After the World Series."

She said it like the playoffs were a given. Harper was engaged to Kevin Rossi, a superstar catcher. "That's optimistic."

Harper laughed. Owen figured she was running her personal life, and relationships, the same way she ran Reliance Software—with total control. If she told Kevin to be in the World Series, the man would be smart to listen.

"Owen, I need a favor."

15

"Name it."

"My au pair, Kim, was driving in from out east and she hit a pothole—the tire and wheel are done. Can you pick her up and bring her to the barbeque?"

The clock on the stove told him he was going to have to hurry. "Ah, sure. Where is she?"

"At the Starbucks on Main Street in Huntington." Making a few mental calculations, he figured he could be there in about 45 minutes if he hurried.

"No problem. Does she need me to do anything else? Is the car being moved?

"Yes, we handled that."

"Okay, tell her to sit tight, have another latte and I'll shower and swing by to get her in a bit."

"You're sure? I'd get her, but I'm picking my mom up at the airport. Who the hell travels on Memorial Day weekend?"

Harper's mama, that's who. Someone else he had to meet. He'd been hearing a lot about Diane Snow.

"I'll see you soon," he said, happy to have something to do.

"Thanks, Owen." There was a pause—which usually meant Harper was thinking. "I'm glad you're back. And that you're safe."

"Thanks, babe. I actually have a scar to show you when I see you."

"A scar! You were hurt?" She kept yelling but he couldn't make out anything she was saying.

"Calm down! It was just a scratch. Three stitches."

"Don't scare me like that! Dumbass. You're good otherwise?"

Wow, this was a softer Harper. He thought Jason and Nate

had been kidding when they'd told him she'd mellowed. Even with all the ranting, he could tell she was really upset. "No worries, I'm good. Still adjusting to the real world, but good."

"Kim was over there. She doesn't talk about it much."

"Your nanny was in Afghanistan?"

"Yeah, but like I said, she doesn't really talk about it."

"It's hard to explain it to people. Some days it's like living inside your worst nightmare. Other days the boredom could turn your brain to soap."

"Well, I'm glad you're back. I might actually have to hug you."

Owen laughed, ready to respond, but Harper ended the call before he could say anything else, probably because she was going on emotional overload.

He felt good. Relaxed. Looking at the clock one more time, he knew he had to get moving.

He had a lady to rescue.

2

OWEN PARKED HIS NEW RANGE ROVER ABOUT A HALF a block away from Starbucks. Town was pretty busy for a holiday weekend Sunday, but then, Huntington was always busy. The shops were trendy and the restaurants plentiful. He couldn't wait to sit at a sidewalk table at his favorite Mexican place and enjoy a cold beer and some great food. He liked the whole vibe, which was why he chose his house on the water in Centerport rather that an apartment in Manhattan. He got enough noise and chaos when he was deployed.

Harper had texted him a quick description of Kim—a little over five feet tall, long, wavy dark hair with some blonde high-lights—so he put up his radar as soon as he stepped inside the coffee shop. After Harper told him she'd been in the military, he wanted to know the Nanny's story. Everyone who served had a story.

Making a quick visual sweep of the place, Owen relaxed a little. It was half full. There were families with kids, couples and a few singles scattered around. It was nice. Safe. No one was trying to kill him.

And that was Owen's story in a nutshell. His last tour made him feel like he had a big old target on his back. In reality, it was probably true. He'd been on an adrenaline high for the last eleven months. Constantly on guard, consistently ready to fight. He guessed his exhaustion was really a crash.

He took a few more steps into the store and looked down the long side where there were even more chairs and tables. There in the back, sitting in an oversized leather chair, was a woman who matched Harper's description.

Harper had said Kim was tiny and she wasn't kidding. From where he was standing it looked like the woman was being swallowed by the big chair. Her head was down, her mane of hair falling forward while she tapped something into her cell phone.

His long legs closed the distance quickly, not knowing what was driving his curiosity. Still a few steps away, the girl looked up and Owen stopped dead. Dark hair, grey-green eyes...beautiful.

Holy shit.

It was her.

It was the nurse who'd collapsed in his arms at the hospital. The one who lost her fiancé, who found out he was cheating.

The one he hadn't been able to get out of his head. The one he'd thought about every damn day since.

He knew she'd left Afghanistan. He'd made the drive back to the hospital at one point and the commander of the facility said she'd gone home a month or so after Albanese died. They were sorry to lose her. According to her commander, she was his best nurse, compassionate, yet tough as nails in a crisis. But everything she'd suffered had rendered her unable to cope. Since she was coming to the end of her tour, they sent her home.

Owen remembered being disappointed at the news. He'd wanted to see her again. He didn't know exactly why.

Suddenly, there were a hell of a lot of questions spinning through his brain. The first was him wondering why the universe was fucking with his head. He hadn't made another move toward her when she stood and approached him. The woman *was* tiny, the top of her head didn't even reach his chin. Wearing a black dress with little polka dots, flat shoes, and a sweater, she looked like the girl you took home to meet your mother.

Her smile was wide, her eyes twinkled. She was a stark contrast to the distraught woman he comforted less than a year ago.

"Owen?" she asked, extending her hand. "I'm Kim Torres. Thanks so much for coming to get me."

Damn.

What the hell was he supposed to say now? *Nice to meet you?* He'd already met her. *Nice to see you again?* Not likely, because it appeared she didn't remember him, and he wasn't about to bring that memory flooding back.

"My pleasure," he managed as he took her hand in his. It was warm, soft. "Sucks about the car."

Perfect. Way to sound like a dork.

"You're telling me. Anyway, I appreciate that you came to get me. Would you mind if we stopped at Harper and Kevin's? I wanted to change before the barbeque."

He thought about her slipping out of that little dress and his brain fogged. Damn, he was in big trouble. "I don't mind. Just tell me how to get to their house."

"It's a bit out of the way. They're in Oyster Bay. Are you sure?"

"Not a problem." She stood there, staring at him, so goddam cute. Smiling. Playing with her hair. Smiling some more. Why was she doing that? Shit. Was she trying to get him to stroke out?

"Are you ready?" he asked.

Her eyes widened. "Oh! Of course. Yes." She grabbed her denim jacket and bag, and he indicated that they should leave through the front door, leading the way until they got to the street and settled into steady pace, side by side.

"It's going to be fun today," she said, her voice silvery, light. Different than what he remembered. "I really appreciate being included in everything."

"From the sound of it you're like a member of the family."

"I hope so." She pushed a lock of hair behind her ear, bit her lip. *Was she nervous?* "I love Anna, and Harper has been a wonderful friend to me."

He took the key fob out of his pocket and opened the passenger door of his big, black SUV. She smiled shyly as she climbed in the truck and Owen wondered what he'd done right.

He didn't know why he was so happy to see Kim Torres again. Maybe it was that they had a shared history. Maybe it was the physical attraction, but Owen felt there might have been something more. He was a smart man, a practical man. He didn't jump to conclusions. He'd been to war; he'd built a business. Yet, he had no doubt that this pint sized woman could take him out at the knees. Normally, that would be a red flag for Owen. He didn't date seriously, and avoided emotional entanglements.

He had a feeling that was about to change.

ONCE OWEN CLOSED THE DOOR, Kim allowed herself to take a breath. "Holy hell," she whispered. Never in a million years did she think she'd be so affected by a man. She had worked in a military field hospital. She'd been engaged to a Marine. Yet there was Owen Kent, tall, broad, gorgeous and Kim had lost her breath. Literally lost her breath.

His eyes were electric blue, bright and with a spark she'd never seen and his dark hair was short, sprinkled with a little gray at the temples. But it wasn't just the looks.

No, Owen Kent was a lot more than an average hot guy.

Harper told her he'd just gotten home from a yearlong tour in Afghanistan, but not much else. But Kim could see it. Owen carried himself like a man who had put his life on the line. Bravery, service weren't just words for someone like him, but part of who he was.

They rode in silence except for the music he'd put on the stereo, and Kim giving the occasional direction. And while she felt comfortable with him, there was a charge in the air, something between them that she couldn't yet understand.

"So," she said. "How have you been since getting home?"

Owen grinned. "Better than many, I'm guessing. I'm okay, but it was a rough year."

"True enough." She knew a lot of guys who came home without limbs or the ability to function in society. For some, war was just too much. "What will you do now?"

"I'll go back to Reliance. If they still have my job for me."

He worked for Reliance? She couldn't imagine Jason, Nate

and Harper not giving a veteran his job back. Not in a million years—she knew they were hiring more vets than ever. "I'm sure they will. They're such good people."

He chuckled. "I'm not worried. If Jason says no, I'll just kick his ass. Think I can take him?"

She was sure he could. The man was a Marine officer. That made him a lethal weapon. "I, uh…"

"Don't worry. I won't leave any visible marks. I worked Intelligence for a few years." He winked. "We're good at keeping things under the radar."

Kim wasn't sure if he was joking or not, and because of that, she decided she shouldn't say anything else. But every time he looked at her, smiled, or winked, she could feel a little pop down low in her belly. Damn.

Fifteen minutes after leaving downtown Huntington, Owen turned the truck based on Kim's instructions and pulled down the long driveway of Harper and Kevin's house in Oyster Bay.

It was a large, ornate Victorian with a huge wraparound porch and gingerbread trim. They'd finished remodeling only recently and had moved their little family, and her from the city as soon as they could. It turned out Harper loved living there and Kim did too. There were quiet beaches close by and there was room to breathe and move. Something she'd never had a lot of. She'd grown up in neat little three bedroom Cape Cod style house in Seaford on the south shore, but four kids and two parents in a small house put privacy at a premium. Now she had the entire guest cottage to herself. Two bedrooms, a big bathroom and blessed, blessed quiet.

"Wow," Owen said, looking at the house. "I never thought

Harper would end up in suburbia, but she did it big. That's some house."

"It's even more beautiful inside. Gorgeous moldings, big open rooms and the kitchen is amazing."

"Cool. Give me the dollar tour." Killing the engine, and exiting the truck, he made his way around the car faster than she could gather her things.

He opened the door for her, smiled that lady killer smile and when he offered his hand, like an idiot, she took it. Good Lord. The man made her ovaries ache.

When he touched her, when he folded his large hand around her small one, her world rocked. More than the handshake earlier, his touch, his scent, his presence made her feel calm and safe. Over the past year, Kim never felt safe, never felt calm. This connection was personal, and Kim had the sense she'd been here before. Been with him before.

"Is something wrong? You look like you've seen a ghost."

She shook it off. "Just a little déjà vu. Weird."

"You want to talk about it?" He held onto her hand and Kim didn't want to let go of the feeling. The déjà vu was strongly connected to him, and as much as she felt compelled to tell him, there was no way she was going to.

Owen Kent represented something, but at this point, she didn't know what. He was connected to her past, a past she really wasn't prepared to share. But he seemed so grounded, so down to earth, that she considered his offer. This was a good guy. One who probably understood what she was going through, but who wasn't going to tell her how to think or feel.

That morning with Tom's family was a hard reminder that for most of her life, someone had been telling her how she should feel about things. Whether it was her family, Tom or his family, everyone had expectations. The Albanese's were a close Italian family, and Tom was the only boy among three sisters. They'd been neighbors since his family moved next door to hers when she was five and he was seven. It was quite possible she fell in love with him then, but it wasn't until ten years later, when they were both in high school that he noticed her as something other than the pest from next door, more than his younger sister's friend. He was everything and he always made sure he had total control of his environment.

That kind of attitude made him a great Marine. He moved up quickly, took charge and if he was afraid, he never let it show. Men like him tended to absorb everyone around them and Tom was no different. He'd certainly absorbed her.

And now his family was trying to do the same thing.

"Kim?"

Oh, shit. Owen was talking to her.

"Are you sure you're okay? You kind of zoned out there."

"Sorry. I'm really fine. I was at the cemetery this morning, I guess my mind wandered. It's nothing..."

She moved toward the house, but Owen caught her hand again and all of that lovely warmth filled her instantly. "The offer is real. If you need to talk, all you have to do is ask. Okay?"

"What, should I just call you up someday?"

"Anytime." His blue eyes locked on hers and she found herself wanting to drown in them. That was some powerful mojo he had. "Nobody understands what you've been through better than someone who's been there, too."

That was true. What surprised her was that Owen was

dead serious about being available, but she also doubted he'd been through what she had.

"Thank you, Owen. But I'm okay." *Liar, liar pants on fire*. It wasn't that she didn't appreciate his offer, but she wasn't going to expose her bruised and battered heart to a perfect stranger. Her family didn't even know the whole story, and right now it was best for Kim if the whole humiliating experience stayed under wraps. "Come on," she said. "Let's get moving. I hear they're steaming a bushel of clams and I don't want to miss it."

That was the way she'd been dealing with everyone, lately. She changed the subject before the emotions hit her before she lost control.

Her reentry was uneventful considering she'd pretty much had a breakdown. Losing Tom was one thing, watching him die was something else, but the cheating put her over the edge because everything she'd known to be true, everything she'd believed, was a lie. Kim was just about at the end of her service requirement when it all went down. When she opted for a discharge rather than another stint in the reserves, no one tried to talk her out of it. The psychiatrist at Bethesda wished her luck.

They knew a basket case when they met one.

It was better now, but instead of going back to her regular job as a critical care nurse, it took months hiding out at a friend's place in Hawai'i for her to feel like she could face her family or Tom's family, and it was awful because no one could really help. She knew her distance was breaking her parents' heart. That her brothers and sisters missed her. But they didn't understand why she didn't want to be around them.

They didn't understand why she didn't go back to nursing. They didn't understand anything.

Because no one knew the truth.

OWEN FULLY INTENDED to tease the crap out of Harper when he saw her. The very sophisticated, urbane, I'll-never-settle-down Director of Operations had gone into full domestic goddess mode. Her house was a showpiece. The kitchen alone was bigger than several rooms in his house and equipped with every possible amenity. Apparently, Harper liked to cook. And bake. There were three large mason jars filled with different types of cookies.

As he walked into the backyard at Meg and Jason's house, he felt almost normal. Looking to his right, Kim practically skipped off when she saw the kids and Owen turned toward his friends, while still keeping his eyes on her. She was so damned adorable.

"There's our missing warrior!" Meg Rossi Campbell, his friend Jason's wife, greeted him with a warm tight hug. Meg and Jason married to protect his niece from a custody suit and stayed together because they were made for each other. Meg, a gorgeous bombshell blonde, had the biggest heart and the most dynamic personality. It took Jason a while to realize how lucky he was to have her in his life and he'd spent every day since that epiphany making her happy. In a few months they would soon be welcoming their third child.

"You should have come over sooner." She slapped his arm and he warmed at the affection. Owen hadn't really seen anyone except his parents and his sister Melinda. "We've been so worried about you."

"I know, and I'm sorry, but I needed some time to settle in. I'm fine."

"Hmmpf," she muttered. "That's what they all say. I guess I have to cut you some slack."

"Thanks," he looped his arm around her shoulder and walked with her toward the larger group. He felt good, happy, as he approached. These people had seen him through some very tough times. Owen, Meg's husband, Jason, and their friend Nate Bayard had known each other over twenty years since they landed in the same prep school English class. They played hockey together, tried to figure out girls and got into plenty of trouble together. They went their separate ways with Jason going to MIT, Nate going to Duke and Owen going to the Naval Academy, but their bond—their friendship—stayed strong.

They couldn't have been more different, but yet, they were more alike than any of them wanted to admit. Driven almost to distraction, the three of them built Reliance into a security software giant that generated billions of dollars.

Billions. He still couldn't believe it. He also couldn't believe when a profile of the three of them appeared in a popular magazine right before his deployment. Like days before he left. He'd caught a lot of shit from his troops for the piece which detailed exactly how rich he'd become. They wanted to know why he didn't buy his way out of Afghanistan.

But the fact was, it wasn't until this very last tour that he considered resigning his commission.

He grabbed a beer and joined the conversation, but found he was stealing looks at Kim whenever he could. He really wanted to know her story. What had she been doing the past year? Why was she a nanny and not working as a nurse?

Jason nudged him with his elbow and nodded toward Kim. "She's nice, isn't she?"

"Yeah, she has a lot of spirit." He had to keep this general.

"Tough loss she suffered."

Owen started to say something and then held back. He didn't know how much anyone knew about Kim's experience, and he wasn't going to be the one to tell them. "How much did she tell you? She doesn't seem to like talking about it."

"She doesn't. She just told Harper that after her fiancé was fatally wounded and brought to the hospital where she was serving, she couldn't go back to nursing. She's a trauma nurse, I guess, and couldn't face it. A secretary at the office knows her somehow and recommended her to Harper for the nanny position. She's been a real asset. Kevin and Harper both love her. She's great with all the kids." Jason pointed at her back in the play area surrounded by children.

She didn't tell them everything. Then he wouldn't either.

"I guess she needed a change," Owen said. "Not a bad idea."

"How are you doing?"

"Better. It took a lot out of me and I've been sleeping a lot more than I usually do. I guess I needed some down time after I got home, but I'm ready to get back to work."

Jason patted his back, glad for the news.

"So, Meg's knocked up again?" Owen asked. "How many are you planning? Eight? Ten?

Jason grinned. "That sounds about right. You need to find yourself a woman, my friend. You have some catching up to do."

Right then, Kim walked over to the cooler and grabbed a soda. "Did you get your job back?"

Jason looked between Owen and Kim, the look on his face telling him his friend wasn't quite following.

"Ah, he's thinking about it." He really needed Jason to pick up on this or he was going to go down in flames.

"Thinking about what?" Shit. Jason was really confused. Damn, he wasn't usually slow.

"Jason, really?" Kim chided. "A vet?"

"We employ a lot of vets. What are you talking about?"

"Owen," she said sweetly.

Owen was standing behind her and he was really touched that she would try to go to bat for him, but he wasn't going to let this joke go without having a little more fun. He got Jason's attention, and finally his buddy seemed to grasp what was going on. He played it up.

"You know, Kim, I need people with a very specific skill set and our friend here was out of the country a long time. I do have a maintenance position that needs filling, though."

"Are you kidding?"

"Kidding about what?" Harper had arrived and Owen got a look a completely different woman that the one he left. She looked softer, happier and she had a baby settled comfortably on her hip. "Hiya, handsome," she said giving him a hug and a kiss. "So what's the joke?"

Kim wasn't shy, she jumped right in, and once again Owen was really taken by the fact that she wanted to help him, but she wasn't going to be so happy in a minute. Not when she found out they were messing with her. "Jason is deciding if Owen can have his job back."

Harper's brows pulled together and her lips turned up at one side. "Is that so?"

"I can't believe he has to think about it…"

"You two are such dirty liars," Harper snapped.

"Liars?" Kim said.

Harper turned to her and shook her head. "Owen doesn't have to ask for his job back."

"He doesn't?"

"No." Harper turned back to him, satisfied, because right then she knew that he knew she was going to throw him under the bus. "He owns a third of the company."

A really big bus.

Kim turned to him with her arms folded, her body language screaming annoyance. She might have been small, but this little pixie was fierce.

"A third of the company?"

"Yeah." There was nothing else to say. He had nothin'.

Harper didn't let it end there. "The big baby hasn't been to work for the last few weeks because he was decompressing on his boat." She bounced Anna on her hip while she eviscerated him. The contradiction wasn't lost on him. "Ready to get off your ass and earn your keep, big guy?"

He ignored Harper and kept his eyes on Kim, whose gaze was intense and unforgiving. He'd have to remember to get even with Harper.

"You poor thing, stuck on your boat." Kim crooned. "How do you get by? Are the billions enough?"

He didn't have a chance to reply because Kim turned on her heel of her little white sneakers, flipped her hair and walked away, back to the kids, while he was left standing there feeling like a shit.

Well, that was fucking perfect.

"You guys have got to stop this tag-team teasing you do. Some people don't think it's funny." Harper adjusted Anna on her hip and Owen would have responded about what happened with Kim, except the pretty little girl cooed and smiled and reached for him.

"Oh, she just saved you, Uncle Owen."

He didn't even think twice and took the baby from Harper, holding her close and relishing the soft, sweet smell of her hair.

Owen wasn't a guy who had a lot of experience with kids. He had a small family, his sister had just gotten engaged, so he hadn't had a lot of opportunities to be around kids. He liked them, but holding the baby was new for him. It was kinda cool. The kid was looking at him with the most intense blue eyes, he could see the intelligence there. It was fascinating to him. This little life had just started and he'd get to watch her grow.

Without warning, Anna's smile bloomed again, this time even bigger, and Uncle Owen was her slave.

SOME MEN WERE SUCH JERKS. Kim supposed it was in the DNA and most of them couldn't help it, but you would think that after a year in a war zone, Owen Kent would have had a little of the jerk kicked out of him. Of course, she knew she was too sensitive, and what had happened wasn't that big of a deal. It took years for her to forgive her brothers for teasing her so unmercifully. But part of what had her miffed was the flippin' dishonesty. What harm would it have been to just tell her he was one of the partners? It's not like being a billionaire is a bad thing.

She let it sink in.

Wow.

Owen Kent. Billionaire Marine. It sounded like the title of a romance novel. What the hell was a guy worth billions doing leading grunts in a combat zone? Kim, still not sure what he was all about, became even more confused because when she glanced over to where he stood, he was cuddling a baby. *A baby.*

And he looked like a natural doing it. Her heart started doing a little maternal happy dance. What was it about women and men with babies? Was it the contrast—the big man and the tiny child? Was it something in our DNA that said *reproduce with this one*? She didn't know, but something inside her moved when she saw Owen babbling to Anna. Something softened, and she found her anger was fading. Damn him.

He turned, and caught her looking. *Of course he did.* And now he was walking toward her, still holding Anna. Once the baby saw Kim she wiggled in Owen's arms and squealed. Yeah. So much for the mad.

Taking care of the little girl had done more to bring her back from the dark place she was in than anything else. No psychiatrist, no medication could do for her what this baby had done. When Owen stopped in front of her, Anna lunged and Kim happily took the child off his hands.

"Come here you beautiful creature," she said. "You made a new friend?" She looked at Owen as the baby nuzzled. "Watch out for this one, Anna," Kim whispered to her. "He lies."

Owen stuffed his hands in his pocket. He deserved that.

"Pictures don't do this kid justice. She's so pretty." He reached out and Anna immediately wrapped her hand around one of his fingers. "I can't believe how much I missed being away."

"That's what happens when you deploy. One of my brothers got engaged when I was on my last tour."

"Are you done?" he asked. It was a common question between those who served. Some people were lifers. They'd stay in the military until they were told it was time to go.

"I'm out. My time was up. I was at the field hospital in Kandahar and saw more than enough. I want to stay on this side of the world."

Kim didn't want to find Owen so likable after he messed with her before, but she did. He had an easiness about him that made her comfortable. He was easy to talk to, mostly because he actually listened, and Kim hadn't found many men who fell into that category.

"You had a bad time?" he asked quietly.

"I'm sure you know the story? My fiancé was brought into the hospital where I was assigned after he and another guy drove over an IED. He died right in front of me."

She took a few steps and sat on a nearby bench, still holding Anna who was peacefully sucking her thumb and dozing off.

Owen kept his distance, gave her space, and that was nice —he didn't overstep simply because they had a common history. But common history or not, he didn't need to know everything. Kim stopped herself before she said too much. Yet, she found she wanted to and that simple fact, that something about him had her ready to unload all her secrets, made Owen different from everyone else. When he looked in her eyes, and she saw nothing but truth and goodness, Kim wanted to tell him everything.

"I can't imagine how that must have been," he said quietly. "I'm so very sorry for what you went through."

Kim's heart clenched. It was hearing his words—so strong and so sincere, that for the first time in ages, she felt her eyes burn. "Thank you."

"You're welcome." He paused, twisted his fingers. Something was on his mind. "I do apologize for not being more upfront about my job situation."

"You were just teasing," Kim said.

"Yeah, but I should wait until I get to know people better before I tease them."

"That might be a good idea." She laughed, feeling the tension that had swelled between them dissipate. "I'm too sensitive. I have three younger brothers, you'd think I'd be used to it."

"I have one younger sister," he shared. "So, I'm very good at it, and Jason and I have perfected the art of the scam."

"Not Nate?" Nate was also a partner in Reliance, but he didn't have the big personality of Jason or Owen.

"Nate? Nah. He wouldn't know how to lie."

Kim giggled and checked the sleeping baby in her arms. She could feel her blood pressure dropping with every soft puff of Anna's breath. "So what do you do for the company?"

"I'm the Chief Information Officer."

"I'll ask again, what do you do?"

He smiled. God, he was gorgeous when he smiled. "I deal with how the company uses technology and implements it. Basically, I make sure everything works and nobody notices."

"So you make sure the technology is invisible?"

He chuckled and finally sat next to her and a little thrill wound through her. "I look at technology to help the business run, using it strategically to support the internal workings of the company. But yes, it should be seamless."

"Sounds complicated. Did you go to MIT, too?" She was starting to feel intimidated by these people. She went to a state university for nursing.

"No, I went to Navy."

"Really? The academy? Wow."

Now she was just flat-out impressed. No one got through any of the service academies without a lot of determination to go along with the brains.

"Yup. Opted into the Marines and they put me to work in intelligence."

He'd mentioned that before. Nervous suddenly, as the urge to bolt overcame her, Kim's foot started tapping frantically. Tom was in intelligence. He did a lot of recon, went on a lot of missions he couldn't talk about. She remembered when he made the move from the Infantry and she couldn't figure out why. It was always something with him. Something harder, something more dangerous. The man was all about the adrenaline rush.

Look where it got him?

Time for her getaway. "I'd better find a place to put her down for a nap."

With the gentlest touch, Owen reached out and ran his hand over Anna's head and down her back. When the tips of his fingers accidentally brushed against Kim's skin, she calmed. Just like that, Owen's touch reassured her.

For a split second there was a flash of something, a memory, or a piece of it...something like the déjà vu she felt earlier when he took her hand. She froze, scared, one side of her wanting him to go away and the other side wishing he would hold her. It was bad enough that his scent, a musky combination of soap and man was making her a little drunk, but now there was something else, something that was spooking her more than anything ever had. She was drawn to Owen, inexplicably so, but at the same time, she wanted to run.

"Hey," he said rubbing his hand on her forearm. "You see another ghost?"

"It's so weird. I can't put my finger on what it is. I don't know."

"Any idea? Is it a flashback?"

"No, not that. I'm not sure what's going on."

He kept his gorgeous blue eyes fixed on hers and it was there again. A niggling feeling that she was missing something. Something big. The corner of his lips twitched up and he turned his attention back to the baby.

"You can't just hold her while she sleeps, huh? You look so comfortable with her against you like that." He was still stroking the baby's hair.

If only she could. Kim loved having the baby in her arms, and loved the way she felt with her. Now, the way things were going, she'd never have kids of her own because she was too afraid of opening herself up to anyone.

"She'll wake up way sooner than she should and a cranky Anna is not fun."

"She sounds like her mother's daughter."

Was this guy for real? He was so tuned into the people around him. How could it be that she liked him already? "She is." Sweet or not, she had to put the baby down. "It was nice talking to you, Owen. Thanks for listening."

"Anytime," he said. With that, she rose and walked toward the house, glancing back once to see the very handsome Marine was still watching her. Kim didn't know what to think about Owen Kent. He seemed perfect, but that's what everyone said about Tom.

She was fully aware of how that turned out.

3

THERE WAS A POINT WHERE THE DAY JUST GOT TO BE too much. Kim loved the Campbells and the Rossis but just like her own family, there tended to be a bit of overload. There was too much concern, too much meddling. So, when Anna had settled in for a nap, Kim decided to take a walk around the grounds. On the far side of the property, behind a row of trees, was an old barn.

It wasn't in bad shape, but currently there were no residents and seeing Meg had her hands full with two kids, a cat, a puppy, a flaky software executive husband, a job, and she was pregnant, she didn't have time for a pony, no matter how much Molly begged.

Perching herself up on the split rail fence, she breathed in the clean spring air. After being in the middle of a desert for a year, she'd never again complain about rain. People could say all they wanted about "dry heat" but until someone had experienced the blast furnace conditions of the southern Afghani desert, they could keep their comments about dry heat to themselves.

She'd been home for ten months and she was still living her days in the hospital there. Still dealing with everything she lost. Talking to Owen earlier had brought on a couple of flashbacks she could have done without, and she didn't know how she was going to get past the memories. Quite frankly she was tired of herself.

Taking care of Anna had been a blessing and curse. She loved the little girl with all her heart, but Kim knew she was using her to hide. Hide from her career and hide from her problems. Finding the job through an old friend of her mom's had been a Godsend.

"You look like a woman with a lot on her mind."

Well if that didn't stop her breathing, nothing would. Owen was approaching her, looking sweet and sexy, his long fingers wrapped around the necks of two bottles of beer. Every nerve ending fired just looking at him.

When he got close enough, she managed a deep breath and reached out when he offered the beer. "Not really. Not if you count admiring everything here that's green as something important."

He chuckled, the rumble resonating in his chest. He understood. He'd just left a place that was barren and brown. Here everything was green and lush. It was paradise for her, and she'd been home almost whole year.

"There's a lot to be said for green," he said as he surveyed the trees surrounding them. Taking a long pull on the bottle he considered her quietly. "You might be admiring the quiet, but your brain never shuts down, does it?"

No. It never did. It was one of the reasons she took the nanny job. Anna took her as far away from the Navy as she could get. Caring for her was peaceful. But when she was alone she relived everything.

"Maybe I have a lot to think about."

"I think we all do."

Kim sipped her beer. "Where were you based?"

"Helmand Province."

"Ah, we were neighbors."

And in her mind, that wasn't a good thing. Helmand and Kandahar had proved the deadliest places for U. S. service men and woman. She was glad the military was going to start to pull out. Fewer people would die.

She wondered if he knew Tom, but decided not to ask. The last thing she needed was one more person telling her how sorry they were she lost such a great guy.

"So, did you come and find me because you need a drinking buddy, someone who appreciates all the green, or to talk about the war? I can handle the first two, but I'm not into talking about the last one."

Talking with him earlier was more than enough. Between the emotions he dredged up and the attraction, Kim's senses were on overload. The beer was good, though, cold, as she took another sip. She focused on little things, the breeze, the feel of the cold bottle in her hand, not the man who was becoming part of her space very, very quickly.

"A drinking buddy works."

He was so full of shit. He wanted to talk.

"Come here often?" he joked.

"Are you serious," she laughed. "That is the worst line."

"It never works, but I keep trying."

"Maybe you need a new line."

"Not my style. And I don't think any line would work on

you, anyway. You're too astute. You'd call bullshit in a second."

"Wow, that's a pretty big assumption considering we just met."

"Am I wrong?"

That wasn't the point. The guy was getting inside her head and she wasn't sure she liked it. She glanced over and he was watching her with those damned electric blue eyes, waiting her out. "Okay. Lately, I've been more inclined to tell people what I think. Life's too short to play games. So, I'll ask you again. Why are you here?"

"Has Harper told you much about me?"

"Not really, why?" She knew some, but it was pretty superficial. Just that he was in Afghanistan, it was his third tour, but not much else.

"I generally get in trouble for one of two reasons. I try to fix everything. *I mean everything.*"

"And the other reason."

"I have rotten timing."

"You already apologized for teasing me. It's fine."

"I know."

"And I don't think I have to be fixed? Do I?

"I don't know. Do you?" He took a long pull from his beer and trained his gaze on her again.

Seeing the way his polo shirt spanned his broad chest, the way his bicep and forearm muscles flexed when he moved, she'd love for him to fix what was ailing her. But that wasn't what he was interested in. He was fishing for information. About her. And she had no intention of giving it to him.

"I'm alright."

"But you're not working as a nurse."

"Nope. Needed a break."

"I bet you were good at it."

"What? Nursing?"

He picked at the label on his beer bottle. "Yeah."

"I really don't want to talk about this."

"Why? I bet you miss it. You love that baby, but being a trauma nurse—that calling is something that's burned in your soul."

"Wow, I guess I am a project. Trying to fix me, Owen?"

"Come on, it's not that. But can you tell me the work isn't part of who you are? I saw you with that baby, sure, but you have an edge."

"Maybe I've changed." A baby wasn't a soldier or Marine with a hole blown through him. A baby wasn't a double amputee. There was something to be said for keeping things on the happy side of life.

"Nobody changes that much." He drained his bottle and challenged her to argue with him. *So Mr. Wonderful could be an asshole? Great.*

What he said might have been true, but she didn't need to hear this. She didn't need to be analyzed by a guy who she'd known for a few hours. People always presumed things about her, about what was in her heart and her head. Everyone thought they knew what was best for her. Her mother told her to get right back in the saddle and go back to nursing. Tom's family wanted her to grieve forever. Everyone had an opinion and it pissed her off. Owen was pissing her off. "I'm going to walk back."

She wiggled her butt and jumped off the fence, but the ground was rutted and Kim, never being graceful, stumbled, landing flat on her rear, and splashing her beer. Not only was she on the verge of losing it because Owen had started to push every button, she just fell right on her ass in front of him. Getting away before this got worse was the only thing she could think about. But before she could stand, he had her hands in his and was helping her up, and then she stumbled, landing with her ass in the dirt. Again. "Oh, jeez. Are you okay?"

Not really. She looked at him. Her eyes burning with the tears she'd been forcing down in the name of a strong front. She couldn't care. Not about herself and certainly not about others. When she did, it ended disastrously. Owen was on one knee in front of her checking to make sure there were no cuts, no other injuries.

"You need to stop running away from yourself."

His voice, his touch, what he said all forced the emotion to spill over. Her voice was strained, small. "But I've gotten so good at it."

"Are you hurt?" Owen helped her up and Kim couldn't resist not only the physical pull, but the emotional one. He was like a magnet and she found herself turning her face into his chest and absorbing the warmth and strength there.

"I don't like you very much right now." He rubbed her back, held tight. "Besides, I'm a basket case. You should really keep your distance."

"That's exactly why I'm not keeping my distance." He didn't mean those words the way they sounded, but something niggled inside her and made her wonder what it would be like to be wanted by a man like this. So smart, so gentle. He kept going. "I told you this fixing habit gets me into trouble."

She let out a watery laugh. "I'm getting that."

She stepped back, trying to get some space between them, but his hands stayed on her upper arms. Moving. Up and down. Up and down. Pressing the heels of her hands against her eyes, she tried to get her mind off what was upsetting her. Of course, Owen was touching her so there was that to think about. *Oy, she had to focus.*

And that's when Kim zeroed in on the fact that she'd had this conversation while she was standing in Owen's arms. It was as normal and natural as anything she ever felt. Like she belonged there.

But she didn't belong and started to step back. Owen, on the other hand, didn't want to let go and pulled her in.

"Not so fast," he said, tilting her face to his. Well, this was humiliating. Using the pad of his thumb he wiped under her eyes. "I didn't mean to upset you. I push too hard. Friends?"

Getting involved with Owen was something she should avoid, even as friends, but there was so much about him that appealed to her. *He* appealed to her, even the part that was an asshole because the guy cared. He really cared. "Sure, friends."

He smiled down at her, all that gorgeous black Irish making her insides clench. "You're not very convincing."

"I'm sure. But don't do it again."

"No promises."

His body dwarfed hers in every way there was. It was hard, honed by battle, and she was sure, a strict regimen of exercise. How they interacted, though, was way too familiar considering they'd just met. But it felt like she'd known him a lot longer. Like he knew her and her secrets.

"This is so beyond inappropriate," she whispered.

"Yeah." But even that didn't stop him, Owen reached around her with one arm, pulling her close. "Don't I know it?

If Harper sees us, I'm a dead man." His words came out on his wonderful laugh. She could get used to hearing that laugh. Growing quiet, the flat of his hand made circles on her back. "It's okay to let people help you, you know?"

It had been almost a year since she'd come home. A year since everything she'd believed in had been taken away. But no one, not her family, not Tom's family, no one thought about her. It was all about Tom's death, all about what she lost because he wouldn't be there to love her. None of the concern ever focused on what Kim was going to do with her life, how she was going to cope. And here was Owen, a virtual stranger, understanding what the people close to her had failed to recognize. She should step away. No, she should *run*, but she didn't. She stayed in his arms because he made her feel safe. And Kim never felt safe.

Still, she fell back on her standard line, she deflected. "What makes you think I need help?"

"Come on, Kim. Be honest with yourself. I know you've been through hell, when are you going to admit it?"

Kim shrugged, hanging on to the last thread of her control. She'd already fallen apart once today. That was her quota. The only thing left was for her to tell the truth and she wasn't giving away how much Tom's death cost her.

"I'll ask you again. Why aren't you working as a nurse?"

"You don't quit, do you?" He raised his eyebrows when she deflected and waited her out. So friggin' annoying. "Fine. I don't think I'm ready. I'm a critical care nurse. It's pretty intense work."

Work she used to love.

She could see the wheels turning in his head and then it looked that he'd decided to let it drop. Kim was thankful because she didn't want to think about the job offer from the county medical center that was sitting on her kitchen counter. It was a good offer. She'd be a charge nurse in the burn unit. Definitely not ready for that.

God knew, Owen was right, she hadn't done much to help herself. Finally finding the courage to wriggle free of Owen's grasp, Kim stepped back and gave him a long hard look. There was a sense of command there. A sense of power that only came with a deep, inborn confidence. She envied him. What must it be like to know exactly the right thing to do? Well, she had to look like she had it all pulled together. *Fake it till you make it, baby.*

"I should get back."

"I make you uncomfortable?"

"I don't know if I'd call it that," she felt herself grin. God, he was so cute and he knew he got to her. The bastard.

She started walking, hoping he'd stay put so the fire he'd ignited would cool down. That was too much to hope for. Within seconds he was next to her.

"I'd like to get to know you better."

"God, you're pushy." She picked up her pace. "I'm sure I'll see you around."

"How about we go out sometime."

Kim stopped and turned. "Look, you've been wonderfully kind, and I appreciate that. And yes, I find you very attractive. But I don't think we're a good idea."

He stared at her for what felt like forever. "Why?"

"Well, if I'm going to be honest, I think you're just looking to get laid after being away for so long. I'm not interested in being a booty call."

"If that's all I wanted there are ten women I could call right now."

Son of a bitch. "On that note..." she started walking again and he caught up, and grabbed her hand.

"I did it again. I'm sorry." He rubbed his hand on the top of his head. "Shit. I meant that I like you. It's not that I'm just looking for sex."

"Ha!" she exclaimed. "You are looking for sex!"

"I'm not dead, Kim and you are beautiful, smart. I'd be lying if I said I wasn't interested, but if anything happened between us, I can guarantee, you'd be more than a booty call."

Skeptical, as always, Kim didn't know what to think. He was a man and men tended to think with a more southern portion of their anatomy.

"You don't really know me, Owen. Like I said, I'm a basket case."

He reached out and took a lock of her hair between his fingers, drawing it out. "I got that part."

"Owen!" He looked toward the patio, which was now in view, and saw Harper standing with her hands on her hips. "Stop hitting on her."

Kim rolled her eyes and Owen laughed. "She can take care of herself."

Kim smiled at that. No one thought she could take care of herself and while Owen's logic was a little twisted, Kim found she liked him, and liked him well enough that if a booty call was what he was looking for, she might not say no.

He was hot as hell. Funny. And he respected her. There was a lot of good passing between her and Owen Kent. It was too bad nothing was going to come of it.

. . .

OWEN WATCHED Kim as she mingled with Harper, Meg, and Caroline, as well their mothers, and wondered how they'd gotten from talking about her work as a nurse to booty calls. He meant what he said. The woman was worth far more than a one night stand, not that he'd ever even get that far the way he kept screwing up with her, but it was sure nice to think about.

He had to get to know her on a different level. This wasn't the crushed woman he held in the hospital last year. No, this woman, while wounded, was a fighter, and he could see she was fighting herself.

He was sitting on the deck with Josh, Nate and Jason and they expected Kevin from his game any minute. It was good, comfortable, and they were all at good places in their lives. Owen realized the biggest changes for him happened over the past year when he was away. Mostly, because he realized that he didn't want to sacrifice one life for the other. The Corps was important to him and he would always be part of the brotherhood, but his focus had to stay with his family and friends and about what good he could do here, not seven thousand miles away.

4

KIM SETTLED INTO HER BUNGALOW AT THE REAR OF Harper and Kevin's house, tired after a long day of hamburgers, sweets, backyard volleyball and kids. It was a good tired, though. A happy tired.

With these wonderful people, Kim was never made to feel like anything but family, and that's why she was so reluctant to give up her job, even though once in a while she missed her nursing.

No one is fully prepared for combat nursing, but before she was deployed she loved the work she did as a trauma nurse in the large county hospital. She never knew what to expect each day and that was part of the thrill.

But she loved Anna and she loved helping her grow up. Harper relied on her in the best way and Kim had to acknowledge she wasn't quite ready to leave this life.

The buzz from her cell phone startled her and Kim cringed when she looked at the caller ID. Her mother. The cringe wasn't for her mom, but it was for the crushing guilt she felt every time she thought about her family. She was ignoring them simply because they still lived next door to Tom's family.

"Hi, Mom."

"Is everything okay?"

"Why do you ask that?" Crap. Were all mother's mind readers? Could they hear feigned happiness?

"You're forcing it. I can always tell, you know."

She did know that. Her mother knew her better than anyone, which was why everything hurt so much. Her parents had mourned Tom, and she just couldn't find the words to tell them what had gone wrong.

Her mother though, was starting to ask questions. Lots of them.

"I had a good day today. The Campbell's throw a nice party."

"We had a nice party. I saw Tom's family and they said you bolted from the cemetery and don't want to see them again? Teresa is crushed. Jenna is so hurt. She feels you're their last link to him. She doesn't understand how you could be so cold."

Right to the point and more than direct. Teresa was Tom's mother and Kim understood she was grieving, but she wasn't above emotional blackmail, either. Her mother didn't seem to understand that piece of it and Kim's back went up. "I don't want to see them and I'm not cold, but I have to take care of myself, too."

"I know, honey. I know."

"Do you, Mom? Because it seems like you only take their side."

"Is that what you think? Why you never come and visit? Why you're always too busy?"

51

"Pretty much. Yeah." Bam. That stopped her mom cold. Kim could hear the quick intake of breath through the line and felt bad immediately.

Her mother was a strong woman. But she was quiet and when she finally spoke, her voice was full of emotion, hurt. "I...I didn't realize."

Did she lie? A lie would almost be worse than the truth. Kinder but not better. "Mom..."

Silence. And a sniffle. More silence. "Okay," her mom said finally. "Maybe you should tell me why."

And that's when Kim's stomach rolled. "It's complicated. I just can't hear about how lucky I was to have Tom in my life anymore. How I'll never find anyone like him ever again. How I should be back working in a hospital. With his family and you guys constantly telling me these things, I just don't want to be there."

"I see."

"I know you loved him, Mom..."

"*Stop*. Stop right now." Kim took a sharp breath because her mother was never harsh. She was, probably, the kindest person she knew, which made this that much harder. "You are my daughter and I love *you*."

For the second time today, her eyes filled with tears. "I know you do. It's been hard." Hard keeping the truth from her.

"Why don't you and I meet for lunch one day," her mother's voice was barely there. "Someplace where we won't run into *people*."

"I'd like that." More than anything because Kim missed her family something fierce. But she still wouldn't tell her everything. It was just too much.

"Is there someone else, honey? Have you gotten involved with anyone? It's okay. I mean, the Albanese's will adjust."

"No, Mom." There hadn't been anyone who had even sparked her interest. Until today that is. Owen Kent got her attention. Just thinking about him, and the way he touched her warmed her from the inside out. The man was completely out of her league, but he was awfully nice to think about.

"No one?"

Her mother sounded hopeful, and Kim wished she could say there was someone, but other than a casual date or two, Kim spent a lot of time alone. "No," she said firmly—pushing Owen Kent out of her head. "And I don't think there ever will be. I don't think I can do it again."

OWEN, Jason, and Nate sat around the outdoor fireplace nursing neat scotches and smoking cigars. The evening was comfortably warm, still not too many bugs. Looking up, the light pollution made it so he couldn't see as many stars, but he'd take fewer stars over being shot at any day of the week.

Owen stretched his legs and took a puff. Relishing the buzz from the tobacco and the single malt in his hand. "They offered me a promotion if I stayed in the reserves," he said.

Jason leaned forward, his elbows on his knees and Owen locked eyes with his best friend. "Lieutenant Colonel? What are you going to do?"

Nate took a sip of his drink, and he and Jason waited for an answer.

"It's done. I turned it down. I told them I'm out once my commitment is up."

Nate let out a breath. "You're okay with that decision? It

used to be you were going to do at least twenty. You only have a few more years before that happens."

"I know, but how many more tours?" He took a long drink from the glass and the liquid burned his throat. "I know they're drawing down, but this last one was enough. I may have to go back in the fall for a couple of months to help with some logistics, but as of the first of the year, I'm out. My separation was approved."

"What happened this time that was different?" Jason asked. "You're not yourself, man. It's like something spooked you."

How did Owen tell Jason and Nate that he was haunted by the pretty little nurse who collapsed against him in Kandahar? That he'd thought about her every day since her fiancé died. That seeing Kim Torres in person again had given his heart a jolt like he'd never experienced. He didn't know if he could.

"I'm ready to settle down, I think. I'm too old to keep trying to prove myself in the field and my life is here. I missed a lot being away. I missed my family and all of you. My parents are getting older and I—" He stopped and thought. "I just don't want to miss anything."

He didn't know why Kim affected him the way she did. No woman had ever gotten under his skin like this, much less one with whom he'd had two minutes of contact. When he saw her today, she was exactly like he thought she'd be. Kind, thoughtful, but still hurting.

When he got back to camp after he'd met her at the hospital, he had the unhappy task of writing condolence letters to the families of the two men who were killed. He looked through Albanese's personal effects before they were shipped out to his family, so he could get some idea of what he should say. There were two other officers who knew him better, and regular Marines who had served with him before, but he felt it was his duty to write the letter.

He found notes and cards from Kim and pictures of her and the sergeant that went back years. In some ways it felt like an invasion of privacy, but in others it gave him insight into the man who was under his command. He had a large close family and he had this beautiful creature who loved him. Tom Albanese destroyed her. Tom's friends told Owen he and Kim had been together since high school. *High school*. The woman he'd been cheating with said Tom was planning on telling Kim it was over.

None of it mattered now, but Kim Torres haunted him. He couldn't forget her even if he wanted to.

"There is something," he said. "It's a woman."

Talk about jumping into the deep end of the pool.

Narrowing his eyes, Jason tossed the stump of his cigar into the fireplace. "Now we're getting somewhere."

"Who is she?" Nate asked. "Anyone we know?"

"Actually, yes." The scotch really burned as he tossed the rest of it back. He was going to need it to fortify his nerves. "You need to keep this to yourselves. I don't want to spook her. I still need to get to know her, but it was someone connected to my last posting.."

Jason and Nate passed a look between them. Something Owen translated as them thinking he was crazy, but being good friends, they would humor him. To a point.

"Someone we know who's connected to… " Jason's eyes flew open. "Kim? Is that why you were sniffing around her?"

"I was her fiancé's commanding officer." He looked into his empty glass picturing that day all over again. "I hadn't been there long when he was killed, but I had to write the letters, contact the family. I knew all about her. Tom Albanese was a lucky man to have her in his life."

"This is officially the strangest coincidence ever," Nate said.

"I had no idea she was Harper's nanny. When I picked her up today, it was like the wind had been knocked out of me. I couldn't believe it."

"What did she say?" Based on the tone in Jay's voice, he was more than just shocked. "You guys were pretty casual today, considering."

"That's the thing," Owen said. "She doesn't know. There was a second when I thought she might have made the connection—she could have heard my name from his family, but it didn't click, so I didn't say anything."

"You should." Nate stood and grabbing a fire iron, poked the logs in the fireplace. "If she does find out, that could get ugly."

It was something to consider, but Owen didn't want to dredge up anything that could upset her. Then again if she found out about his link to Tom—to her—if she found out he'd read her letters and knew details about her relationship with Tom Albanese, who knew what she'd do.

"I can't get her out of my head. I hate what happened to her. Now that I've met her in person...I don't know." Owen was keeping it vague because he was holding back the most important part of the story, the part that had brought him to his knees. He felt a crazy protectiveness where she was concerned. He was completely at her mercy. Yes, he sounded like a complete candy ass, but he didn't really care.

Jason and Nate were leaning back in their chairs, quiet.

They didn't respond. They didn't tell him to grow a pair or man up. They sat quietly, until all he heard were the giggles of Jason's children filtering through the open windows from inside the big house.

"What are you going to do?" Jason's voice was quiet. Serious.

"No idea. I knew she was from the island. Part of me wanted to find her, but I knew that was..."

"Creepy?" Nate asked.

Yeah, it was creepy. Which was why he hadn't done anything about it. He'd been home for weeks, he had the means to run an extensive search and background check, and he hadn't even Googled her. "Well, I didn't. But then I walked into that Starbucks and there she was. I don't usually believe in signs or fate, but I don't know if I can ignore that."

"You can't," Jason said. "Sometimes things like this happen subtly, but this is right in your face. You can't ignore it."

Nate stubbed out his cigar. "You really like this girl?"

"It's different," Owen said. "There's something about her that wrecks me. Maybe I've just cracked." He scrubbed his face with his hands. "This is my PTSD."

"Don't be a fucking drama queen," Jason spat. "You obviously have some kind of, I can't believe I'm saying this, link, with her. Somehow, some way, it happened. So, stop crying in your drink and do something about it."

"Like what?"

"Holy shit." Now it was Nate's turn. "Ask her out. Take her to dinner or something."

"I said I'd like to get to know her better. She didn't think it was a good idea."

"You're just going to give up?" Jason asked.

Owen blinked in disbelief. "As a rule, when a woman says no, I accept that she means no."

"She didn't say no, though, did she?" Nate asked.

"I think I pushed too hard. Asked too many questions."

"You do come on a little strong," Nate mused. "You'll see her again. Take it slow. But first, say you're sorry for being a dick."

"I wasn't a dick."

"Yes," his friends said in unison. "You were."

Owen could feel the testosterone seeping out of his body. Kim had messed with his head and she didn't even know it. If he had any chance, ever, he had to apologize to her first. "I guess I have to find her number."

Pulling his cell phone from his pocket, Jason swiped his fingers over the keypad . In a second, his phone buzzed. Owen, in turn, put it in his own phone.

He'd been dreaming about this woman for a year, and now she was there, in his life and Owen had to get the nerve up to do something about it. But this wasn't a mission or even a business deal. Kim Torres represented something that scared the living shit out of him. For the first time since he committed to Navy when he was eighteen, Owen was looking at something that could affect the rest of his life and he had no idea how to handle it.

He really was a candy ass.

His hands moved slowly up and down, and Kim arched into the rock hard body, feeling his warmth through his clothes. Lips. His lips were trailing over her throat and down her chest, and when he pushed open her shirt, the cool air flowing over her breasts made her gasp. He did the most wonderful things with his mouth, and the feel of his tongue on her nipples was exquisite torture. Her hands held his head, his dark hair was softer than she thought it would be, and his eyes which were the most brilliant blue, flashed at her with mischief when he looked up at her. God this was perfect. He was perfect. "Owen," she whispered.

Bzzzzz. A fly? Was there a fly in here? Bzzzzz.

Kim moved her hand to swat at the fly, but she hit the wall behind the couch and started awake. She'd fallen asleep.

And she was dreaming. About Owen.

Dammit. Why did she have to wake up? Her dream was the most vivid she'd ever experienced. It was amazing and so was he. There was no denying it. Kim hadn't been able to get Owen out of her head all day. Now it seems he'd be with her all night too.

If only.

Bzzzz. Yeah, not a fly. It was her phone. Picking it up off the table, she saw four text messages. She pressed the icon and her heart just about stopped.

Hi, Kim. It's Owen. Ohmigod. *I know it's late, but first I want to apologize if I came on too strong today. My intentions were good, execution not so much.*

She scrolled to the next message.

I wanted to let you know I'm going to call you tomorrow to invite you out to dinner. ;)

Unless you really hate the idea and then you could tell me not to call.

But I hope you won't do that.

Kim pressed a hand to her chest and smiled. He was too cute. He was a badass Marine intel officer and the man was flirting with her.

She hit reply and started typing. Then she stopped.

She'd been here before. That feeling of being swept away by a guy who was strong and self-assured. She'd believed in him without question and lost herself, but she wasn't a teenager anymore.

Based on her dream, Kim was already too attracted to Owen for her own good. If she was giving it all up in her subconscious after one day at a barbeque what would dinner do to her? This was a bad idea, even if he was dream worthy.

Everything about Owen attracted her. His looks, his voice, his brains. There wasn't one thing she could find that put her off. Well, except when he pushed her buttons about the war. And even then she was only mad because he was right about her. After they'd talked by the barn, he backed off. Instead, the conversation they had over burgers was about his business, about her job taking care of Anna and a little about her experience in the Navy. He asked very specific questions rather than anything about her feelings, which were such an unholy mess they scared her on her best day. But Kim had to admit, she'd never met a man who had such a great sense with people. He must have been a wonderful commanding officer. There was no bluster around him, just quiet confidence. It was heady. What surprised her was that when she was with him she felt safe, secure, and Kim knew she could never rely on a man to provide that again. No. She couldn't trust him, even if she wanted to.

Even if her heart was aching to do so.

Moving her thumbs, she started typing the message. *That's nice of you, but I don't think dinner is a good idea. There's no need to call.*

Send.

Her heart broke a little as the bubble appeared in the conversation and closed the door on the possibilities Owen represented. Standing, Kim decided it was time to go to bed. She left her phone on the table where she wouldn't hear it.

OWEN STARED at the screen when her message came back. He couldn't believe it.

Still not sure what to say, he shook his head and then glanced up at Jason and Nate. "She said no."

"Seriously?" Jason said. "No?"

"Wow." Nate rubbed the back of his neck. The bastard was pushing down a laugh. "Has any woman ever said no to you?"

Once in a while he might get turned down, but not in recent memory and in a lot of cases, women asked him out. Whether it was the uniform or the money he made, he was never short of offers. He dated here and there, but no one stuck. No one held his interest or made him feel anything. Over the past year, Kim was the only woman he thought about and he didn't know why.

Owen shrugged his shoulders. Obviously, Kim wasn't as into him as he was her. It was odd, though. He was generally a better judge of people and based on her reactions, all the body language, she liked him.

"Are you going to give it up?" Nate asked.

Again Owen shrugged. "She's been through a lot."

"Yes," Jason said, "But you could be what she needs, man. Make her, I don't know, a mission objective."

Owen laughed. "You're such an asshole. A mission objective? How does Meg live with you?"

Nate jumped in. "You're a master strategist, Owen. Figure her out."

"See the hill. Take the hill," Jason declared loudly.

"Oh, my God," he muttered to himself. "Did you hear me before? No is a complete sentence. She said NO."

Owen hadn't considered that if he ever met Lieutenant Kim Torres in the real world, getting to know her wouldn't be easy. That was all he really wanted. Okay, that was a lie. He wanted to kiss the woman senseless and he'd felt that way since he'd seen her in the coffee shop.

"She uses the gym at Reliance a couple of days a week." Nate shared. "She brings the baby to Harper in the afternoon for lunch and works out."

"Is that so?" Okay, so maybe he could run into her. It was a possibility.

"It is," Jason said. "But be careful of Harper. She's protective of Kim, so she might run interference if she catches you sniffing around."

"Good to know."

It was all good information, but any move Owen made would ultimately be driven by Kim. She was calling the shots whether she knew it or not.

5

KIM OPENED THE DOOR TO HER COTTAGE TO FIND
Harper holding a basket of bagels and wearing her snarkiest
grin. "You have coffee?"

"Uh, yeah. Sure."

Glancing at the clock on the wall, she saw it was eight
o'clock in the morning and for a second Kim wondered if she
was late for work. But remembering it was a holiday she had
to wonder what her friend was doing in her kitchen. At least
she brought food. Kim was starving.

Harper may have been her employer, technically, but when
she came to work for the software executive almost a year ago,
they bonded immediately and became friends. Harper was no
bullshit, and she appreciated that Kim was pretty much the
same. Now, though, the woman who could terrify a room full
of executives had trained her gaze on Kim. "I need answers,
missy."

Kim had selected an everything bagel and was slathering it
with cream cheese. Her diet was going to hate this, but she
was craving carbs. She always craved carbs when she was

63

stressed. "You want to tell me what the hell you're talking about, or are we game playing this morning?"

"No games," Harper said. "What's up with Owen?"

Kim was just about to take a bite of her magnificent bagel creation, but stopped when Harper posed her question.

"Owen?"

"Yes, he asked you out and you said no."

Kim closed her eyes, annoyed, and put the bagel on the small plate that appeared in front of her. "He asked me less than ten hours ago. How did you know?"

"Jason told Meg, Meg texted Kevin and Kevin told me this morning."

Leaning back in her seat, Kim folded her arms. This was the price of being part of a big, close, extended family. "Oh, my God. You people have to stop."

"Why did you say no? Don't you like him?"

"What if I told you it was none of your business?"

Harper tossed her head back and laughter pealed out of her.

"That's what I thought." Kim adjusted her position on the kitchen stool, leaned forward and took a breath. "I do like Owen, he seems great, but I'm not ready."

"It was just dinner. You've gone out to dinner with men before."

"Harper, don't push me. This is different."

Harper poured some milk into her freshly brewed coffee, and took a seat on the other side of the island. "Is it? How?"

"He's a Marine. Been there, done that."

"He's not your fiancé and it seems to me he kinda gets you. You two seemed pretty interested in each other yesterday."

"Harper..."

"You like him. That's why it's different."

That was exactly why she couldn't see him. She'd only known him a day and she liked him too much for her own good already. "I'm cautious. Generally when something seems too good to be true, it usually is." Tom certainly fell into that category.

"Owen is as good as he seems. He's a bit of a stiff, but he's a good guy. You don't get better."

Kim considered her fingers, paying particular attention to her bare ring finger. For so long she wore Tom's ring and in the end it brought her nothing but pain. The thought of getting involved with anyone, even casually, scared her to death.

"I don't know Harper...it's not a good idea. What if things go south? You guys are close and I don't want to be in the middle of anything."

"Oh stop. If I haven't messed things up with those three bozos, you certainly aren't going to do anything."

Kim had been front and center to the drama that unfolded when all Harper's secrets came out--from the baby she hadn't told Kevin about to her country bumpkin pedigree. Still, she wasn't going out with Owen.

"He's not going to give up, you know. He likes you."

"He barely knows me! How can he like me?"

"Oh, girl, the same way you can like him. There is serious chemistry between you and Major Kent. I could see the sparks flying."

Major Kent. The name rolled around in her brain. It caught on something and then let go. She had been having these odd feelings where Owen was concerned. Beyond liking him, which she did, Kim felt like she was missing something. It didn't matter. She'd made her decision.

"I'm not getting involved Harper and I'd appreciate it if you wouldn't encourage him."

"Even if I think you're being a dumb ass?"

"Yes, even then."

They ate their bagels quietly and it was the silence that finally got to her. She hadn't bared her soul to anyone since coming home. She'd been broken since last year and finally she was starting to feel whole again. Owen let her see how much work was still left to do. Kim grabbed a napkin and dabbed her eyes. "I just don't know if I have it in me," she whispered.

Harper looked up from her breakfast. "What? A relationship?"

"A relationship with a man like him. I know I'm projecting. We barely know each other, but there's something about him Harper, something I can't identify that tells me he could own me and I just don't know if I can give up my heart to someone again. I don't know if I'll ever be ready."

Harper reached across and took her hand. "It's just dinner."

"You see it as just dinner. For me, it's not. It's more. With him it could be more. I just know it."

"Really?"

"You know how you said he's a good guy? I could see that the minute he walked into Starbucks to pick me up. He's kind. He's smart. He's sweet. He's..."

"He's hot. He's really freaking hot." Harper added the final quality with gusto.

"Says the woman living with the Baseball God." Kevin

Rossi was a perfect male specimen, and Harper called him the Baseball God because it pissed him off. And there was nothing she liked better than pissing off her fiancé.

"Yeah, but even I can't deny that whole strong, silent warrior thing Owen has going on. Damn." Harper paused. "Is that it? Is it because he's like your fiancé?"

"Owen couldn't be more different from Tom. They're alike in some ways, sure, but in others he's totally different." In the important ways, she hoped.

"So what's the problem? Something else is bothering you."

Kim pushed her hair back and blew her nose. "I didn't tell you everything about the day Tom died."

Did she do this? Only a handful of people knew the truth about what happened. Could she tell Harper?

"What happened?"

"Tom was burned on something like sixty percent of his body, including one side of his face and neck. He had a massive belly wound. I can't imagine the pain he was in. He was conscious when the brought him in. He talked to me."

Harper squeezed her hand. "Oh, honey..."

"It wasn't just that I was there. I watched him suffer, Harper. He told me he was sorry and that he loved me and then he died."

"Kim, I had no idea. I can't imagine how you've handled it."

"Anna helps. She helps me forget. But there's more to the story."

Harper stayed still, focused on Kim, so she continued. "I left the treatment bay and walked into an open area right outside the ER. I think I threw up in the garbage pail. I don't remember. I do remember that I was sitting on the floor for, I don't know how long exactly, for a while. It was so hot. Like a hundred and ten degrees that day--even air conditioning didn't help. Hell on Earth. I heard a vehicle pull up and thought we might be getting more wounded, when I saw a Marine military police officer running down the hallway right toward me. It was a woman and she shouted at a medic asking for Tom."

"I don't understand."

Kim nodded. "I didn't either. I stood, it took me a bit because I was shaky, and then the medic told her Tom had died. She broke down. The grief came pouring out of her. It seems...it seems she was his girlfriend. I was right there, having just watched my fiancé die, only to find out he was cheating on me."

"Oh, God. Oh, Kim." Harper hopped off the stool and walked around the island, hugging her friend from behind.

"I was in shock after that. My head felt swollen, almost fuzzy. I don't remember much else. Apparently, I collapsed against another Marine who was waiting for treatment, but then my friends shuffled me out of there. I only stayed in country another couple of weeks; I was no good to anyone, so I was sent home."

"You amaze me," Harper said. "To lose someone you love and then to find out—"

"That I was a fool? That he played me for a fool?" she cried. "I hated him. I didn't want him dead, I didn't want him to suffer, but I was glad I never had to see him again. Does that make any sense? I was broken, humiliated...I still am. No one knows except for a few people who were there and now you." Tears were flooding her eyes and tracking down her cheeks. There were so many she stopped trying to dry them.

"I haven't told my family and I haven't told his. In their eyes, he's still the dutiful, perfect Marine—a hero—and I was lucky to have him."

"You're carrying this alone?"

"Pretty much. This is why I can't go out with Owen. I can't. I do like him, but I don't want a relationship. I can't handle one."

Harper squeezed her tight. "I'm so sorry."

She nodded, relieved she'd finally told someone what happened. But at the same time, she was sad because she'd closed the door on something that might have been great. Tom was a ghost who would never leave her. He'd never let her rest. Never let her trust anyone. Never let her love again.

Harper held on and Kim thought about the people she cared about, the ones she really needed, and while she may have felt bad for Tom's family when she cut them off yesterday, she'd done the right thing. Her family, however, didn't deserve the way she'd treated them.

She was the oldest of six children and she'd been blowing off her parents and siblings for the better part of a year. One of her brothers had gotten engaged. Her youngest sister was graduating from high school next month. Kim was going to celebrate with both of them.

She couldn't pursue anything with Owen, but she could reclaim her family. That was something.

"THEY HAVE, hands down, the best waffles on the planet." His sister Melinda tucked her auburn hair behind her ears and patted her belly. "Let's take a walk and burn off some calories."

69

Owen didn't need to burn off any calories because he'd already run five miles today, but he liked spending time with his sister. Maybe she could help him figure out his Kim problem.

"What's on your mind, big brother?"

His little sister wasn't so little anymore. She was a tall, gorgeous, twenty-nine-year-old award-winning photojournalist. To say the woman had attitude would be an understatement.

"Just settling in. I'm going back to work tomorrow."

"That's good. You've never been one to hide out for too long. The routine will help."

"That's what I was thinking. How are the wedding plans coming?"

His sister had been engaged for three months and according to his mother, she and her fiancé still hadn't set a date. Owen suspected there was trouble in paradise. "Mel?"

She took a big breath and then the words shot out in a burst. "I'm going to break it off. I don't want to marry him."

Owen let it sink in and once he processed it, he wasn't surprised. Not setting the date was his sister's way of resisting. "Okay. Why?"

Generally speaking, he liked her fiancé Alex, but he suspected his sister had a good reason for wanting to end it.

"He wants to change me." She paused and shrugged. "He said my work is too dangerous."

"Your work is dangerous. But you were doing it, and successful, when he met you. It's not like it's a surprise."

"I know, right? He said if we're going to start a family I'd have to give it up."

"He might have a point there." He couldn't see her embedded with a military unit if she was pregnant.

"Yes, but he wants to have kids right away. I want to wait a couple of years. I'm only twenty-nine!"

"Have you talked to Mom about it?"

"No." She shuffled along the pavement like a little kid. "She's going to be disappointed."

Owen reached out and looped his arm around her shoulder. "The only thing Mom and Dad want is for you to be happy."

"I know." Melinda leaned her head on his shoulder as they walked. "What about you? Don't you have someone special so the pressure is off me? You are the first born."

"There's someone I'd like to know better, but she's not interested."

"Not interested? Is she slow?"

He kissed the top of Mel's head. Almost six years younger than him, his sister turned out to be an incredible woman. It was too bad for Alex he was going to lose her. "She's had a bad time of it. Lost her fiancé in the war. It hasn't been easy."

"Oh, and here you are, fresh from combat. That's going to throw up some red flags."

The military service was the most obvious deterrent, but Kim was sporting scars no one could see. "She's still hurting, but I like her. She was a Navy nurse, has a good heart. You'd like her."

"You may have to be patient," Mel said. "Do you see her often?"

"I could." He wanted to. "She's Harper's nanny."

"Nurse to nanny. Interesting."

"I think I should step back for a while. Give her some

space. Get my own life back in order."

Owen was doing his best to get back into some kind of routine, like Mel said. Going back to work tomorrow would definitely help. After living in close quarters with so many people for all those months, his house, which was at first a blessing, was now a curse. Since going to the party at Jason and Meg's house yesterday, he wasn't so thrilled about waking up in the quiet.

He'd been up at dawn, the sun breaking over the harbor and flooding his room with light. He thought about what he had to do today, and other than finally breaking down and getting some groceries, he'd done everything.

Over the past week, he'd stowed his gear, cleaned, and locked up his personal weapons, and hung his uniforms in the spare room closet. He was going to see his parents, too.

That morning, he was more reflective than usual. He'd laid back on his bed and stretched his arm over his head. His life had become a fucking to-do list. He'd looked at Kim's text at least a dozen times since last night, and he hadn't been able to get his head around her response. He'd open a text to her and then close it. He didn't want to be a pain in the ass, but he wanted to know why she felt the way she did. Then the text came from his sister, the only other crazy person who was awake at the crack of dawn on a holiday asking him to meet for breakfast.

He used meeting her as a reason to get his ass out of bed and ran five miles before even arriving at The Shanty in Northport. Getting sore and sweaty was just what he needed because otherwise he was going to explode.

Ever since seeing Kim yesterday, he'd needed to blow off some steam. He'd dreamed about her last night and woke up wishing she was there in bed with him because, as his raging hard on told him, he'd like nothing better than to make those dreams a reality.

The elbow he felt in his ribs made him look down at his sister. "Penny for your thoughts?" she asked.

Not a chance. His thoughts about Kim were way too dirty to share with anyone, especially his baby sister.

They'd traveled up and down Main Street and were almost back where they started their walk. That's when he heard it.

Barking.

Yelping.

More barking.

Setting up on the town green by the harbor, was a local rescue agency. Apparently they were having an adoption fair. A dog. He needed a dog.

He tugged his sister's sleeve. "Let's go look."

Mel looked up at him and smiled. "Yeah?"

"Yeah." As they got closer, a dozen puppies and young dogs contained in small fenced in areas playfully yipped and barked at the passing pedestrians. He had no idea what he was doing or what kind of dog he wanted, but he figured if the right dog was there, he'd know.

"They're going to want details about what you'll do with the dog when you're at work all day."

Owen stopped and thought for a second. "I'll take it with me."

"Really? Can you do that?"

"I own a third of the company," he said, smiling. "I can do what I want." And he could. He'd never do anything that would cause anyone harm, but he knew there was lots of evidence showing that having a dog in the workplace would be a good thing. It would be good for morale. And stress reduction.

They wandered around the pens and he saw more cute puppies than he could handle. Finally, he was approached by one of the organization's volunteers. A petite blonde woman, named Elena smiled and picked up one of the little fuzz balls for him to see. "This is Sheba. She's a Golden-sheepdog mix. Very sweet—around four months old."

Sheba was adorable. Very cute, but he could see all that gold fur sticking to his dark suits. He kept looking and out of the corner of his eye, he saw a little black flash. Turning, he saw it again. In one of the far pens was a little black dog going vertical. He walked over and saw a pink collar around the puppy's neck. She wasn't very big, and she wasn't what he would call a pretty, but as she sat there, her long tail thumping against the grass, he knew. Turning to the volunteer, he motioned her over. "What can you tell me about this girl?" The puppy was looking from him to the volunteer and back again. Alert, aware—*smart*. She was waiting patiently, still wagging her tail and damn it if the dog didn't look like she was smiling.

The volunteer hooked a leash on the dog and lifted her out of the pen. Owen crouched down and the puppy wiggled right over to him. "This is Casey. She's a Lab mix. Based on her bounce we think she's mixed with some kind of small terrier. Maybe Beagle."

"Hey, Casey. Hey, sweetie." The dog's ears were flat against her head and she was getting right in Owen's face giving him lots of kisses. Then she sat and flopped on her back. "She's ten months old, spayed, has all her shots and is housebroken."

"Will she be big?"

"We're thinking this could be as big as she gets. She's about forty pounds. Loves to play catch. She's very affectionate, as you can see."

"What do you think Casey? You want to come to my house?"

Mel was standing behind him. "God, she's got you wrapped around her paw already."

"Totally."

"Are you his wife?"

"No, sister," Mel responded. "He's not married."

"Are you going to be available to take care of her, sir?" the woman asked.

"Yeah, I work home from time to time, but I can bring her with me to the office. Everyone will love her there."

"Oh." Elena looked skeptical. "That won't be a problem?"

"Nah," He nodded toward Mel. "I reminded my sister, I own the company. The dog is perfect."

He filled out the paperwork and got a list of supplies. He tripled the requested donation and gave the volunteer his business card. "Please let the director of the rescue know, if she needs anything, please reach out to me. I'm happy to support the work you all do."

Elena looked like she'd hit the adoption jackpot. Not only did Casey find a home, but Owen also planned on making sure the rescue had all the funding they needed.

He picked the little dog up and smiled at his sister, who, it appeared, was wiping a tear from her eye. Casey licked his chin and snuggled into him.

This little mutt was sure going to make things interesting.

6

He did what the rescue volunteer said and bought the dog a crate, but Casey lasted all of ten minutes in it when it was time to go to bed. Owen had to admit, she was a really good dog. She found a spot at the end of his king size bed and stayed there all night. He'd brought her to his parent's condo for dinner and his mother and father really took to her, although his mom couldn't resist getting in a dig about needing a human grandchild.

As he got ready for work that morning, Casey walked around his room moving between the bed, the floor and walking outside on the deck. The ride to the office took about forty minutes, and again, the dog just went with the flow. He wished he could get some of his employees to be so adaptable.

Pulling into the Reliance campus, Owen marveled at the expansive building. When he left for his last tour, they were just starting the interior work on the converted shipyard. The shell was there, but there was no landscaping, no personality. Both he and Nate questioned Jason's idea to move the company base from New York City to the coastal Long Island village, but he had to admit the place was impressive.

Owen saw the reserved parking sign—in a camo pattern—that said *Reserved for the CIO.* He smiled and finally admitted to himself how much he missed the work and the people who made this place more than a business. Being in the corps was in his blood and when he'd left, to help his friends with the start-up, he didn't know how he'd adjust. But once they got into things, when the program started selling, when the business really started to grow, Owen loved it. Parking, he took Casey's leash and walked down the path that went between the harbor and the building, past the basketball court and the daycare playground, and entered Reliance.

Looking around the reception area, the place was still quiet, but he saw a familiar face at the desk. Carol Lusardi was an old friend of his parents' who had been Reliance's receptionist since they opened a real office five years ago. She'd taken the job when her husband passed away and she didn't want to be stuck home alone.

"It's about damn time you showed up here, you rotten kid."

Coming from behind the desk she captured Owen in a fierce hug, "Thank God you're home safe. Tell me you're done with it."

"Almost." He looked down and Casey was sitting. Waiting her turn.

"Who is this?" Carol bent down and scratched behind her ears. "New mascot?"

"Yeah. I figured I needed to do something to make the place home. It's my first time at the new office."

She grinned. "That's right! Do you know where your office is?"

Owen looked around the spacious lobby surveying the wall of floor to ceiling windows looking out onto the water. There were corridors coming from each side, and he didn't know which one to choose. "That would be no. Do all the rooms have views like this one?"

"Not all, but most. Wait until you see your office."

"You've got me a little nervous."

Again Carol laughed, lightening his discomfort. And there was plenty of that to go around. This company was one third his, he helped build it from nothing, but he didn't know anything that was going on, and hated feeling so out of the loop. He didn't even know where his office was. A big problem in his book.

"Come on." She motioned him to follow her and then looked at the dog. "You, too, Missy."

BY MIDDAY it was like he'd never left. His office was part of a suite that included Jason's and Nate's offices, the conference room, a kitchen, and a central area where their assistants had desks. Casey made friends, travelling from desk to desk and office to office. She was pretty well behaved considering it was her first day too.

His assistant, Marla, had gone to a local pet store and bought bowls, dog food, dog treats, toys, and a big bed for the pup, while Owen took in his new space.

Carol was right to warn him.

The room was huge, with a private bathroom, a bar, a sitting area with large leather club chairs and a desk that should have its own zip code. Meg had decorated it tastefully, as always, with muted tones and perfectly coordinated everything. Nothing too ornate or girly. What touched him was that she'd had a half a dozen photos of him, Jason and Nate framed and scattered around on shelves and tables. She never failed to recognize the importance of their friendship.

"Did you really get a dog?"

He looked up from the departmental quarterly reports he was reviewing to see Harper standing in his doorway. That made him think of Kim, who he'd been able to get his mind off of a little, as he helped Casey settle in. Of course now that he had thought about her, he remembered her scent and the softness of her skin and his body responded like the traitorous bastard it was.

"Yes, I did. She's awesome. I believe she's learning to use the copy machine right about now."

"You are too funny. What are you going to do with her if you have to go away again?"

"My parents and my sister said they'd help out. And that's if I even have to go. I'm out, completely, at the end of December." He'd only told Jason and Nate that his separation had been approved.

"Seriously?" Harper sat in the chair facing his desk.

"Yeah. I'm done."

Harper made a face. He wasn't sure what the face meant, but she'd never been able to hide her emotions.

"What?" he asked.

"Nothing. Well...I heard you asked Kim to dinner."

"Not really. She told me not to bother. I didn't pursue it."

Harper stared at him. Hard and then leaned back in her chair and folded her arms. "You like her."

He leaned back in his chair and steepled his fingers. "I wouldn't have wanted to ask her out if I didn't."

"Yeah, but it's more than that. You really like her."

Owen looked around, lifted the papers on his desk, opened a couple of drawers and closed them.

"What are you doing?" Her grin ticked the corner of her mouth.

"I'm looking for my homework. We've obviously gone back to middle school and I don't want to get in trouble."

"Smart ass. Look, I'm just watching out for her."

"Have I done anything to indicate she needs protecting?" Owen was thinking about all kinds of things Harper could protect her from, but that was just his dirty mind working overtime.

"No. For what it's worth, I think she likes you, but she's gone through a lot."

"I'm aware. She told me some of it." He didn't let on that he knew the story firsthand. If anyone was going to know his role, and what he knew, he'd tell Kim first.

"What do you know?"

This was really rubbing him the wrong way. He didn't like talking about Kim with Harper. He knew why his friend was being protective—Owen came from a world that caused Kim a lot of pain—but that didn't mean Owen was going to give up Kim's secrets. Harper shouldn't either.

"You know what? That's between me and Kim. What she went through is personal and I'm sure you know way more than I do, but it's not for me to talk about."

Yeah, that was Major Kent talking. Every once in a while, his officer training took over and he didn't care about Harper's value to the company. He was her boss, he didn't think the conversation was okay, and he had no problem letting her know. "I think we're done here," he added for good measure.

The pure shock on Harper's face told him she had no comeback. That was a rare occurrence, and he wished he could have enjoyed it more, but the satisfaction of leaving Harper speechless was shadowed by his concern for Kim.

"Alright then." She stood, straightened her skirt, and smoothed her hair. "I'd better get back to my office. Kim is bringing Anna in so I can have lunch with her."

Thank God he had a good poker face. Just knowing Kim was in the building made his heart twitch.

Harper was almost to the door of his office when she turned and tipped her head to the side. "You should really check out the gym we put in. It's got everything."

"I heard. I'll go later." He returned to his papers, pretty much ending the conversation. He hadn't realized how pissed he was.

He heard a yap from outside his office and Casey ran toward Harper who gasped when she saw her. It was love at first sight. "Okay, she's cute as hell." The dog sat, but not still. Her tail was thumping and she was scooting around on her butt. "Hello, baby girl," Harper cooed. "How are you?"

"Everyone loves her."

Harper directed her attention back to Owen when the dog had received sufficient attention and flopped on her bed in the corner.

She snapped her fingers. "Now I remember why I came down here. You distracted me." Harper said flatly, remembering she was pissed. "I thought you might be able to help."

"What is it?"

He leaned back in his chair and motioned for Harper to sit down, which annoyed her even more.

"There have been some issues with the veterans we've hired. We're up to almost thirty. You know that H-R tries to be proactive with regard to mental health issues, stress reduction, substance abuse and even some of the financial and family problems they've had since coming home."

"Right. There's a problem?"

"Helen, the social worker who's handled this kind of thing in the past, is a little overwhelmed. It's not that she doesn't want to help, she doesn't have the contacts she needs to provide the services our employees require."

Helen was a lovely Danish lady of seventy-five who worked part time making sure the company's employees were tended to emotionally. Everyone was always so worried about physical fitness, they tended to forget about everything else. Owen of all people knew if your head wasn't screwed on right, your body didn't matter much. Still, even he hadn't thought about the very specific problems that the veterans would have and that Helen would be overwhelmed.

The issues were different. More and more vets came home, but those who returned often came with multiple physical or emotional issues. More than most health care professionals would be able to handle.

"We need to find a liaison, someone who can connect us with people through the VA. They have programs, but getting through the maze requires someone who knows the system."

"That's a good idea," Harper said, making a note in her tablet. "I'll see if there's anything I can do, but in the meantime, we have to figure something out. One of our new hires, great guy, is a below the knee amputee. He has a new prosthetic he wants to work with and he's having trouble getting therapy services."

That didn't sound right to Owen. He didn't need to use the VA, and he wasn't going to clog up the system when he could take care of himself, but the guys coming home were supposed to be priorities.

"Helen doesn't know who to contact. She's trying to act as an advocate, but she's hitting a wall."

"Alright. Let me think about this and see what I can find out."

Nothing made his blood boil more than when veterans needed help and couldn't get it. He flexed the hand he'd injured a year ago, feeling the tension rise through his body. Pretty soon he'd have a rip-roarin' good headache.

"Why don't you go work out or something?" Harper suggested.

"Yeah, maybe." It wasn't a bad idea. It might help him work out the problem and get Kim out of his head. That was a win-win right there.

"It might help you blow off some steam."

"I'll go in a while. I have a few things to finish."

"Now is a good time. It's a nice day, so it's probably quiet."

"I get it, Harper. The gym. I'm a little busy."

"No." She slapped her hand on his desk. "You really need to check out the gym soon." Harper looked at her watch. "Like in ten minutes."

It took another second before Harper's constant nudging made sense. Kim was there and she worked out when she brought Anna to see Harper. While that certainly would lift his mood, she'd sent a pretty clear message that she wasn't interested. Harper needed to back off.

"Look, I get what you're trying to do, but I'm not going to force myself on Kim just because you think it's okay. I do like her, but I also respect her wishes. Maybe, since you consider yourself such a good friend, you should do the same."

"But..."

"That's all."

Harper stood there tapping her foot. "Excuse me? Was I just dismissed? Kim is my friend and I have every right to discuss..."

That was the last straw. Owen stood, placing both hands on his glass topped desk and leaned forward. "You are out of line. I suggest you drop the subject."

Harper's heel was tapping furiously and her face had turned an amazing shade of red. She finally spun around and left the office, pushing past Jason and Nate as she went.

"Whoa. What did you do to Harper? She looks upset." Nate sat in the big leather chair by the window and immediately started tossing a baseball he'd found on the end table.

"I'm not going to coddle her like you two. She's going to check her attitude at the door. I respect her ability and her ideas and I will never interfere with anything she has to say about this business. But she is not going to interfere in my personal life. Not at the office."

"She's used to speaking her mind." Jason walked to the window and snagged the baseball from Nate.

"If it has to do with company operations, I'm all ears." Owen watched the two of them. At this point Jason was playing keep away with the baseball. "Is this what you two knuckleheads did while I was gone?"

Nate stood and grabbed the baseball when Jason

misjudged. "No, but we did break the foul shot record," Jason said.

Owen rolled his eyes.

Nate walked over and put the ball on Owen's desk. "You might want to extract the stick that's jammed up your ass, Major. Profits rose fifty one percent when the new software released a few months ago."

"Employee productivity also rose," Jason added. "*And* we broke the foul shot record."

"Sorry," Owen said. "But I'm not apologizing to Harper. I don't need her to tell me how to run my life."

"Does this have to do with Kim being here?"

Owen shrugged. "She's not interested. I'm giving her space."

"Space," Nate said. "You're giving her space?"

"Yes."

The dog trotted into his office and sat between the three of them, looking at each one in turn. She picked up a ball of her own from the floor and dropped it at Jason's feet. "I don't think it has anything to do with space." He picked up the ball and with a flick of his wrist, sent it flying into the reception area. Casey tore off, there was a scream from one of the secretaries, something crashed, but Jason kept his focus on Owen.

"You are such a little girl."

"What?"

"You stand there like you're such a badass, but you have no idea what to do. You're interested in Kim, you want to let her know that you are, but you're too scared to try. Blame Harper if you want, but she cares about you, asshole. Maybe you could return the favor instead of hiding behind your fucking honor."

"If a woman turns me down, she turns me down. That's it. It has nothing to do with being scared."

"Well, if that's it, then she'll know for sure you don't give a shit." Nate walked to the door. "I'm going to eat and then run the numbers for that sales proposal. Meeting at three?"

Jason nodded and followed him, leaving Owen to process what Nate had said. This thing with Kim should have been easy. Why wasn't it fucking easy?

Of course he wanted to go to the gym. He wanted to get Kim to go out with him. But he was the only one who'd witnessed what she'd gone through and no matter how much he wanted to, he'd need something from her. Some kind of signal or sign that he could make a move again.

He gave a shit. He'd been thinking about Kim Torres for a fucking year.

But he also knew what she'd suffered. He knew it on a personal level. And that changed the game. So while his friends gave him advice, Owen was going to follow his instincts.

7

K IM STRETCHED, STILL A LITTLE SORE FROM HER workout, when she heard the sound of the Harper's SUV pulling in the driveway. It would only be a few minutes before Anna would zero in on Mama's voice and wake up from her nap.

Kevin had left for his game, and Kim had had an hour of blessed, blessed quiet to read. So she took the crime thriller she'd been absorbed in, grabbed herself a cup of coffee and went out to the deck.

The gardens at the house were really coming together. There was a crew on the western side of the property planting about twenty hydrangea bushes. They were going to look beautiful but right now there was too much noise to read.

She could look at one of the very hot landscapers all day long. His name was Antonio and he was from...she didn't know. Which was good because then she could make up a fantasy life for him. Let's see, he was an orphan, but his mother died leaving him with the challenge of getting an education and working to help his eight younger siblings from

Costa Marco (made up country) get to America to prosper in their own right. Cue patriotic music.

Whatever. He looked amazing with his shirt off.

She heard the footsteps on the deck stairs. "I'm loving this view today," Kim said. "Thank you for these landscapers. Especially the tall guy over there. His name is Antonio, but don't get your hopes up, we're destined to be together."

"That's too bad for me then." *Owen Kent.* She'd know that deep, gorgeous voice anywhere. She'd spent the last three days kicking herself that she hadn't said yes to his dinner invitation.

"Shit."

"Hi there." He came around and parked himself on the other chaise. "May I landscaper watch with you?"

"I can't imagine that would be much fun for you."

"I don't know. I get great pleasure knowing women aren't nearly as evolved as they want us to believe they are. I mean objectifying the landscapers? I thought better of you."

"Are you here for a reason, Owen?"

"I came to see Harper. Being able to tease you a little has been an added bonus."

"Well, I'm glad you're enjoying yourself but Harper's not home yet." Kim picked up her book, pretended to read. It was hard to do with a couple of hundred pounds of lethal man less than two feet away. "You can go. Dismissed."

"*Dismissed*? I believe I outrank you, Lieutenant Torres."

Kim's stomach dropped. How did he know that? "I don't remember telling you my rank."

"Oh. I guess someone mentioned it."

"I guess." The conversation trailed off.

"So, do you expect Harper home soon?"

"She should be. Why?"

"I…" He hesitated. "I have to apologize."

"Apologize? That would mean you'd have to admit fault."

"I'm not the asshole you seem to think I am."

She didn't think he was an asshole. Not at all. But right now Kim had the upper hand and she was going to take it.

"What did you do?"

He rubbed the back of his neck. "I shut her down like she was a green recruit. The woman was not happy."

"Oh, no. I bet she wasn't. I'm surprised you lived to tell the tale."

"I'd like to think I could protect myself against a hundred and thirty pound woman with no special training."

"Oh, Harper wouldn't make a frontal assault. She'd get you quietly. No warning."

Owen smiled, then laughed as he thought about what she said. "I'll watch my back."

"You'd better." Kim reached for her drink and realized she'd been rude, in more ways than one. Just being around the man made her crazy. "Can I get you anything? Iced tea, water, a beer?"

"Water is good. Thanks."

"Coming right up."

She was happy for the chance to slip away for a second. Just being with Owen was messing with her head a little. He was nice. He screwed up and he wanted to fix things. That was a good guy right there.

And the look of him, good Lord. She'd never seen a man wear a suit like that. It was a medium grey, and the pants and jacket were tailored to hug his physique, from his shoulders to his long powerful thighs. The black shirt he wore with it was well fitted and looked soft and expensive. He was the picture of success right down to the scent of his cologne, which lingered, teased, but didn't overpower.

Again, she thought about the other night. Why had she told him no? Dumb.

She got his glass of water, and returned to the deck. He'd removed his jacket and tie, rolled up his sleeves and gotten comfortable on the other chaise lounge, sitting back, and stretching out. He was typing something into his cell, and looked up when she closed the door.

"Thanks." He took the glass from her and she watched his Adam's apple bob up and down as he took a long drink. "That's perfect. Did you find you were really thirsty when you got home? Like you couldn't drink enough?"

"No. Are you a sugar junkie? Maybe diabetes runs in your family?"

"No. I think I just want water because of the way the moondust settled over everything. I always felt like I was eating it."

"You probably were." The moondust he was talking about was the super fine sand that coated just about everything in Afghanistan and in some places was a half a foot deep. Tom used to complain about how it could seep into a weapon and cause it to jam if the soldier or Marine wasn't meticulous about keeping his weapons clean.

"It's probably just a psychological response. Because I'm not screwed up enough."

Kim reached out and placed a hand on his forearm, feeling the hair brush her palm. "We all come back with demons. If yours is that you're thirsty, I think you should take it and keep quiet."

He nodded, a flash of humor crossing his face. "I guess you're right."

"How is it being back at Reliance? I mean other than putting Harper through her paces?"

"It's...relaxed. I think it's going to be more of an adjustment than I anticipated."

"You've been living in a very rigid environment, that's understandable."

"The culture has changed at Reliance. The move out of the city is great, don't get me wrong, but it's become even more loose than it was. It's going great, profits are up, but I don't know where I fit."

Was she reading him right? Did Owen need to talk? "You're the only one who wears the whole suit thing, right?"

"It's my business. I think I should look like I care."

"It wasn't an indictment, just an observation." She'd been observing a lot at Reliance over the past six months, and compared to Nate and Jason, she could see that Owen was a stiff. A smart, gorgeous, sweet stiff, but still a stiff. On most days Nate was dressed in khakis and a button down. Jason went from business casual or a suit on meeting days to his Sponge Bob pajama pants when he went into flaky geek software designer mode.

"Nate told me to get the stick out from up my ass."

"Do you have a stick up your ass?"

He looked at her, incredulous. "I'm a Marine. I have the mother of all sticks up my ass."

Shocked at first, it only took a second for Kim to dissolve into laughter at not only the way he said it, but the way he could be so self-depreciating. Owen was laughing too and in that one quick moment, Kim felt like she'd actually made a friend. It was nice.

There was a little noise on the baby monitor sitting on the table between them. Their heads turned in unison at the sound. "The princess awakes," Kim said.

"Hey," Owen said rising, "Can I go get her? Will she flip?"

Kim didn't know. From what she saw at the barbeque a few days ago, Anna loved him to the point of pushing her own mother away in favor of her Uncle Owen.

"I'll go with you. Just in case you're not her guy anymore."

"I don't know if I'll be able to handle that. Rejected by two beautiful women in less than a week? It might be more than I can take."

Oh, now she felt bad. Mostly for herself. "Owen, I'm sorry, but…"

He pressed his index finger to her lips and stepped in. "Don't apologize. I shouldn't have rushed you."

"It wasn't that. I'm a big chicken."

"A chicken?"

"You're, um, a little intimidating. And I'm out of practice."

"I'm intimidating?"

"Yes."

"Oh. I've never been called intimidating."

"Don't get me wrong, there's this vibe around you, it's not something I can identify, but remember I know what you do."

They were walking inside the house and Owen stopped and turned her to face him. "The last thing I want is for you to feel at all uncomfortable. I'd like to get to know you better, but how about this? If you want to go out with me just tell me to "ask." Then I'll know it's what you want."

"I appreciate that, but…"

"I'll grow on you, I promise."

That wasn't what she was worried about. If anything she was worried he already had.

They reached the home office where Anna was standing in her pack and play, bouncing up and down at her knees. When the baby saw Owen she let loose with squeals the likes of which Kim had never heard.

"Is that my best girl?" He asked before scooping her into his arms. Anna hugged his head and giggled when he rubbed his stubble gently on her palm. He locked eyes with the child and Kim could see he was totally in love.

If that didn't just do her in, she didn't know what else would. Bottom line, she would totally have his babies. Like tomorrow. Forget Antonio.

"She really does love you." Kim ran her hand over the baby's back and loved the way she nuzzled into Owen, rubbing her face against his neck.

"I never thought about kids. Now I do."

"You know that's from the war, right?"

"What, the baby?" Now he looked very confused. It was cute.

"Paying attention to kids. Wanting kids of our own. I became a nanny to get away from the war."

"Has it helped?"

She tilted her head back and forth indicating it could have gone either way. "Yes and no. I know I've been running, like you said the other day. I will have to stop, eventually. I wonder if I'll ever have a family. If I'll ever have the nerve."

"You will."

"I hope you're right." He smiled down at her, still holding Anna close and looking like an ad for Daddies-R-Us.

"Well, isn't this cute." Harper's voice cut through the soundtrack that had begun playing in her head. The "walking down the aisle" soundtrack that took her to a very happy place. Owen was starting to look like he could be part of that fantasy if she let her guard down long enough for it to happen.

"Here let me take her so you two can talk."

"Talk?" Harper said. "We don't need to talk. I have nothing to say to Major Asshole here. Now give me my baby."

She pulled Anna from Owen and the little girl objected loudly, reaching for her new

favorite uncle. "Ahh. Mama. Ahh"

"Kim, please show Owen out. I have to calm her down."

"Do you need me anymore tonight?"

"No, you've had a long day. You can go."

Kim was a little surprised to be sent out, and she looked at Owen and shrugged. He followed her and walked her to the kitchen.

"Thanks for putting up with me. I don't know how this is going to go with Harper."

"Good luck." His proximity was disorienting. She had to get out of there. On one hand he was absolutely gorgeous and so very appealing, and she'd love to give him some moral support, but on the other, she knew he could wreck her heart without even trying. No. Owen was a bad idea. Even though he was a really good one.

"Maybe I'll talk to you," he said, hopeful.

"Yeah, maybe."

"You're around Reliance a lot, right?" He was fishing for information and Kim was flattered to be sure. Seeing Owen was no hardship, but it was dangerous..

"Occasionally." *Like three times a week. She was so getting caught in that lie.* He was close and he smelled so damn good. Lord, the man was addicting. *Get out. Get out of there.* She grabbed her backpack and smiled. "Bye, Owen. See ya."

And there she was…running again.

HE LIFTED a hand as she went out the doors to the deck, down the steps to the stone path to her cottage. It was a good distance from the house, but not so far that he couldn't watch her make the walk. He was supposed to have a date that night with a woman he'd been seeing before he'd left for duty. She'd heard he was home and called.

He'd cancelled before he left the office. He didn't want to date. He didn't want to hang out and pretend to have a good time wining and dining other women when the one woman he was interested in didn't want him.

"Oh, my God. Are you still here?" Harper walked right past him, onto the deck and plopped her little pink bundle in a saucer like exercise thing. Anna immediately started to squeal with joy. Not one to give up until his objective had been reached, he followed her onto the deck.

"Mother of God, save me," she prayed in exasperation.

At least she said something. She'd barely spoken to him since he'd talked to her like she was a dumb jarhead, and if nothing else he had to repair their working relationship, because she was too important to the company to lose. She just had to keep his personal life out of the discussion. Somehow he had to get her to understand he had his reasons.

When he'd been there the other day, Kim told him the back deck was the favorite spot on a nice day and he could see why. There were mature trees, lots of open space. It was peaceful, which he found so interesting considering Harper's kinetic personality, but it must have had some calming effect, because that's when he saw his badass director of operations singing to her little girl, who was bouncing in that little saucer like thing. He guessed it was fun. For babies.

Harper turned and grimaced when she saw him and then, quickly moved to get the baby out of the contraption she was in. Yeah, that wasn't happening. Harper was bolting into the house.

"Oh, no," he said blocking her way. "You're going to let me apologize."

"Do I have to salute you when you do?"

"No. I guess I deserve that."

"You bet your ass you do. I think what pisses me off most is that you think you're the only one who cares about Kim. You're not. I've known her longer than you, she's my friend— she's like family, for God's sake—and I thought I was doing something nice for you. Giving you a chance to get to know her."

"And now?"

"Now? Now you're just an asshole who doesn't deserve the time of day."

"Right." He sat in a chair near the outdoor fireplace and crossed his legs. Lord knew, he had this coming. On the topic of Kim, he knew he was right, and he wasn't going to budge – she was off limits for now – but he shouldn't have treated Harper the way he did. He should have been more under-standing. Instead, he got his back up and turned into Asshole number 1. She was going and going, railing at him about every one of his personality defects and including a few she'd made up and Owen let her. He deserved this and more.

Owen bent down and made his finger crawl over the tray in front of the baby. God she was cute. Harper glared at him while he talked to the baby. Yeah, that got him in hot water.

"Are you listening to me? You start this conversation, but now you pretend like I'm not here?"

He nodded at Harper. "You're right. Carry on. I'm listening."

"Carry on? Fuck you and your carry on. I'm not one of your soldiers, Owen."

"Marines. And you shouldn't curse in front of your daughter."

She sputtered at his warning about Anna. It was funny, but she was still pissed.

"Marines. Whatever. Don't command me."

"Harper, I'm sorry. I know you only want to help, but you have to understand my need to keep some distance."

"Maybe..." She tapped her heel up and down on the deck, frustrated, angry. "Maybe I could...try."

"I was an ass, like you said—"

"I said a lot more than that."

"You did. Please, let's put this aside? I'm really sorry."

She hesitated and plopped next to him on the nearby sofa. "I'm still pissed."

"Understood."

"I'm not going to make it easy on you." She was scowling but he could see the twinkle in her eye.

"I wouldn't expect you to."

8

It was so dumb. Kim had known Jenna Albanese since the two of them were five years old. They'd walked into kindergarten hand in hand, had told each other every secret, had discovered boys together and when it was time, Jenna put Kim, who had been in love with Tom forever, right in her brother's path. Kim felt sick about the way their relationship had crumbled over the past year, but in truth, it shouldn't have surprised her. Her life was a mess.

So, inviting her oldest friend to meet her at Starbucks so they could talk shouldn't have been a big deal, but it was. It was a really big deal and the first step to Kim getting her life back.

Making Tom's family responsible for everything she was feeling wasn't fair and she'd known it for a long time, but it was a safe place to hide out while she got up the nerve to face her problems. She'd lashed out a little over a week ago at the cemetery and it took her a while to realize she was blaming the wrong people. The only person to blame was Tom. And since he was gone she had to find a way to let the anger go.

Talking to Jenna could only lead to something good, so Kim reached out.

Now she was early, sitting at a table outside Starbucks and watching the people go by. She loved the dynamic between families and couples. Mothers with their children, young people, old people. Everyone had a story. She'd spent some time on Memorial Day talking to Caroline Rossi-Campbell, Meg, and Kevin's sister, about her romance novels and she said her stories came from real life. Just looking around Kim could see that material was everywhere.

"You look like you're hatching a devious plan."

That voice was a like a gentle caress. Warm, soft, deep. Kim heard herself sigh, long and low, before looking up into Owen's smiling face.

"What's that line from the movie? I think I'll have what you're having?"

Realizing she might have looked orgasmic there for a second, her face heated and her hand shot out slapping his arm in response. Owen laughed, full and strong, sinking into the seat opposite hers.

"That wasn't nice," she said.

"I don't know, you looked pretty pleased with yourself. What are you drinking?"

"Just a mocha." She didn't want to tell him it wasn't the sweet drink that elicited the response but a very sexy Major whose voice sounded like a long hot night.

"Come here often?" He asked, his smile wide.

Kim burst out laughing. God, it felt good. She couldn't remember the last time she laughed like that. "Are you going to try your bad line again?"

"I've been practicing. I have more."

"Oh, no," she said with a chuckle.

"Are you religious," he said taking her hand. "Because you are the answer to all my prayers."

"Oh, God..." she snorted.

"Did that one work?" he asked hopefully.

"No!"

"Okay. Another one." He leaned into her and wiggled his eyebrows. "I'm not a photographer, but I can picture you and me together." He offered his cheesiest wink. Kim was laughing so hard that her stomach hurt. Mostly it was the delivery. He cornballed it up with every line, each one going more over the top.

"You should have been an actor," Kim said.

"I want to be your socks," he moaned, clutching his chest.

"My socks?" *What the hell?*

"Your socks, beautiful lady, so I can be with you every step of the way."

The laughter that broke from her chest was so pure and true, Kim collapsed onto the table. Her belly trembled, she gasped for air, her sides hurt. Owen was laughing along with her and they were drawing looks from everyone passing by, but she didn't care. It was perfect. This was such simple fun, and she couldn't remember the last time she'd laughed like this. Just laughed.

The wheezing, the gasping for air, finally subsided, only for her to break into giggles again. But then she looked at Owen, who was happy and smiling and the sheer beauty of the man forced the breath from her chest in a whoosh. Bam. Just like that.

It was true. Sitting there in jeans and a button-down, his blue eyes sparking with life, his ruddy skin flushed and his smile wide and bright, Owen Kent was breathtaking. And he'd given her one of the happiest moments in the past year just by making her laugh. There was something very sexy about that.

"You are a lunatic," she said.

"Yes, but you loved it."

"I did. Thank you. I needed a laugh."

"Anytime." He sipped his coffee and locked his eyes on her. "So what does bring you here today?"

"I'm meeting a friend for coffee."

"Ah. A date, maybe? Should I be jealous?"

"Uh," Kim bit her lip loving that he might care enough to be jealous. As it was, she was still regretting telling him no for dinner. Over the past week, she hadn't been able to stop thinking about him. "No date. She's my oldest girlfriend."

"Yes, she is and I do consider this a date because she's been effectively blowing me off for the last year, so it's a very big deal. Jenna Albanese." Jenna stuck out her hand.

The color that had brightened Owen's face just a second ago drained as he shook Jenna's hand. "A pleasure. I'm Owen. Ladies," he said while rising. "I'll leave you to your reunion. Kim," he winked at her. "See you around."

He walked away, and even though Kim was happy to see Jenna, she was really sorry for Owen to leave. Until she got to watch him go and was able to admire everything about the man from his broad shoulders to his trim waist, to the way his jeans hung on his hips to his very, very fine ass. "Damn," she whispered.

"Damn is right, sista." Jenna was watching with her, just like old times. "Who was that hunka' burnin' love?"

"He's a friend of Harper's, the woman I work for."

Kim turned and Jenna gathered her into a hug. "It's about time you called me."

"I'm sorry. I've been having a tough time lately."

"I got that a few days ago at the cemetery. I wish you'd talked to me. You know you can tell me anything. No judgment."

"I know, but I don't want to put you in the middle with your family. Things are hard enough already."

"You are so stupid about this stuff. Let me get a coffee and I'll be right back."

Jenna trotted off and that left Kim with a few minutes to think. She thought about her friend and she thought about Owen. Her side still ached a little from the laughs they shared and she had to admit, he was getting harder and harder to resist. Almost to the point of distraction. She'd vowed he wouldn't get to her, but in a few short days, he'd started to break down the wall she'd built around her heart.

And it was crazy. It was too fast. He was too much, but everything about him felt right. From the bickering to the laughs to the wicked chemistry. She liked him. And she kind of wished she'd let him ask her out.

She zoned out remembering the dream she had starring her, Owen, and her bed. It was vivid, beautifully so, and she held onto every detail because even in her dreams, he made her feel cherished.

It was crazy. She was obsessing and he'd probably let the idea that she was s total basket case settle in and was looking at her like a project. A fixer upper.

He was a god. Rich, confident, and in total command.

Kim was a hot mess.

"You look upset. We haven't even talked."

"I'm thinking. I think way too much lately."

"Well stop it!" Jenna took a seat adjacent to Kim and put her giant frozen drink on the table. It was full of caffeine, chocolate, whipped cream and calories, and Jenna didn't care. It's something she always envied about her friend...her ability to stop thinking and just enjoy life.

And if she worried about the calories, it didn't show. Jenna Albanese was one of those women who was completely happy with how she looked. Her straight nut brown hair hit her shoulders in a neat blunt cut. Her skin was olive toned and flawless, and she had curves to spare. She didn't have to wear a lot of makeup because her bright green eyes were surrounded by inky dark lashes.

Jenna was a natural beauty, inside and out--there was nothing overt or flashy about her. Men loved her natural easy going manner, and women couldn't find fault because she was so damned nice.

Kim had really missed her.

"Now, tell me about the guy." *No, no, no.* She couldn't have zeroed in on Kim's interest in Owen already. She met him for a split second. Which was probably long enough for Jenna.

"What guy?" Well, she had to try. It was pointless to hide it, but she had to try.

"What guy? Seriously? Mr. Tall, Dark and Do-Me-Right-Now. You look like you want to eat that man for dinner."

"No." Kim started twisting her napkin. "I don't know why you'd think that. I barely know him."

"Oookay. You keep telling yourself that." She took a long pull on the straw in her frozen drink. "So, how is your job? I want to meet the baby and see your place. Do you love it?"

"It's been good to separate myself from things, so yeah. Harper is great to me and I love the cottage where I live."

"You were in the city for a while, weren't you?"

"Yup. I was an Upper West Side nanny, now I'm a Gold Coast nanny."

"Well aren't you the hot commodity?" Jenna laughed and Kim raised her coffee cup.

"It's good to be wanted. I like the routine."

"I'm glad you're enjoying it." Jenna, who was an Art teacher, lived and breathed her work, much the way Kim had when she was a nurse. "I know everyone thinks you should be throwing your scrubs on again, but take your time. Especially if it puts you in contact with guys like that. Holy. Shit." Jenna fanned herself. "Are you sure you don't want to tell me about him?"

Kim leaned back in her chair. "There's not a lot to tell. I like him, but I've also probably blown my chance. He asked me out and I said no."

"Here I always thought you were a bright child…"

"That's not funny."

Jenna raised an eyebrow. "Why would you say no to him? Even if it was just for sex you should have said yes."

"That's a terrible thing to say."

"Why? Do you mean to tell me you don't need to get laid? You totally need to get laid."

Kim had to agree, she did, but the last person she expected to hear it from was Tom's sister. And just the suggestion brought all kinds of hot and sweaty thoughts about Owen right to her head. There was no doubt in her mind, the man would be excellent in bed.

But right on schedule, there was a flash of fear, of doubt,

and then there was the stinking disloyalty she felt toward Tom and his family, even though she shouldn't. Kim pushed the desire down, pushed thoughts of Owen out of her head. For about ten seconds.

"I vote we get pizza and go to your place."

Jenna was keeping things light and casual, but Kim brought all that to a screeching halt.

"Does your family hate me?"

That brought quiet. And Jenna was never quiet. Kim could see she was formulating a response that was honest but wouldn't hurt Kim. "They don't hate you. Not at all. My mother is angry though. She thinks you're hiding something. Are you?"

"Hiding something?" Oh shit, oh shit, oh shit. This was bad. The way Jenna was looking at her, she thought her mother was right. "You know, pizza is a good idea. And you can help me with something. I'm thinking of buying a new car and there's a dealer nearby with specials for the military."

"Not going to answer that question?"

"Nope."

"I'll get it out of you later. Let's go car shopping."

OWEN WAS ACTUALLY a little worried when he heard Anna had a bad ear infection. The child had him completely wrapped around her little finger. Kevin was still on a long road trip and he knew Harper must have been going a little stir-crazy. With her mother out of town, and Kim obviously out for the day, Owen decided to stop by. He'd been trying to mend fences with her since the blow-up the week before, and sure enough, when she answered the door looking like she'd lost her mind, he was glad he'd made the trip over.

He took the cranky baby, who was now distracted by someone new, and that allowed Harper to shower. It was all she needed to restore her sanity.

Sitting on the deck with the baby now napping, Owen sipped a beer and was happy they seemed to have restored some balance to their relationship.

"Are the road trips tough?"

"This is a long one, and my mom is on a cruise, and Kim is seeing her childhood BFF, so it was kind of the perfect storm. Usually, I handle it, but I was a sloppy mess on the phone with Kevin right before you got here. Is that why you came over?"

"Nope. This was just Uncle Owen being awesome."

A low rumble from the front of the house caught his attention. Someone with a muscle car just pulled up to Harper's house. His testosterone would know that sound anywhere. "Are you expecting someone?"

"Just Kim. She went out with her friend like I said."

"I know. I saw her at the mall."

Owen made the walk around the house and stopped dead to see Kim and her friend Jenna ogling a shiny new Mustang. It was low-slung, bright red, and mean-looking. He also saw the letters GT. Yeah, this was a badass car.

"This isn't usually what girls bring back from shopping trips."

"No?" Jenna cocked her head. "Maybe you've been hanging out with the wrong girls."

He motioned with his hand toward Kim, who was now sitting in the car pressing buttons. "It seems I know the right one now."

That brought a grin out of Jenna Albanese. "She's the best person I know. Life dealt her some shitty cards."

"I know. We've talked a little."

"She told me." That piqued her friend's curiosity. It seemed her fiancé's sister didn't hate the idea of him. Good to know. Maybe he had an ally.

"Owen? What are you doing here?" Kim had finally looked up from the dashboard.

"I came by to talk to Harper, but it seems now I'm here to get a ride in your new car. Wow." He leaned in the window and surveyed the interior. "This is a hot beast."

"Once I test drove it this afternoon, I was sold. They had everything ready in an hour."

"Come on," Jenna was standing there holding a pizza box. "Let's go to your place so we can eat and gossip about this man without interruption."

"Um, ah…oh."

"You talk about me?" He moved closer, but Kim seemed frozen in place, her eyes locked on his. "I'm flattered."

"Only in the most general sense," she replied.

Owen felt himself smile as the blush grew across Kim's face and crept down her neck. Knowing he was on her mind made this a damn good day.

And he had no intention of letting it go. Leaning in, he brushed his mouth over her cheek and settled by her ear. "You can talk about me as much as you want. But you can also talk to me. Whenever you want."

There was a little whoosh of breath and a soft sigh that escaped her lips, just like the one he heard earlier when they shared some laughs over coffee, and if her friend hadn't been there, Owen would have taken Kim to her cottage and tried to get a few more of those little sighs out of her.

"I have to go." Kim got out of the car and closed the door. "Good to see you."

"Yeah. Nice car. Good luck with it."

"Thank you."

"Whoa! Nice ride!" Harper walked out front and smiled, but Kim just waved and made her way down the path to the cottage with Jenna, not stopping to talk.

"What was that all about? Or am I not allowed to ask?"

"You can ask. I may not answer, though."

"You are an ass, you know that?" Harper stood next to him, arms folded, pretending to look at the car.

"I do my best," he replied. After a couple of beats, he glanced over. "Harper, I understand her in ways you can't possibly know. And for that you should be thankful, but you have to let me handle it my way."

"You're not telling me something."

"You're right, I'm not." He wasn't budging on this.

She hesitated, but then patting his arm, Harper turned and went toward her house. "Okay."

"Okay?"

"Don't hurt her, Owen. Because then I will have to kill you."

"Noted."

KIM OPENED the front door of the cottage and Jenna did a slow spin when she entered the great room. "You don't pay rent on this?"

"Nope."

"Whoa. It's nice."

"I love it. It's beautiful. It's quiet and it's up to me how much contact I have with the family. If I want to go hang out with them at the house, I can do that. If I want to be by myself I can do that too."

"Are you by yourself a lot?"

Kim thought about it. For a person who grew up with a ton of siblings, family, and friends who were always in her house, she was, and it wasn't like her. "More than I should be."

Jenna put the pizza box on the kitchen counter and turned, pressing her back into the granite. "You don't have to tough this out by yourself. I know you've heard this from a lot of people, but it's true. Especially with me."

"I know. The situation is a mess, and Tom was tied in with so many people. I needed to get away from him and the memories."

"Come here and sit." Jenna motioned to a bar stool at the kitchen island. Swallowing hard, Kim settled in, forcing down the tears. Habit had been keeping her from sharing what was in her heart, but then she thought about how free she felt when she told Harper the truth.

Grabbing for the box of tissues on the counter, Jenna handed them over, more than likely sensing that this wasn't going to be fun.

"You never had to cut me out. Never. I know you were being brave for all of us. I know you were trying to protect my family, especially my mom."

Oh, God. What did that mean? "How do you…"

"How do I know? I've been waiting for months for you to tell me what went on. Now I'm going to tell *you* everything."

"Jenna…"

"No. Just listen. Six months after we lost Tom, I got a message from one of the guys in his unit, Mike Anderson. Nice guy. From Ohio, I think."

"I know Mike." He was a nice guy. He was getting married in a few weeks if she remembered correctly.

"Apparently, he and Tom were close. Went to Boot Camp together and ended up on the last tour together in Afghanistan. He was with Tom before they loaded him into the helicopter." Jenna grabbed a napkin and dabbed at her eyes. "Tom told him Mike he had to see me when he got home because that would be the only way I'd find out the truth. That you would try to protect the family."

There was nothing to say at this point, so Kim's mission was to avoid eye contact.

"I know there was someone else. He told his friend to tell me everything. And he wanted you to know," Jenna's voice broke, the grief straining her. "He wanted you to know he did love you, and that he was sorry. He knew you were going to find out…and…and he was so sorry."

"I did find out. Maybe twenty minutes after he died."

"Oh, my God."

She launched into the story in a way she never had before. What had happened to his body, the details about his death had Jenna crying quietly. "That was bad enough. That he held on for so long was unbelievable. He shouldn't have survived even for a little while. He was in terrible pain." Remembering his last minutes were the worst. "He told me he was sorry. At the time I didn't know why."

"Oh, God…"

"Your mom keeps pressing me about what he said and

what he did. If he had last words. I can't tell her these things, Jen. I can't. I can't tell her about the other woman. There's no way. She lost her son, her baby...I can't tell her anything that will sully his memory."

"I know. But she's onto you. And you need to see your parents and your brothers and sisters." Jenna walked over and gave her a strong hug. One filled with warmth and gratitude. "Thank you for taking care of him and for protecting my mom. You are, without a doubt, the bravest person I know. But it's time for you to take care of yourself."

"Hardly. I don't know if I'm coming or going. I feel like my whole life has been turned upside down."

"Trust me. Most people would have unloaded the information and been done with it. Not you. You just bear it for everyone."

"I'm still scared though. Of pretty much everything. I get that Tom was sorry, I appreciate what he said, but I'm still hurt, Jenna. He hurt me."

"And now there's the new guy. And you're not sure you're ready."

Kim slumped down. "He's made me think about things I never thought I'd have to face again."

"He's gorgeous and he's into you."

"He's nice too, you know? A really good guy."

"He looks successful. I'm assuming one of the big fancy Range Rovers I parked my Bug next to is his."

"He's very successful." That was the understatement of the century. The bottom line was Owen had it all going for him, Kim just wasn't sure she had the nerve. "I need a drink."

Nervous breakdowns went well with red, so she pulled a pinot noir and two glasses from the wine rack. Never one to mess with wine, she uncorked it and poured it in record time.

Taking a well-filled glass, Jenna sipped. "What are you going to do about him?"

"Owen? Probably nothing."

"Again...why?"

Kim took a deep breath and walked around the room, finally settling herself by the front windows. She had a great view of the yard all the way to the deck and there she could see Kevin, Harper, and Owen playing with Anna and talking. "He could be something, and I just don't know if I could handle him. He's different."

"So are you. And you've never been one to dodge risk. Everything you do is about risk," Jenna said.

"Never with my heart. Tom was safe and look where that got me? Am I really ready for Owen? This is new territory for me."

"Honey, every time the sun comes up it's new territory. You have to decide if you're going to live or simply exist."

9

Kim wondered if she pushed herself hard enough, she could do a marathon or a triathlon. As she hit her stride on the treadmill in the empty gym, she thought about herself running and running and the thought of doing what she was now doing for three hours on a road, with hills, made Kim wonder if she should just stick with Yoga or Zumba or something. Kim was never a hard core athlete and she never had to watch her weight, but since she'd been home, she'd been eating a lot more and she wasn't as physically active as she'd always been. Being a nanny kept her very busy, but it wasn't like being a trauma nurse. So three times a week she brought Anna to see her mommy at work and Kim used the gym. It had been a hopping place in the colder months, but now that the weather was warmer, people were opting to hit the basketball courts or run on the special path the guys had had installed around the building.

She had twenty minutes of running to do and then she'd hit some machines. Music was playing through her earbuds, she was getting a nice sweat going and then her stomach lurched because in walked the object of every fantasy, Major Owen Kent.

She hadn't seen him in a few days, and she'd discovered that she liked crossing his path.

Holy crap. He wore a grey sleeveless t-shirt and had on a pair of workout shorts that had USMC emblazoned on one leg. His biceps bulged and on one arm he had a tattoo—the Globe, Anchor and Eagle that was the symbol of the Corps. Owen wasn't bulky. His muscles were defined, long and smooth. He looked powerful, dangerous. And Kim's ovaries jumped up and down screaming for her to do something. God, she wanted to.

He walked over to the treadmill next to hers, hung his towel over the hand hold to the side and smiled. "Hey," he smiled. "Come here often?"

But then she remembered she was pissed at him. Apparently, he'd gone on a date. And she was mad and jealous and it didn't matter that she had no right to be. Turning him down had been a dumb thing to do, but at the time it didn't seem like it, and now, he was right there, being gorgeous, and nice and reminding her that she was an idiot.

Trying to be cool and not wanting to break her stride, Kim nodded and kept running. She was getting a little out of breath and wouldn't have been able to say much even if she wanted to.

He started out at three miles per hour and quickly kicked it up to six, keeping pace and not even holding on to the rails. The thumping of his feet on the belt was hypnotic. But still, Kim noticed she wasn't keeping up. It annoyed her, and what got her even more angry was when he started talking.

"You like to run?"

She scowled. He was being polite with the small talk. Or it could have been a real question. She didn't know. Second guessing herself was becoming tiresome, but it seemed with Owen, that's all she did.

"I love having a facility right in the building," he continued. "Convenient."

Again all she could do was nod. Kim pushed the button on the treadmill and upped her speed. He wasn't even straining, and she would have said something about him being a showoff, but she couldn't breathe. She might have actually thought about doing him real harm when he looked over at her display and chuckled. "That's a nice jog."

Jog! She was on the verge of cardiac arrest. He was still keeping a steady pace and then he kicked it up a little bit more. Kim didn't know how much more she could take, but Owen was just breaking a sweat. She, on the other hand, was drenched. Everything was sticking to her, her hair was slipping out of the tie and heat was pouring off of her. When she got a stich in her side that almost blinded her with pain, Kim couldn't take it anymore.

She hit the safety stop and doubled over. Holding her midsection, she was out of breath and miserable. Taking her water and stepping off the treadmill, the first thing Kim wanted to do was get away from that instrument of torture. That part was easy.

But there was no getting away from her burning lungs and she chastised herself for being so damn competitive. Especially with someone like Owen. The man was a professionally trained warrior; he was in top physical condition.

She was not.

Still bent over, the stitch was subsiding, but her breathing hadn't steadied yet. And there was a good chance it wasn't going to when she felt a large, gentle hand between her shoulder blades.

"Come on. Let's sit you down." Owen took her towel and her water bottle before guiding her to a bench on the side of the room. "Over did it a little?"

Kim wheezed and gasped for air, nodding.

"What were you thinking?"

How did she answer that? *I wanted to be a badass and keep up with you?* No. That made her sound childish. Still, it was the truth. "I thought I'd try to keep pace with you." *Better.* "For fun. I didn't think." She sounded like a frog with the hoarse voice, and weird little hiccups of air. *Ribbit.*

He held out her water bottle, his smile sweet, his concern genuine. "Take a sip."

"I'm fine, Owen. Thank you." It was such a lie, in addition to really taking a stupid risk, simply being around him was muddling her brain.

Because the universe was cruel, he sat next to her on the small bench. His hips settled next to hers, his broad shoulders taking up so much space. She hated it. *She loved it.*

Even with a sheen of sweat glistening on his arms and face, he didn't look like he'd even exerted himself. He looked...hot. And as he inched closer and brought her hand up for another sip of water, Kim breathed in. His scent made her dizzy.

With her eyes closed she leaned into him and only possibilities filled her mind. His arm looped around her shoulder and she wondered if she was oxygen deprived because rational thought was completely gone. He was so kind to her. Why didn't she want to see him? Oh right, she'd heard he went on a date with someone else.

"Look at me, Kim."

Her eyes opened and his face was close, so close to hers, who could blame her if she moved that final inch and kissed him? His lips looked so soft, his eyes were so kind.

"I'd really love to kiss you." *Oh, God*. Had she said that out loud?

She felt that low rumble of a chuckle, the one that let her know he was there and close. She could totally get used to him being close. "That's a nice thought, but let's first focus on getting you on your feet."

She took another sip and the fog started to lift.

His hands wrapped around hers and without any effort, pulled her to her feet. She was steady, no wobbling, except in the area around her heart.

"Okay?" he asked. "Feel like you're going to pass out?"

"No, um, I might die from embarrassment, though."

His smile bloomed, revealing a small gap between his two front teeth, making him more handsome, if that was possible. "Why are you embarrassed?"

Kim steadied herself as Owen's hands settled on her shoulders. "I, uh, I wasn't myself there for a second."

His eyes locked on hers and Kim honestly felt like she might be going down for the third time. "I shouldn't have said anything about kissing you. That wasn't appropriate."

"No? I kinda like the idea." The way he was standing, holding her, she wasn't going anywhere and for some reason it wasn't a bad thing. He moved closer, his big body pressing against hers, the smell of sweat and man turning her brain to mush once again.

Kim rolled her eyes and scooted away from him, sipping her water rather than making eye contact or talking to him. Once her breathing started to settle, she figured she could make a graceful exit and go get Anna. Stealing a look, she saw Owen slumped against the wall tapping one finger against another. He was watching her. His gaze steady, unwavering and if she had more nerve, she'd jump him. If only.

She heard a phone go off and looked around for hers, but remembered it was in her bag back in Harper's office. Owen however, reached into the pocked of his shorts and pulled out his.

"Yeah...uh, huh....right. shit. I can't believe this is a problem. Why can't he get what he needs?" The volume of his voice was going up— he was upset about something. "No. I'll figure it out. Yeah. Okay." He ended the call and seemed lost in his own thoughts before he turned his attention back to her. "Sorry."

"It's fine. You okay?" she asked.

"That didn't seem okay to you?" he said with a smirk.

"Not exactly. What has you so upset?"

"Angry is the word."

"At me?"

He reached out and squeezed her hand. "No. Not you."

Kim was more than a little relieved to hear that. She'd really made some big mistakes with this guy, and he deserved better. "Can I help?"

His brows pinched together and he turned his body so he was facing her. "You know what? You just might be able to."

"What, help?"

"Yeah. How much do you know about the VA?" Owen's eyes were still and serious. This was important to him.

"I know it can be a mixed bag. People can get really tied up in red tape, but the benefits can be lifesaving." It was the truth. The VA had, in some cases, the best equipment available. The newest technology. But there were so many veterans in need, of all ages, access to services was often difficult.

"I have one of those red tape issues with a new hire. Amputee. He's having trouble getting therapy."

"What? That's bullshit."

"Bullshit?"

"Totally. Come on," she said. "I need a phone. I'll have your guy in therapy tomorrow morning."

OWEN HAD NEVER SEEN anyone transform the way Kim had. She'd gone from sweet nanny to bureaucratic ball-buster in a matter of minutes. He brought her to an empty office in H-R, introduced her to Helen and got the go ahead from the employee to speak on his behalf, and Kim went to work.

It had taken her two phone calls and fifteen minutes to clear up the problem.

"In the future, remember that guys who've just come home, who were involved in any of the recent conflicts get preference. No waiting. Nothing. They get bumped to the top of every list."

Helen nodded. "I didn't know *dis*," she said in her accented English. She was really a sweet person and was so relieved someone could get the right help. "I'll call you next time. You can tell me who I have to get angry *wit*."

Owen folded his arms. "Helen, do you know how to get angry?"

"You stop," she said while giving Owen the side eye. "Or I'll practice on you."

The last thing he needed was his social worker getting all badass on him, so he put up his hands in surrender.

Kim grabbed a piece of paper, scribbled something before handing it to Helen. "My number. Call me if you need me to get in touch with someone."

Man, he wished he had permission to use that number. "Thanks, Kim. I appreciate it."

"My pleasure. Sometimes just getting out of the phone extension loop at the VA is a challenge. Forget talking to someone. But your guy is all set up and he should be feeling better soon."

If Owen didn't find Kim appealing before the problem with the VA, he would have after. There was something really special about a woman who would drop everything to help a perfect stranger. But that's exactly what she did.

"I'd better go get Anna, so I can get her down for her nap."

"I'll walk you." Owen wanted to take advantage of every second he could with her.

"Helen, it was nice meeting you." Kim shook her hand and Helen smiled sweetly in return.

"It's lucky you two met. It will be a great help to all our employees who have special circumstances." Helen retreated to her office and Owen found his hand drifted to the small of Kim's back as he guided her out of H-R. The best part, she didn't resist.

Once they were in the hallway, though, he stuffed his hands in his pocket because he wasn't about to press his luck, but he did want to thank her for helping. The way she worked got him thinking. There was so much they didn't know about navigating benefits for their returning veterans, that he thought they might have to hire someone to do just that. It's something he'd have to explore with Harper, and soon, because it was too important to let go.

Kim was adjusting the bag on her shoulder and she quickly looked up at him and smiled. His heart stopped. Right in his chest, it stopped. Thinking about what she said in the gym, Owen wanted to kiss her till they both couldn't breathe. "Thank you for everything," he said.

"I'm glad I could help. I couldn't believe the runaround the poor guy was getting."

"I know. I think I may have to hire someone to help Helen just with those cases."

They walked a little longer and he notice they'd both slowed down, taking their time getting back to Harper's office.

"You really take care of your people here, don't you?"

"They're the most important part of the company. If we don't have happy employees no one will be successful. The philosophy's been working for us so far."

She smiled. "I'd say so."

They stopped at Harper's office door and he peeked inside. Her secretary was on the phone and he could see Harper's stiletto clad feet propped on the edge of her desk.

"You didn't have to walk me back. I knew the way." She smiled at him again and Owen felt seventeen.

"Yeah, but I'm still finding my way around.

"How has it been, being back and everything?"

"Not bad. I'm settling in. Like I told you last week, it's going to take me a while. But in some ways it's like I never left."

"That's good." Kim kept her eyes locked on his. "I meant what I said about helping out. Helen can call me..."

"I know. I appreciate that."

"Hey!" Harper walked out to reception area of her office, and he felt Kim back away from him just a little bit. "I hear you solved the VA problem. Amazing work."

"It barely took any time," Kim said. "Let me get Anna so I can get her down for her nap."

"You're too late." She folded her arms and shrugged. "Kevin came by. He finished his workout early, so he took her to the park. You, my friend, have the afternoon off."

"Off?"

"Yup. Go get some lunch. Get a pedicure. Go shopping. Do something fun."

Owen didn't miss the hint Harper had just dropped right in front of him. "You know," he said. "If you're hungry, I'd love to take you to lunch. To say thank you and to get your take on the problem in general."

Harper poked Kim in the shoulder and he really wished she'd stop pushing so hard it. "I don't know..."

"Just lunch," he said. "I really do appreciate what you did for us. It's the least I can do."

"Okay. Lunch." Kim may have been happy. He couldn't tell, but she'd said yes and that was a start. "Harper, may I use your bathroom to change and freshen up?"

"Of course. Take your time."

She looked back at them suspiciously as she made her way into Harper's office and once the bathroom door closed he looked at his friend and raised an eyebrow. "How often does Kevin come and take Anna to the park?"

"If I ask him he does." She reached out and patted his shoulder. "You're welcome. Try not to scare her off. Okay?"

"I'll do my best." He had to take a deep breath. "She was really something on the phone today. Confident, quick and had the people on the other end eating out of her hand. She was you. Only nicer."

"I'm going to ignore that." Harper's scowl quickly dissolved into a grin.

When Kim came back into the room, wearing jeans and a pretty pink top, which scooped low in the front, Owen realized he had no idea where he should take her to lunch. And he had to think about the dog. *Shit.* "Let's walk back to my office, I have to check on a couple of things before we eat."

"No problem. But if you're busy, we don't have to go."

"Oh, no. No backing out. I want to take you out."

"You know, I think we're even." They picked up a good pace on the way to his office. "You did keep me from dying in the gym. I mean. There's that."

"You weren't going to die." Owen snorted.

"It's possible," she continued sweetly. "I saw a white light. It was coming for me."

"I think you might be getting a little dramatic." She was funny, too. Could the woman be more perfect?

"No, it was terrifying." She put her hand on his arm and they stopped walking. "You saved me." The words were like a song. Sweet, musical.

"I like saving you." He meant it, as his hand captured hers.

Kim probably could have used that as an excuse to take off, but she didn't. Instead she went up on her tiptoes and for a second he thought he might get that kiss she'd mentioned, but the woman went one better, she got close to his ear and whispered two little words.

"*My hero.*"

And that pretty much brought Owen to his knees.

He would have kissed her right in front of everyone if they hadn't been pounced on by a very energetic black dog.

"Oh! Oh, she's so cute!"

"This is Casey."

"Oh, my gosh. Who does she belong to?"

"She's mine," he said.

"When did you get a dog?"

"Last week. There was an adoption fair in Northport and she and I hit it off. She's really pretty good. But this is my problem. I invited you to lunch and I don't know what to do with her. I feel funny just leaving her. Everything is still new."

"You are one of a kind, aren't you?" Kim bit her lip and then squatted down to pet the dog. "There's a really cute little lunch shop about a five minute walk from here. They have outdoor tables and I've seen people there with their dogs. It's not fancy, but it would solve the problem. We could eat and you wouldn't have to leave her."

"Are you sure? I wanted to take you someplace nicer."

"It'll be fun. And it will be good for the puppy to socialize."

If he hadn't started falling for her already, he would have right then. He was standing on a very slippery slope, looking down at the most beautiful girl petting his dog and solving his problems without a second thought. Yeah, he was in deep trouble. "Okay. Sounds good."

She extended a hand to him this time so he could help her

up, and once he had her hand in his, he didn't let go. "I need to get her leash."

"Okay."

"It's in my office," his voice had gone low, throaty.

"Okay." Kim didn't resist when he pulled her through the reception area and into his office closing the door behind her. Owen was used to making split second decisions, and he wasn't about to second guess his instincts now. As soon as the door clicked shut, he pulled Kim in and his lips came down on hers.

THANK GOD, he kissed her.

Kim had been hoping, but she never thought it would happen here, or now, or ever for that matter. She only hoped. So much for being annoyed. Apparently, she didn't really care if he was seeing anyone else.

But it was a bad, bad thing because getting involved with a man like Owen was dangerous. A man who could make her feel, could make her believe and could break her heart.

But he felt so good and his mouth...his mouth was perfect.

Owen's fingers threaded through her hair and he held her head steady as he took gentle sips. Testing, tasting, and teasing her into more. Everything in her went soft, warm and her hands reached up and wrapped around his neck partly because she wanted him closer, but also because she had to hold on. She had to keep from slipping into a fog brought on by his scent, his body, his hands, and his wonderful mouth.

The kiss was sweet, sensual, full of promise, but Owen was careful with her, not to pushing her too far. He moved his mouth over hers, lingered over her cheek, behind her ear.

Feeling his hands cradling her face, Kim opened her eyes and looked at the man who could mean everything. One kiss. One perfect kiss and she knew he was what her heart had been missing. It was strange. A year ago she felt like her life was ending. Now, with Owen, she felt like it could begin again.

"Owen," she whispered. "You aren't seeing anyone else?"

"I was supposed to go out with one woman, but I cancelled. Why?" his voice hummed as he nuzzled her hair.

"Just wondering."

"I'm not seeing anyone." He tilted his head back and considered her, his eyes narrowed, but a smile teased the corner of his mouth. "Is that why you've been acting like I had the plague? You thought I was dating?"

Yep. Plague was a pretty accurate assessment. "You're handsome, rich and you did mention you could get sex whenever you wanted…"

"I did say that. Not my best moment."

"It was not." God, she had to shut up before she said something stupid. "I mean, um…"

Owen pressed his forehead against hers. "Listen, I'm not seeing anyone else. The only woman I'm interested in seeing is you." His words could not have been more perfect. Or more terrifying. "So, whatever's running around in your head, forget it."

"Okay." she said. "Still want to go?"

"Yeah. I have to change." His voice was husky, warm and Kim thought about the kiss. That panty-melting, soul-stealing kiss. She wanted more, and she took it.

Grabbing his head and letting her fingers travel to the back of his head Kim pulled him in and this time when their lips connected there was nothing sweet except the taste of him. She caught his tongue in her mouth, his breath, his essence as he wrapped his arms around her and pressed her into him. She could feel every muscle of his body, every bone, and the hard length of him pressing into her belly. The heat was so intense, so raw, that if he suggested skipping lunch and staying there to make love, she might have said yes. Everything about him made her want to throw every promise she'd made to herself to guard her heart right out the window. There was passion here. She'd say it was lust, a need for mutual release that drove them, but the way he touched her, the way his fingers threaded through her hair told her there was more. More than she ever dreamed.

Finally, taking a deep breath, Owen stepped back and dropped his hands to her shoulders, his thumbs gently grazing her collarbone. "We shouldn't have done that."

"Probably not, but it was pretty great."

He let out a big breath and smiled, lighting him up from the inside out. "Oh, yeah. But now you're all I'm going to think about."

What kind of miracle was that? Kim hadn't felt like anyone was thinking about her for the longest time. For the first time in a year, Kim felt lighter, happier. Sexy. Free.

She never wanted to pin her happiness on a man again, but being with Owen felt right. And since Tom had died, nothing had felt right.

10

KIM PICKED UP HER CELL PHONE AND CHECKED THE time. Just after eleven. Did she take the chance? Opening a text, she found Owen's number and typed.

Hi.

She already wanted to take it back. Even after their kiss and their lunch, she still didn't know if this was the right thing to do.

Hey, is everything okay? He responded.

Yeah. My brain just won't turn off. And I'm hungry. Contemplating a diner run.

Oh, please take the hint. Please.

Want company?

Yes!

I'd love some.

After that they worked out which diner and what time and the texts ended. Kim sat up in her bed and wondered if this is what Jenna meant about really living and figured she'd find out the next time she saw her friend and filled her in. In the meantime, she had a date. Kind of.

There was something coming alive inside her because of Owen Kent. She hadn't spent a lot of time with him, just a few days, really, but the effect on her life had been nothing short of amazing. He made her look inside herself, he made her laugh. For the first time in a year, she felt things. Good things.

Sometimes Kim wished she had the nerve to be just a booty call, it would be so much easier than being the girl who needed a relationship, who needed love. Still, she didn't think anything would ever be that simple with Owen...they passed having that kind of relationship the first day they'd met.

She'd had that with Tom. He'd loved her and he'd told her over and over, almost to the point of it not meaning anything. He always said it when they made love—even during those early fumbling times on the beach, and later when their love-making was frenzied because they hadn't seen each other in months, he always told her he loved her.

Except the last time.

And now she knew why.

Pulling fresh jeans and a sweatshirt from her drawer, Kim wondered what the hell she was doing meeting a man at a diner at midnight.

She didn't know. But she was happy. And that had to mean something.

OWEN NEVER REALIZED how much he missed certain things while he was away. Diners were one of them. So many of them dotted the island. They all had similar elements, the endless menus, the dessert cases filled with impossible looking pies, cakes and sweets, the bottomless coffee cups, but each one had its own personality, too.

Now, sitting in one that had been retrofitted with a fifties-style mirror finish on the outside, he waited for Kim and wondered what he'd done right for her to have texted him and casually mention her plan for a diner run.

The woman had him tied up in knots. He'd been wondering for a year what would happen if he saw her again. If he was able to get to know her. And now he knew. He was distracted, horny and wondering if he could possibly be falling for a woman he only knew for a short time.

"Hey there, Marine. You come here often?"

He looked up to see the woman in question looking cuter than should be legal. She was in a pair of jeans and a green college sweatshirt from one of the big state universities. Her hair was loosely pulled away from her face and he didn't think she had even a stitch of make up on which made her even more beautiful. Her delicate bone structure was highlighted by her clear, smooth skin. Owen had noticed her eyes changed depending on her mood. The first few times he'd met her they were greyish-green, stormy. Today, they were more olive with flecks of amber. They were bright, happy. They were her.

"Does that line ever work for you?" he joked.

"Never." Kim tossed her purse onto the seat and slid into the booth across from him. "I should not be hungry because I ate what feels like a pound of pasta earlier, but I am. I can't decide if I want breakfast or a burger."

He laughed. The woman was funny and had a hell of a lot of spirit. And apparently a hell of an appetite. "Where do you put it?"

"I've always been a big eater. I could eat my brothers under the table."

"How many brothers?"

"Three and two sisters. All younger."

"Six of you?" There were families with six kids? That was like something out of the fifties.

"In a four bedroom house with two bathrooms."

Owen tried to think about the organizational nightmare of eight people using two bathrooms. Then he thought about his own upbringing, which he always saw as comfortably middle class. Now he realized he grew up more than comfortable.

"You said you have a sister right?"

He wondered where Kim's energy was coming from. At first she seemed really happy, but watching her movements, her eyes, she seemed nervous and he was wondering if there was something wrong.

"Yeah, Melinda. She's younger than me."

The waitress came by and Kim ordered a huge breakfast special that would have fed a couple of hungry infantrymen. Owen settled on nice hearty omelet.

"So, what had you craving diner food in the middle of the night?"

Kim's face froze and dropped. "Nothing in particular. Why?"

"I'm not sure. I'm just getting the sense something is eating at you." She looked away and Owen hoped he hadn't shut the door before she'd even said anything.

"My friend Jenna, who you met last week, is my fiancé's sister. I methodically cut people out of my life after I got back. It was dumb. But seeing her and talking to her about things was hard. I guess I just needed to talk to someone who would get it, you know?"

"I'm glad you texted me. First, because you don't have to deal with shit like this on your own, and second you kept me from messing up my kitchen cooking myself something."

Kim was squeezing lemon into her tea when she absently said something that just about put Owen into the ground. "You can always come to my house. I love to cook, I don't do it enough."

It took a couple of seconds for her to realize what she'd said. "I mean, um. Well."

"That's a nice invitation. Thanks. And if it means I'd be cooking for you I'd consider that a good reason to mess up my kitchen."

"I'd love to help mess up your kitchen." Did she just say that? Shit.

Yeah, that did it. He was as hard as a rock. She'd said something perfectly normal, and the next thing you know he was imagining doing her against the kitchen table. Hot, sweaty, dirty sex against his kitchen table.

Kim looked up having realized what she said. "I'm so sorry. I do that all the time. I say things and they come out all wrong and not that I...oh...I should stop talking."

She was embarrassed and he didn't want her to be. "You do have a way with words," he laughed. "It's not a secret that I like you. A lot. It's also been a while for me. I'm not one of those guys who finds a willing body on base."

As soon as he said it he regretted it because he could see she thought about her own situation. He was still keeping a lot of information from her and he wondered if this would be the time to tell her about his connection to Tom, but he didn't know what it would do to them, if it was still too soon, so he kept it quiet.

Their food was served and quite literally what was placed in front of Kim was enough for three people. The woman might have weighed a hundred and ten pounds, but she really did pack it in. He liked it. Generally women ate like birds around him. He didn't know how they survived.

They ate in silence, the minutes passing slowly, until he heard her clear her throat.

"Owen?"

He looked up and her eyes sparkled. "Yeah?

"I like you too. A lot. But I don't know what to do about it."

"What do you mean?"

"I was with Tom since I was fifteen. He was my one and only boyfriend. I'm totally lost. What do I do? I'm not a kid. I'm a grown woman and I know what I want, but I don't want to be too *easy* either. Do people even say that anymore? Easy? I'm totally out of my element."

"I'd never think you were easy. You can make whatever choice you want."

Kim took another bite of her home fried potatoes, thinking while she ate. "I think I'd like it if we got to know each other better. But I want it to be a Harper-free and a war-free zone. I want us to get to know each other and not have interference from the outside. I love Harper, but she'll look at this like it's her project."

"Okay." He didn't disagree with her on that, but he could handle Harper if he needed to. "So we keep it quiet. Anything else?"

"One more thing."

"What?"

She looked up and made eye contact. Went deep. He felt the warmth of her eyes, glowing hot with flecks of gold. She drew in a long breath, and when she bit down on her lower lip like a shy schoolgirl, he almost lost it.

"I want to mess up your kitchen."

His brain skidded to a stop with sound effects worthy of a Saturday morning cartoon. Brakes were squealing, there were crashing noises. "Excuse me?"

Kim leaned in, a strand of her hair, escaping from the elastic that was keeping it back. It fell forward and curled around her face. "Take me home. Take me to bed, Owen."

He felt like he'd just been hit in the chest. "Jesus. Are you sure?"

At this point he could barely focus because Kim was gently stroking her fingers over his hand. Her touch was overwhelming him and he quickly threaded his fingers through hers.

"I want you, Owen. I know it makes no sense and I don't understand it, but ever since I met you my body has been screaming for you."

"I'm glad I'm not the only one. I thought I was going crazy. I'm analytical. I work problems for a living. How I was reacting to you made no sense." It hadn't made sense since Afghanistan, since the first day he held her.

"I can't stop thinking about you, but I want this to stay between us. Okay?"

He nodded. "Are you finished?"

"Yes."

He got the waitress's attention, paid the check and the two

of them were out by the cars within minutes. "Should I follow..."

Owen didn't listen to what Kim was asking, he simply hauled her in and covered her mouth with his. The contact was a flash point. Combustion. Heat. Owen hadn't ever felt like this when he kissed a woman. He'd never fit like this, had never instinctively known what she would like and how she would like it. He pressed Kim back against his truck, grinding his hips into hers and feeling her push back. Her mouth opened for him and he slipped his tongue inside tasting tea and lemon and her. She was beyond anything he ever expected. Soft, willing, responsive.

"I want you inside me," she whispered.

The woman was talking dirty. Owen felt like he'd just died and gone to heaven. "Anything you want. Anything."

He felt her smile against his mouth. He was falling a little in love with her simply because she wasn't a shrinking violet, and knew what she wanted. He wasn't going to lie and say he wasn't happy she wanted him—he was more than happy to bury himself in that tight little body, but her nerve was as big a turn on as anything.

This woman was made of steel and wasn't going to allow herself to be the victim to anyone.

They were still kissing when he heard a pounding. Looking up, Owen saw the diner's manager banging on the glass cursing at them in another language...Greek maybe...telling them to get lost. That was fine by him. The sooner she was in his house, in his bed, the better.

"Get in your car and let's get directions to my house in your GPS."

He got the address in, kissed her goodbye, and left, driving way too fast because he had to get home first. He just hoped she didn't change her mind, ignore the GPS, and go home.

KIM COULDN'T BELIEVE she was on her way to Owen's house with the sole purpose of having sex with him. She thought about the timeline, about the actual days he'd been in her life, but that didn't matter. Sometimes your heart just knew. And her heart knew this wasn't just sex. Something was going on between them.

She made the turns down the dark roads into the area known as Little Neck and came to a driveway with the right number. Her GPS indicated she'd arrived at her destination and she pulled in.

The house was illuminated by floodlights, as was the path that clearly led to the water. The house wasn't large, but it was beautiful. A typical coastal home, two story, with cedar shakes and white trim. There were flowering shrubs and a rolling lawn that went right to the beach.

It was stunning.

Once she parked she saw Owen leaning against the rail on the porch. He stood there bathed in light from a fixture near the door, his hands stuffed in the pockets of his jeans, his dark hair mussed. He was so handsome, waiting there for her, she felt her heart start to race. The newness of all this coupled with the easy comfort she felt when she was with him was a little overwhelming. She always thought feelings like this took time. Her parents had known each other for years before anything developed between them. The same with so many couples she knew. For this to hit so hard and so fast was thrilling and a little scary, but as Jenna said, she was never one to back away from something scary.

She went to him, allowing him to gather her close as soon as she stepped on the porch. Settling into his arms, Kim laid her head on his chest and let his scent, one that was woodsy and warm, surround her.

"I was worried you would change your mind."

"No, but I'm nervous now that I've had time to think about this. It's all happening so fast and what I'm feeling is so intense."

"I know." He pulled his head back and looked down at her. His blue eyes were grayer in the dim light, but still danced with life. "If you don't want to…"

Kim pressed a finger to his lips. "Stop. I want you. I may be nervous about what's developing here, but I have no doubts."

He kissed her then. Sweet, lingering. First just a touch of his lips. Gentle sips, brushes of contact. She could taste mint —he'd brushed his teeth—and Kim let her hands travel up and up to settle on his neck, pulling him closer and letting the kiss deepen. It did. Tongues tangled, and with that she felt her heart start beating steadily with his. This wasn't the fiery kiss they'd shared in the parking lot; this was slow, tender, and far more dangerous.

This kiss was about their hearts, not just their bodies, and what was to follow could change everything.

A breeze caught her hair and caused Kim to shiver. "Are you cold?" he asked. "Let's go inside."

He took her hand and brought her through the door to be greeted by a wiggling mass of black fur. "There she is."

Kim squatted down and rubbed the dog up and down her neck.

"Hi Casey. Hi girl. She's so quiet."

"We woke her up." He crouched down with her and the puppy rolled onto her back. "She's settling in and she seems to like me..."

"She's sweet." Kim rubbed her belly and the pup twisted her head trying to lick her hand. "And you're easy to like, aren't you sweet girl?"

"She is. Everyone at the office is completely taken with her."

"I love that you bring her with you." The soft spot she saw in him, was such a contrast. That was probably a good part of what was so appealing. Having the dog close by at work was proof of Owen's mushy heart. He wasn't such a big, bad Marine after all.

"It's good to be the boss. Or one of them at least."

Content, Casey stood and went back to her bed on the far side of the kitchen, while Owen drew Kim up. He kissed her as soon as she was close enough. This time there was heat as his mouth took her and his body pressed so close she could feel his very impressive erection against her belly. "So, are we going to mess up the kitchen like we said?" She loved the wicked glint in his eyes when she reminded him of their conversation at the diner.

"As much as part of me would love to bend you over that table and do you right now, I'm taking you to my bed. I'm going to make love to you so hard you never want to leave."

"*Owen.*" Kim wondered right then if she'd made a mistake, she knew this encounter was risky, but he'd just raised the stakes, made this matter. When she'd first thought about sleeping with him, Kim thought it would be a way to deal with a very intense mutual attraction. But now, he was talking about forever. About wants and needs and the thing was, with very little effort, she could fall for him. She was pretty much there.

He picked her up and she wrapped her legs around his waist as he carried her through the house. She nuzzled his neck, loving how he felt, how his arms banded around her, the long powerful stride she could feel as his hips shifted. Everything about his body was controlled, strong. *Hers. It was hers.*

Owen flipped on the light and Kim glanced around. The walls were a rich blue and the furniture was crafted from simple, dark woods. A chest of drawers stood in the corner, and night tables flanked either side of the bed. There was also a large flat panel TV mounted to one wall, and there were two armchairs in one corner facing the TV. Simple, comfortable. The dominant piece of furniture was a large four poster bed. But the most striking feature were the French doors that led to a deck overlooking the harbor. Large windows flanked the doors creating almost a full wall of glass. Simple drapes framed the windows and the doors.

The space told her a lot about the man. That he liked things functional and easy. That he liked to be connected to his environment inside and out. He was a billionaire and while this wasn't a space just anyone would have, it wasn't ostentatious or overdone. He wasn't about ego or showiness. Pretty much everything about him was perfect.

He eased her onto the soft mattress and hovered over her, looking sweet and menacing at the same time. "I have no idea what to do with you first," he ground out.

"You've been thinking about this?"

"Since I met you."

"I've been dreaming about you." *Oops, did she say that?*

"Yeah. Want to fill me in? Maybe I can make those dreams a reality." He grabbed the band of her sweatshirt and pulled it over her head, exposing her to the cool air. Then he went for the button on her jeans, working it and within a few minutes her jeans were on the floor. He'd shifted her so she was in the center of the bed with only a pink thong and her very skimpy bra covering her. He on the other hand was still fully clothed which did not seem fair.

Until he touched her and then Kim didn't give a shit about fair. All she cared about was how she felt, what his hands and mouth were doing to her. "Mmm…"

His mouth had just brushed her nipple. "My bra…"

"What bra?" He brushed his hand up her back and with a snap the bra was off. He smiled at her and even though she'd pretty much lost control of the situation, she had never felt safer, or more protected in her life. If she had any doubts about being with Owen, the look in his eyes told her she had nothing to worry about.

"You're very sneaky," she said pulling his head down for a kiss. A sweet, tender kiss.

"I won't hurt you. I promise."

"I know." Working the buttons on his shirt, Kim couldn't wait. She couldn't handle not seeing him, feeling his skin against hers. He rolled his shoulders and she pushed the shirt up and over, allowing her to feel his long lean muscles, the soft hair on his belly.

"No more waiting," she whispered.

"Kim. I…"

"No games. Just us. It's time."

It's time. Those words hit him right in the heart because it was time. He'd known from the first moment he'd held her in that hospital in the desert—grieving, broken—that he would be her lifeline, her protector, if she ever needed him. And now he could be so much more. Friend, lover...the possibilities staggered him. Suddenly, Owen saw himself as a husband and father when he thought those things had passed him by.

He knew was getting way ahead of himself. But the woman in his bed was the vision that kept him awake at night for almost a year. He'd never believed in soulmates or fate. He believed relationships were built on common ground, not chance encounters.

Yet here they were. On the verge of something profound, and it could all go to hell in a hot minute. The secrets he was keeping could hurt her, and he knew he should get things out in the open. They had to have a clean slate. Pushing himself up on one arm, he moved back from her.

"Kim, I should tell you something." He could not believe he was doing this. He wanted her so bad it hurt.

"Owen," she pulled him close and held fast. "Sex now, talk later," she whispered.

"But..."

"Shhh. I'm okay. I want this." She kissed him softly. "I want you."

That was it. Owen couldn't hold back anymore as she helped him out of his jeans. Sliding them over his hips, her hands were warm, soft against his skin. He'd follow her advice and talk later.

He watched her face as their skin made contact. The charge was electric, but it was more than just sex. More than he ever experienced with any woman. Being with her was the reason he cared so much, worked so hard, and risked his life for his country. Everything he ever did, had sense and purpose now because of her.

She rained gentle kissed over his shoulders, tenderly stroking his back and neck. He opened his nightstand drawer and grabbed a condom, and she helped him roll it on.

If she was nervous about being with someone new, he couldn't tell. She was warm and giving and all Owen wanted was to deserve her.

He entered her slowly knowing it had been a long time, but she was wet and ready and they came together with an ease that belied reason. "You feel perfect," she whispered. "God, Owen."

She was perfect. Hot and tight, he felt her wetness close around him. Each movement sent shockwaves through his body. Had sex ever been this good?

He moved slowly and Kim responded, first with a steady rhythm, then the pace picked up. Their bodies worked, perfectly in sync, and every sensation, every movement intensified the response. She was eager and generous. He felt her breathing quicken, her gasps and sighs were like music. "Oh, Kim. It's so good."

She wrapped her legs around his hips, pulling him deeper inside her. "Owen," she whispered. "Look at me."

He didn't realize his eyes were closed, and when he looked down his heart damn near stopped. She was focused on his face. On his eyes.

"Watch what you do to me, and never second guess that this needs a chance."

He did as she asked. Her body, slick with sweat, was his. Claiming her, burying himself deep inside her. He drove hard, and he watched as her eyes fluttered shut, her back and neck arched and she locked her legs and arms around him. He felt her body spasm.

"Owen, I…" her words caught as the orgasm hit and she flew up and over. She shuddered while her body clenched around his dick, the spasms bringing him to his peak. He finished with one strong thrust, calling her name as his world making sense for the first time in forever.

The last year in Afghanistan had been nothing but heat and death. It had been hell, but finally, looking at Kim he saw the only reason he needed for having gone. It may have been hell, but the angel he'd found there had delivered him.

KIM STOOD in Owen's kitchen sipping coffee at oh-five-hundred hours because she had to get home in time to start her day with Anna. Kevin was still away for one more day and Harper's schedule at Reliance was packed full, so Kim was going to have a very busy week. Hopefully, she'd find some time for Owen.

The last thing she wanted to do was leave his bed. Their night had been perfect and all Kim could hope for was that he wanted to give this a chance as much as she did. Feeling his arms slip around her from behind was probably the best thing that was going to happen to her the rest of the day.

"You have to leave?"

"I do. Anna is up by seven-thirty and Harper has to get ready for work."

She turned in his arms. He was sporting some very sexy stubble, to go along with his t-shirt and running shorts. "Working out?"

"I'm going to take a run before I go to work. I have meetings all day so I won't be able to use the gym."

"You're so disciplined, but it's good. You need your stamina," she teased.

He leaned in and nibbled he ear. "Is that so? Have plans for me, do you?"

"I wish I could see you today," she moaned. Loving the little pings of electricity that shot through her wherever they touched. "It's a busy day."

"Same. But I can stop on my way home." He leaned back and looked in her eyes. "We can mess up your kitchen if you want."

Kim grinned and kissed him. "That sounds like a plan. Bring me Chinese food around seven and I'll be your slave."

He laughed out loud. "This is getting better and better." He stroked her cheek. Suddenly tender. "I had fun. I loved being with you."

"Me too. I was nervous, but you made it perfect."

He was rubbing her upper arms, keeping it easy. Everything with Owen was easy. She stood on her toes and kissed him. "I have to go. Harper is going to be all over this."

"Don't let her push you around. It will be fine. I'll be thinking about you." He kissed her again. "All damn day."

"Same."

Owen crated Casey before grabbing his phone and walking

Kim out to her car. He gave her another kiss for good measure. "Text me when you get home."

"Okay. I'm sure there's no traffic on the road."

"Still." He kissed her again.

"You need to stop kissing me."

He considered her for a few seconds. "No. I don't think so." And he kissed her again. "I'll call you later."

"Okay." Finally able to leave, she thought about how one event, one chance meeting, could change everything.

TWO AND A HALF HOURS LATER, in Harper's kitchen, Kim sat sipping her second cup of coffee when Harper flew in and stopped short. Kim looked up at her boss's crooked grin. *Fabulous.*

"So, young lady. You let dawn kick you in the ass this morning. Out all night, were you?"

Huh? "Am I supposed to check in?"

"And we're defensive."

"Maybe a little. Sorry. I'm not used to answering for my whereabouts."

"I don't mean to pry, but I feel—I don't know—responsible for you.".

"I've been to war, Harper. I promise I can take care of myself."

Harper's face dropped, shocked and more than a little surprised at Kim's response. For a spilt second, she actually looked contrite. "You're right, of course. That was out of line. But we're friends, so I'm going to be crossing that line when I feel it's necessary."

"We are," Kim said. "But if you want me to take what you

145

say in a friendly manner, please phrase it like a friend, not like my mother. Okay?"

"Oh, I..."

"I've always had people telling me what to do, Harper. Trust me, I've seen shit that would bring you to your knees. I don't need anyone telling me what to do anymore."

"I'm sorry. You're right. If you want to talk..."

"I'll let you know."

"I may be late tonight. I have a meeting at 4:30."

"On the calendar. You said not to plan on you until at least seven. Is that still correct?"

"Yes."

"Anna has an appointment at the pediatrician on Wednesday at four o'clock. Do you want to take her or do you want me to?"

"I think I can do it, but can we keep it open?"

"Sure." Kim was marking each item in her iPad, so Harper could see she was serious about her job. But this was a job. She loved Anna, and Harper and Kevin were great friends, but her life was her life.

"Don't be mad, Kim."

"I'm not. Not really. Please try to remember I'm here because you trust me with Anna. I value that, but you also have to trust me with my own life."

"You're right."

Kim took a deep breath having run out of mad. She was tired from being up all night with Owen, but she wasn't a kid and she wasn't going to make excuses for her choices. Especially when one particular choice made her vibrate from the inside out.

Harper took Anna from her highchair and sat with her at

the kitchen table while Kim cleared the dishes. Her phone buzzed in her pocked and she peeked. The text from Owen, a simple *Thinking about you* made her smile.

"I think he's falling for you. Hard."

"Excuse me?"

"Owen."

"I don't know, Harper. He doesn't know me that well." Such a lie. He knew her very well. Intimately. It wasn't all mind-blowing sex, they talked. They talked about everything. It had never been like that with Tom. She and Tom, they had known each other for a long time, but there just wasn't that much to talk about. With Owen she opened up and her soul just spilled out.

"I can't put my finger on it, but he's protective of you. I love you like a sister, and he came after me with a vengeance when he thought I crossed the line. He's never done that before."

Kim sat across from her at the table. "I really like him. I do. But I need you to do something for me."

"What?"

"Stop talking about it."

"But…"

"No. Owen and I have to figure this out on our own. We can't be a project, Harper, no matter how much you want us to happen you have to let it grow on its own."

"Okay. For you. But don't take his crap."

"I won't." She gave Anna's foot a squeeze. "I'm going to throw a load of laundry in, do you need me to do anything for you?"

"No. You know you don't have to do the laundry. We can hire someone to do that."

"I don't mind doing the baby's laundry." She started to move toward the laundry room. "Will I definitely be done by seven tonight?"

"It's probably going to be six thirty, but seven is safe. Why?"

"Because I have an…appointment." *With a very hot Marine.*

Harper nodded. "Well, your *appointment* won't be here before me. He's running the meeting."

"Ah."

"He's a good guy, and I hope it works out. Is he making you happy?"

"So far, yes. I'm keeping my eyes open, but so far, it's good…it's just happening very fast." *Why was she talking about this with her? God, she had to shut up.*

"Sometimes, fast is good," Harper said as she bounced the baby on her knee. "It keeps you from thinking too much."

11

OWEN THOUGHT ABOUT HIS NIGHT WITH KIM *all day long*. He wondered if he'd moved too fast, if what he was feeling wasn't some response to their shared experience. Was he imagining the connection? Was he thinking too much?

Yeah, he was thinking too fucking much.

He liked her. He wanted to be with her. End of story.

Owen was never one to overanalyze. He weighed facts, evaluated, made up his mind quickly, and had good instincts. Now, granted, Kim was messing with his head, his heart, and his libido, but still, he liked being with her.

That night, he called her and picked up Chinese at a little place everyone at work had recommended. She sounded tired —he knew he was. Considering they'd both gotten little sleep the night before it was a wonder either of them was still standing.

At this point, he'd be happy to have dinner with her in front of the TV and let her curl up against him while he watched a ball game. He pulled into the driveway and parked, and miraculously, there was no sign of Harper on the deck. As he walked down the path, he could see Kim outside. She sat on a double chaise on the patio that was tucked against the side of the cottage. He had to give Harper credit. They spared no expense on the place. It was beautiful.

As he got closer, he noticed a book in her lap, but his gorgeous girl wasn't reading, but was, instead, fast asleep. He'd spent at least an hour watching her sleep when she was cuddled in his bed the night before. He decided then, that he didn't think he'd ever get tired of looking at her. He knew her father was Portuguese and her mother was Italian, and the combination gave her the creamiest skin, the most beautiful hair. Owen let one finger brush down her cheek and she stirred ever so slightly. He did it again, and she turned her face in such a way that he could place a soft kiss on her lips. Nothing hot. Nothing dirty.

He did it again and this time, Kim's eyes fluttered open and she smiled under his mouth and stretched. "Mmmm." Her arms came down around his neck and Owen sat on the chaise, facing her, their hips touching. He leaned in, loving how close he could get, and gently kissed her again. Owen caught her scent which was a mix of baby and fresh air and felt like he'd come home. He could do this all day.

"How long have you been here?"

"Only a couple of minutes. I was tempted to let you sleep, you must be exhausted, but the food's going to get cold."

"Ah, we can't let the food get cold."

She grabbed his tie and gave it a tug. "You look so handsome in your suit."

"Yeah? You like the executive look? Because I get a lot of shit for being too uptight."

"I. Like. You."

"A very good thing."

He kissed her again softly, relishing her warmth, her taste. He wanted to absorb all the tiny details. The want for her, the need, welled up inside him.

"Owen, do you know what my kitchen is equipped with?"

"What would that be?" He tucked a lock of hair behind her ear.

"A microwave. An appliance known to be excellent at reheating food."

Yeah, he could love her.

Without another word, Owen swooped in, grabbed Kim while she squealed and threw her over his shoulder.

"Oh, my God! Ahhhh!"

"Quiet, woman. Grab the bag," he growled as they passed the table where he'd left the Chinese food.

He walked into her house, Kim still giggling while she deposited the food on the kitchen counter, all while Owen kept a firm hold on her delicious ass. Kim may have been tiny, but she wasn't skinny. She had gorgeous curves and soft hollows everywhere. He'd loved exploring them the night before.

He found her room and tossed her on the bed with a nice big launch. She bounced and let out a full, expressive laugh. Owen loved how playful she was, and how her smile lit him up from the inside out.

He held himself over her and she reached up and gently stroked a scar that ran from behind his ear and across his chin. It was the tiniest gesture.

"What happened?"

He hesitated because they were supposed to be leaving the

war out of their relationship. "Are you sure you want to know?"

She nodded.

"My first deployment. I was in a knife fight with insurgents we found hiding in a cave. It was a long time ago."

She was examining every inch of it, her gentle touch calming his burn, but not his desire. He still wanted her, maybe even more, but it was different. Her fingers moved, shifting and settling on the back of his neck, where she began to knead and stroke the tension from the muscles.

"Your muscles are like rocks. Tough day?" she asked.

"Just the usual, but I guess I'm still adjusting. There was construction work going on near the office today. It was so loud…"

She understood. It took months for her to stop tensing every time she heard a loud car, or a helicopter overhead. Forget fireworks. That was hell on earth.

"Come on. Off with that shirt and lay on your belly."

"What?"

"You need to relax. There's plenty of time for fun."

Owen pushed off the bed, skeptical, took off his tie and shirt, tossing both on the chair in the corner. The break forced him to take in her space. It was predictably feminine, but not so much so that he felt like he would be swallowed by flowers or anything. All the colors were neutral, ad calming. He expected that was by design. "You know I'll relax if I have a screaming orgasm with you."

"It's not the same thing. Come on." Kim sighed, smiling as he stood there.

"What?" he asked.

"I could look at you all day, you're so beautiful."

"You're just trying to make me forget about the sex," he grumbled.

"Why would I do that?" She was kneeling on the bed, patting the space next to her. He laid on his stomach and Kim ran her hands over the skin of his back. Stopping in different spots where he guessed she was examining more scars.

She started working his muscles, starting at his neck, where she kneaded and pressed the tension away. He may have wanted to do other things with her, but he couldn't deny how good this felt. The woman had great hands. His skin warmed where she laid hands. Owen let himself get lost in her touch, and his body slowly relaxed.

"You let this one get infected." Her voice was small as she stroked a scar on his side. He knew that one well. "What happened?"

"You're going to be disappointed." He smiled into the quilt.

Kim leaned over and pressed a kiss to his cheek. "Tell me."

"I was fourteen. Jason, Nate, and I were trying to get pictures of a woman who swam naked at the beach every night."

"You little pervs. Go on…"

"Well, we got the shots, but she saw us—she and her boyfriend Vito. He was a big guy who wore a straw hat and smoked a short stumpy cigar. He didn't look very athletic, but the man could run. He chased us and we went under a chain link fence, except I misjudged and something tore open my side."

He felt a charge when she ran her finger over it. "It was a mess. I didn't tell my mom and before I knew it, it was infected."

"I bet it hurt like hell when you had it taken care of."

"Oh, God, yes. I thought I was going to die. The nurse who cleaned it out was very thorough. For about six months I told my mother if I got so much as a hangnail."

Kim dug into his back with her fist and after a few more minutes he started to sink into what she was doing. He only felt her hands, the soft quilt beneath him, and the occasional brush of her hair. She was administering long, lingering strokes to his muscles and he wished he could stay here forever.

THE LOW, sleepy rumble that vibrated under her hands told Kim her patient had definitely relaxed. "He sleeps."

Rising from the bed she kissed his cheek, and he shifted position but there was no doubt he was out cold. The air conditioning made the room a little chilly, so she draped a soft throw over him, and again he moved, settling even more into sleep.

"Oh, I can go days without sleep, he says." Glancing over her shoulder as she left her bedroom, Kim giggled. "Big, bad Marine." But then, without any warning, Kim's heart lurched just looking at him. "I think I could fall for you, Owen," she whispered. "Please go easy on me."

OWEN ROLLED AND STRETCHED, feeling something very soft float across his shoulders and when he sat up and got his bearings, he realized he was in Kim's bedroom. The sad part about that revelation was that she wasn't with him. The thorough massage she'd done on his back and neck had put him right out, and his best guess is she'd known that's exactly what would happen.

He didn't know what to make of it. She'd covered him up and let him sleep, not wondering if he was going to spend time with her. She only thought about what he needed.

There were so many ways someone could be selfless. Owen guessed Kim was an expert. There was light coming from the living room, so Owen threw on his shirt to see if he could coax a beautiful lady back to bed. He walked out of the bedroom, following the soft light to Kim. Once he got to the entrance of the living room, he saw her sitting on the sofa reading. Her finger was twirling a lock of hair and everything about her was serene, peaceful. He had already gotten used to her.

Thump, thump.

He knew that sound.

Thump.

"What is it, girl?" Kim said. And then, on cue, Casey's head popped up over the back of the couch. She saw Owen, her ears pinned back and all he could hear was the furious thumping of her tail.

"What the…"

"Oh, look! Your daddy's awake."

The dog vaulted over the back of the couch and made a beeline to Owen. He was stunned, to say the least. What the hell would she do next?

"You want to tell me about this? How long was I asleep?" He checked his watch. Three hours.

"You asked your sister to take care of her?"

He nodded. "She had a layover between her assignments

and she crashed at my place." "Well, she called and I told her you were sleeping."

"You answered my phone?"

"I saw a text come in from her and all it said was SOS. When she called, I picked up. Are you angry?"

"No." He'd crouched down and was rubbing the dog's belly. "Go on."

"Mel got a call, a last minute assignment somewhere in South America, and she had to fly out. I told her to bring Casey here. I didn't want to wake you and the puppy couldn't be alone too much longer. She's so little."

"My sister was here?"

"Yes." Kim had left her place on the couch and was walking towards him. "I like your sister. Again, are you angry?"

He was frozen in place and a warmth spread through him. Kim was truly amazing. "She's good people. I'm sure I'm getting the third degree about you as soon as she gets back. To answer your question, I'm not angry."

"Good. As soon as I picked up your phone, I knew I shouldn't. I mean…"

"It's fine. I don't have a secret life." He had plenty of secrets, though.

"So, umm," Kim said stepping into his space. He really liked it when she did that. "Casey has a leash, a bed, food, and I have bowls she can use. You wanna sleep over?"

Reaching out, Owen pulled her in. There were no words for the simple kindness she'd shown. She let him sleep. She took care of things for him. He liked it.

"I would love to sleep over. Harper won't mind the dog?"

"I checked. She's fine with it."

Kim had thought of everything and Owen was counting himself mighty lucky. "Did you eat?"

"I was waiting for you." Taking his hand, like they'd been together for years, she led him to the kitchen. If any other woman had tried a stunt like this, he'd swear she was looking for a ring. But Kim was doing what she felt was right. Taking care of people was just who she was.

The kitchen table was set for two and she'd transferred the food to dishes. Casey hopped up on a chair in the corner of the living room and curled up like she'd been here forever. He should have been twitchy, the scene was so damned domestic, but he wasn't. He was relaxed. Comfortable.

He was crazy about her.

Owen had returned home from his deployment with a deep urge to settle down, a need to be with someone long term. He'd dated so many women, had so many failures, it was hard to believe that his instincts about Kim, from the very first second he saw her, had been right all along. Everything about her, everything he ever wanted was right here.

He didn't know what he should say or do. There was a part of him that thought they should slow down, mostly so she had time to decide what she wanted. They were caught up in this frenzy of emotions, and he didn't want Kim to feel rushed. On the other hand, he wanted to ask her to marry him.

He was out of his damned mind.

They sat across from each other sharing plates of Mongolian beef and savory dumplings. The room was quiet except for light piano music playing from a little speaker on the counter. It was like they were a family. And it felt strange. Good, but strange.

"You want to tell me what has you furrowing your brow?" Owen looked up from his food to find Kim with her chin resting in her hand and her eyes locked solidly on him.

"I'm just thinking."

"I got that. About what?"

Owen leaned back in his chair, wondering how he was going to say what he wanted to say without sounding like an ass. "I suck at relationships."

"Okay. Why?" Folding her hands on the edge of the table, Kim sat up needle straight.

"I'm probably going to screw this up at first, so bear with me, okay?"

She nodded.

"I suck at relationships because I'm, well, I'm kind of an asshole." She was about to say something, but Owen held up his hand. "I like things my way. I'm a control freak. I think I know better than everyone else, regardless of the subject or situation. Right now, I don't know what to think about us. I'm flying blind."

"I can understand that."

"Yeah? I don't want to rush anything, you know, in case you aren't ready."

"I see." She nodded again, her eyes cast down. "In case I'm not ready. Hmm. You weren't worried about that when you were screwing my brains out last night."

He put his fork down. "I knew I was going to fuck this up. I love being with you. But you've been through a lot…"

"How do you know what I've been through?" She cut him off so quickly, he felt his throat close as her eyes bored a hole into him. "I've told you some things, but there's a lot you don't know. What has you making those kinds of assumptions?"

Tell her! His inner voice screamed. *Tell her now!* He had a chance to come clean, to tell her he did know everything, but he didn't. "You're right, and maybe that's part of it. I like you. A lot. You're smart, funny, beautiful. Your damn near perfect."

"I like you, too. But I'm not perfect. You are, however, right about the asshole thing."

"I know."

"Can I tell you where I stand?"

He nodded.

"I don't know what to think about us either. I've been on three 'dates...'," She moved her fingers in air quotes. "...since I've been home." The last time I went on a first date that led to anything, I was fifteen. It's possible we jumped into bed too soon, and I realize I probably overstepped with your sister and the dog, but all I have is my gut. You have lots of experience with relationships and I'm a novice. I'm sorry if I did something that made you feel uncomfortable."

Damn. She thought he was angry.

"You didn't overstep." He stood and rounded the table. "I'm not used to someone else taking care of things for me."

"I can understand that. We were going to keep things quiet and now your family knows. If you want to slow it down—"

He cut her off before she could say anything else. "I'm taking you out on Saturday night."

"Out? Out where?"

"Dinner. Some place fancy and expensive."

"You don't have to..."

Owen crouched down and took her face in his hands.

"We're going out. I want to. I'm not keeping this quiet. I want to shout from the rooftops that we're seeing each other."

"Okay." Her smile bloomed and his stomach knotted. She'd put her faith in him, trusted him. Now he had to earn that trust.

12

KIM WAS GOING ON A FIRST DATE.

A first date with a guy she'd already slept with, which would probably cause her mother to stroke out. But Owen wasn't content to keep their relationship quiet and Kim was enjoying the fact that she had someone new in her life. That was kind of a miracle.

A bigger one was that she thought she could be in love with him. Which was ridiculous, but there it was.

He was taking her to an upscale, five-star restaurant and Kim had no idea what she was going to wear.

But with one phone call, that all changed. Not two hours later, her mother and two younger sisters showed up on her doorstep. None of them had seen where she was living, so the visit was just as much about letting her family back into her life as it was about getting ready.

She was so nervous about she thought she might get sick. Harper was working on a special project, so she'd gone into the office for a little while that morning. Kevin was off until the afternoon, so he'd claimed a daddy day with Anna, which left Kim hours to think about seeing Owen. And really, it wasn't only about Owen. It was about going on a date. The first real date she'd been on in years.

There were two very important things going on here. First was the fact that she was going out on a real, honest to goodness date, but the bigger part was that she was going out with someone other than Tom. Something she thought would never happen.

Her bedroom looked like a department store dressing room on sale day. Clothes were thrown everywhere. Unfortunately, nothing was right. This past year, Kim had spent most of her time in jeans or yoga pants. Before that she was in scrubs most of the time. The time she and Tom had together wasn't spent going out to fancy restaurants—they didn't go out anywhere. They were simply trying to keep up with each other.

Owen not only represented a new chance at love, but a whole new life.

Her mother walked into the bedroom and put her hands on her hips. Lucia Torres took no crap from anyone, especially her six children, but her heart was as big as the ocean, and Kim was in need of her mother's help.

"You have a problem," she said.

Kim nodded. "He told me I should dress up. I was so dazed, I just said okay not even thinking that I didn't have a thing to wear."

"Not a problem." Her sister Joelle walked into the room and dropped a garment bag that looked to be stuffed to bursting on her bed. She made a slow turn around the room and nodded. "This is very nice," she said. "I love the open living area out there. I wish my apartment had this much space."

Joelle, whom they called Joey for short, was twenty-six and a rising star on Wall Street. She looked just like Kim, with long dark wavy hair and grey-green eyes, and unlike their other siblings, who were all tall, she was short. Coupling that with her exceptional and expensive taste in clothes, she was a one woman styling team. And a lone miracle, until her seventeen year old baby sister Olivia walked in the room. Olivia was going to Yale in the fall and personified the term beauty and brains. Between them, Kim started to feel a smaller glimmer of hope that her outfit wouldn't be a complete disaster.

Her mother was leaning against her dresser with her arms folded. "You said there was no one else. That was a little over a week ago. What changed?"

What had changed? "He was persistent. " *And perfect.* "I've never been a believer in chemistry, but it seems we have it. In spades."

Olivia sat on the bed next to Kim and grinned. "Tell us about him."

"His name is Owen Kent. He's the chief information officer of the software company Harper works for and he's a Marine officer. Reserves. He just got home a little over a month ago."

"He's a Marine?" Joey pursed her lips and unzipped the garment bag. "Honey, you really want to go there again?"

"I didn't think so, but he's not a lifer, like Tom. He has a career outside the corps. Did I mention he's a billionaire?"

That got their attention. First there was silence. Then seeing all their faces wash with shock was worth their meddling. "Whoa," Olivia said. "A billionaire? With a "B?"

"That would be a yes. He founded and built Reliance Software with his two high school friends."

"Reliance. They're the biggest player in the field of financial security software. He's a billionaire a few times over is my guess." Joey pulled a blue dress out of the bag. "Nice work! A billionaire. Let's knock his socks off."

Her mother sat in the chair in the corner of the room and watched as her sisters found Kim the right dress and shoes and helped her with hair and makeup. It was like they hadn't been apart all these months. It made Kim vow she wouldn't separate herself from her family again. As she stood in front of the mirror and adjusted the skirt of the navy blue jersey dress, she smiled. It was perfect. Modern, feminine, sexy, the dress had a softly draped cowl top that let her show a hint of cleavage and an asymmetrical skirt that showed off her legs without being too short. Olivia had brought a pair of strappy high-heeled sandals and some chunky jewelry, and when Kim caught a glimpse of herself in the mirror, her nerves ebbed. She had to admit it. She looked good. She didn't look over done, but she didn't look like her normal nannying self either. Kim looked pulled together, sophisticated.

She hoped Owen would notice.

"Hellllooo?" Harper's voice came drifting through the house.

"We're in the bedroom," Kim called.

"Hey, I heard you're going out on the town." Harper entered the room, looking every bit the executive with her slim skirt and silk top. Well, you couldn't count the bunny slippers on her feet. Harper always kicked off the five inch heels as soon as she walked through the door and put on the bunny slippers Kevin gave her when they moved into the house. "Hey there, everyone. I'm Harper."

Her friend shook hands with her family and then when the introductions were done, stood back, hands on her hips and gave Kim a good once over. She held up her index finger and indicated that Kim should turn around. Once the fashion show was over, Harper nodded. "Very nice. Owen's gonna die." Harper shot a smile at Mom. "I can't wait."

"So, I look okay?"

"You look better than okay. That dress is perfect for you. You're gorgeous."

Kim nodded and breathed out. "What time is it?"

Olivia looked at her phone. "Seven fifteen."

"Owen is always early," Harper said. "But we do have enough time for a glass of wine. Kevin just put the chicken on the barbeque."

Harper left the room, and grabbed a bottle of Pinot Noir and some glasses. "I just opened this and thought I should bring it by. A little liquid courage never hurt, right?"

Kim would take whatever she could get, but she had to remember not to have more than one glass when she was out with Owen. She got silly when she was drunk. She didn't need to be silly. But who knows? Maybe that's exactly what she needed.

"So, Harper. What can you tell us about this man?" Her mom went right to the point. She didn't know what she was going to do with the information, but it warmed Kim's heart to feel her mother's protectiveness.

Taking a long drink from the glass in her hand, Harper smiled. "Owen is one of the best people I know. Strong, honest, smart. He's an excellent businessman and a better friend. He'll take good care of her."

"We've heard that before," Joey said under her breath.

Kim let her sister's words sink in. "What do you mean?"

"I mean Tom may have loved you, but he didn't know how lucky he was to have you. I get the feeling things weren't as perfect as you wanted everyone to believe."

"I didn't know you felt that way." All those years she was with Tom, her family never said a word about him.

"I don't want to talk badly about him now, I mean the man's gone, but don't sell yourself short, Kim. Don't. I don't care if Owen is a billionaire. If he doesn't treat you like a princess, like he's the luckiest man in the world because you're with him, drop him."

"You deserve the best, my girl," her mother said. "I wish I could stay and see him. I could tell a lot by the way he looks at you."

"You can stay. Come have dinner with me and Kevin. There's plenty. You three can get a look at Owen, and he'll never know."

"Harper..." that's the last thing she needed. Kim was nervous enough. Although the thought of showing him off to her family was really appealing.

"Oh, I don't know," her mom replied. "That's so sneaky."

"It's perfect," Olivia said. "I want to see the guy. Is he hot?"

"Smoldering. Tall, dark, built. He's taken to sporting a lovely scruff."

Joey nodded. "I wanna get a look at that."

"Wonderful. I'll go set some extra places at the table. He'll never know."

"You aren't going to fool him, Harper." Kim had only known Owen a few weeks, but he had a first class bullshit detector. He'd figure out something was going on.

"Don't you spoil our fun," Harper drawled. Every once in a while, Harper channeled her mother who came from the Deep South. Usually, when she was trying to be charming. "Come on ladies, let's get this place set right and I will introduce you to my delicious baby and her daddy."

Joey leaned in and whispered in Kim's ear. "She's hot stuff and I cannot wait to see this guy. But I mean it—be the princess."

Hugging her sister, Kim was happy. For the first time in a long time, she was really happy.

"Okay, as I suspected, he's early. Kevin texted me. He just saw Owen's car pull in."

Kim walked everyone to the door and giggled as they scurried up the path, past the pool to the deck at the back of the house. It left her with a few minutes to gather her thoughts.

OWEN PULLED his car alongside the house and parked his new Aston Martin next to Harper's SUV. He'd gotten hell from his sister two weeks ago when he took delivery of two cars both with price tags that could feed a third world country. The Rover was practical. It would get him and the dog to and from work in any weather. This car, though. This was his toy and it was one of the completely outrageous luxuries he'd allowed himself since coming back. Sure, he had his house and a sailboat, but compared to how he could *afford* to live, Owen was happy with his relatively modest lifestyle.

Kevin stepped out of the backyard and shook his head at the car. "A Vanquish? You bought a Vanquish?"

"Why do people have a problem with this?" Owen reached in and grabbed the bouquet of flowers from the back seat before he closed the door.

"I don't, I'm jealous. It's fucking hot."

Owen smiled. "It's unbelievable. I've never driven anything like it."

"Taking Kim out?" Kevin had now assumed the big brother posture and Owen was impressed with how loyal people had become to Kim in such a short amount of time. He knew she was special and that was playing out in the way people tried to protect her.

"Yeah, just dinner. I thought we'd head to Huntington."

"Harper's worried."

Owen took a few steps toward the path that led to the backyard and thought about what he should say. He stopped. Turned. On one hand he wanted to ease Kevin's mind, who would, in turn, ease Harper's. It unnerved Owen himself, because deep down, he didn't understand why or how he'd come to feel so strongly about a woman he was still getting to know. As to whether or not this whole situation made sense wasn't for him to decide. It was for her. Owen was going to give Kim everything he had, and hope she'd feel the same.

He couldn't explain what happened to him in that hospital a year ago. He was a guy who led with his brain and made decisions based on facts that had been carefully analyzed. Sure he liked his fun, the car he'd just pulled up in was proof of how much he liked fun, but his heart was never involved. Now it was.

"I'm not going to hurt her. I care about her. A lot."

"She's like family. Be careful."

"Count on it." He knew there was something else he needed to say, but it was the kind of leap Owen never thought he'd make in his life. "I think she could be the one."

"Seriously?"

"Yeah. There's a lot we still have to work out, but I've never been more serious in my life."

He'd start working things out tonight by telling her that he'd been Tom's commanding officer. He couldn't avoid it and while some may have called the collision of their worlds coincidence, he believed it was fate. And since he'd never believed in fate before, that was something worth paying attention to.

As Owen walked down the path to the cottage, he spied Harper with three other women on the back deck. She waved and smiled. "Hey there, Owen. Have a good time tonight."

He waved back and wondered why the older woman who was sitting with her was scowling at him. He glanced at the two younger women and one of them made him do a double take. Interesting.

KIM JUST FINISHED PUTTING the last of her clothes away, in record time no less, when she heard a knock on the door. Making one last check in the mirror, she took a deep breath and applied a quick coat of lip gloss. This was going to be a fun evening. They'd go out. They'd have a nice meal and some conversation. It would be fun.

Then Kim opened the door, got one look at him, and wondered how long it would take to get him into her bed.

"Wow," he said. "You look beautiful."

"Thank you." He handed her the flowers, and she felt heat rush to her cheeks. The gesture was so wonderfully sweet and innocent, and there was nothing sweet or innocent about what Kim wanted to do to him.

"You brought me flowers."

"I would have brought you the whole flower shop if I could, but no bloom compares with the bloom on your cheeks."

The delivery was flawless, but the twinkle in his eyes told her she was being played. "Another cheesy line?"

"I've got a million of 'em."

Kim groaned, but loved their running joke. She loved that they had something that was theirs, even if it was something so silly.

He took the flowers from her and laid them on the counter as he turned Kim to face him. Owen's hands, which were roughened from a year in the desert, gently cradled her face. She didn't resist. Didn't hesitate covering his hands with hers. When they first met, she thought her reaction to him was lust, but looking into the deep blue of his eyes, seeing the emotion there, her heart told another story when it cracked open and let him in. It was too soon, she knew it, but there was no stopping what they were about to start. It might be a mistake, but it was a risk Kim was willing to take.

Owen dipped his head and finally their kiss sealed what they'd been heading toward. She'd only known him a few weeks, but it felt so much longer—like forever. Like he understood all she'd gone through, and he gave her exactly what she needed.

His lips gently teased hers, coaxing her deeper and deeper into him. When she eased her arms around his neck and pulled him down, pulled him in, everything exploded like a sunburst. She felt the muscles of his shoulders bunch, his fingers threaded through her hair as he held her so he could make the kiss count.

He left her mouth and nipped along her jaw and neck and Kim let his name go on a breath. For that moment, that place in time, he totally owned her, but she could feel in his touch, in the way he held her, there was a desperation and her hold on him was just as strong, maybe stronger. He was a big man —controlled, commanding, intimidating—but for the first time, Kim saw the power was in her hands.

"Owen?" She took his face in her hands and held him, gazing into his eyes. "What is it?"

"I need you like I need air." His hands settled on her waist. "I don't think you understand what you mean to me."

"I do," she whispered before kissing his brow, his cheek, his lips. The stubble on his cheek was rough as she ran her hand over his face. "Let me get the flowers in water. We should go. I think...I think we both have to get a hold on what's happening between us."

Owen rested his forehead against hers and breathed out, taking her hands in his. When he tilted his head back a grin ticked at the corner of his mouth. "You're right. I don't know what got into me."

"It's me too. You do *something* to me, and I don't understand it."

"Maybe it's lust."

"I thought about that, but I don't think this is just about sex. Do you?"

"No..." He smiled, mischief twinkling in his eyes. "But we could find out."

"Later, I promise." Kim giggled and hugged him close, loving how she felt when his arms closed around her.

"You're right. We can't with your family sitting on the deck with Harper, pretending *not* to be your family."

She laughed. "I told them you'd figure it out. Harper's like, *'Nah, he won't.'* But I knew you would."

Owen let go of Kim long enough so she could settle her bouquet in water and fix her hair and lipstick. "You knew I'd spot your family?"

"I did. Harper totally underestimated you."

"She often does. Who's on the deck?"

"My mom, my sister, Joey and my youngest sister, Olivia."

"Ah. Are they checking me out?"

"Probably. I'm sure Olivia will have a lot to say about you. Joey is more cautious. "

"I guess you field all types when you have a big family. Was it fun? All those siblings?"

"Tons. It's also insanity in a bottle."

He laughed, deep and full, perching himself on a barstool near the kitchen island, he pulled her between his legs and kissed her forehead. Kim's heart smiled.

"We have to go so there's enough time for me to meet your mother and still make our reservation."

Had she heard him right? "You want to meet my mom?"

"Of course I do. And your sisters."

Now her heart was singing. Talk about doing everything right. "Oh, okay."

"Is it a problem?"

How could she tell him it was one more thing that set him

apart from every other guy? He knew, instinctively, that her family was important. "No." She kissed him. "No problem at all. You really are perfect." Another kiss. "Let me freshen up and we can go."

He gave her butt a gentle smack and Kim loved the affection and familiarity that went with something like that. Looking in her mirror she made sure she didn't have sex hair and that her makeup didn't look like she'd just had a wicked make out session. Then again, what the hell?

HE LEFT the cottage holding Kim's hand and feeling settled, content. The past few weeks had him thinking he might have been crazy. He didn't lose control of his feelings like this, he didn't jump into relationships with both feet, yet he couldn't help feeling that with Kim he was right where he was supposed to be, that he knew she was the one the minute he laid eyes on her a year ago. They walked up the path and he smiled when he saw Kevin shooting him warning glances while Harper tried to look casual with Kim's family. Kim had told him about how they'd come over for a fashion intervention and then Harper invited them to stay and spy.

When they stepped onto the deck, all conversation stopped. Harper smiled, and turned on her affected Southern charm. "Hello there," she drawled. She wasn't really from the south, but her mother was and that was enough to have Harper sounding like she was the reincarnation of Scarlet O'Hara. "Well don't y'all look nice," she said. "Ready to leave?"

Kim nodded. "Yes, but Owen thought he should meet my family before we left."

Harper leaned back and folded her arms. Kevin didn't miss a beat. He pointed at his fiancée with the tongs he was using to turn the chicken and smirked. "I told you he'd get it."

Owen extended his hand to her mom, not giving Harper the chance to comment. "Mrs. Torres, it's a pleasure. I'm Owen Kent."

"Mr. Kent."

"Please call me Owen. Ladies," he said to her sisters, "I knew you were all related because there's no mistaking the resemblance." He turned his attention back to Mom. "You have lovely daughters, ma'am."

"It's very nice to meet you, Owen. Now that the weather is getting warmer, you'll have to come home with Kim for Sunday picnic."

He didn't know what Sunday picnic was all about, but he wasn't going to say no. "I'd love that."

"Good. We'll look forward to it." Her mother stood and hugged Kim. He wasn't sure, but he thought he heard her whisper *Keeper* in Kim's ear. "I appreciate that you stopped to meet me. I really do. Thank you."

He nodded before leading Kim off the deck, threading his fingers through hers. Once she settled into the seat of the Aston Martin and he got into the driver's seat, she lunged at him, wrapping him tightly in her arms. "What?"

"Thank you. You made her so happy. Thank you."

"It wasn't anything. Just trying to do the right thing, but I'm glad it made you happy."

"I've known you for such a short time, but you think about me. Like I matter. Thank you." She leaned over and gave him a peck on his cheek.

Of course she mattered and she'd been mattering to him

for longer than a few days. He released her hand and she sat back, buckling her seatbelt. Her faith in him was comforting, but he couldn't help feeling anxious. He'd do his best not to let her down - he just hoped she still felt that way when she found out what he was hiding.

13

OWEN PULLED INTO THE PARKING LOT OF GRILL, A very upscale steakhouse right on Huntington Harbor. Kim had been here in the past for drinks with friends, so she knew that it had atmosphere to spare. The main dining rooms faced the harbor and there were a series of outside decks that housed a bar, seating, and tables for outdoor dining.

He pulled forward and slipped the valet a couple of bills before he'd even parked the car. He pointed to a space right in front, telling the young man that he'd prefer his car to be parked right there.

"Worried about the car?"

"It's worth it to me to tip the kid now to keep the car safe. I don't do the rich guy thing often, but I do it with my car."

"What happened to your Range Rover? I thought it was new?"

"It is. When I got home I splurged and bought both. I never do that. Jason has three houses and a friggin' yacht. Nate has a house in the Hamptons that's big enough to house a whole platoon."

"It's not an indictment. I'm just wondering."

"The car is visible and flashy, that's not me, but I love the damn thing."

She couldn't argue with him. Nothing about Owen was ostentatious. He worked hard, served his country. She guessed a car was something that made him happy. "So what kind of car is that?"

"It's an Aston Martin."

"Like James Bond?"

Settling his hand on the small of her back as they walked toward the restaurant, Owen smiled at her. "Yeah."

Kim couldn't resist teasing him. Especially when she could do it in a British accent. "Kent. Owen Kent."

"Stop." he laughed. "I don't need you doing this to me, too."

"Excuse me?" Kim and Owen turned to see a middle aged man leaving the restaurant point to Owen's car. Owen stopped and she could see he puff up a little. Such a guy.

"Yes?"

"Is that an Aston Martin Vanquish?"

Owen smiled like a kid showing off a new toy. "It is."

The man turned to the valet standing next to him and cast a glance toward the shiny black vehicle. "That's a quarter of a million dollar car."

"No shit?" The valet said.

The kid's eyebrows shot up and Kim wondered if hers did too. A quarter of a million dollars? Glancing at Owen, the flush creeping up his neck told her he was embarrassed.

It didn't take much either. While it was obvious he loved the car, then showiness made him uncomfortable.

The man, who was in a silky black shirt and grey pants

folded his arms and gave Kim the same kind of once over he'd given the car. "Hot car and a beautiful girl. Money sure does buy happiness."

That was a new one. She'd been called a lot of things, but no one ever insinuated she had a price tag. Part of her wanted to give the guy a piece of her mind, but Owen handled him perfectly.

"Yeah, the car I could buy. It's a cool machine, but the lady here?" He took her hand and kissed it. "I'm just lucky on that one. Real lucky she'd have me."

Well if that didn't just make her want to drag him right back home. The exchange didn't last long after that. Any interest Owen had in talking to the man evaporated when he made the comment about money.

Owen had lots of money. But Kim was getting the sense he wasn't all that comfortable with it.

They were escorted to an outdoor table with a gorgeous view of the water. It was very warm for the middle of June, and she was happy they could enjoy the perfect weather. Boats dotted the harbor and bobbed up and down on the gentle ebb and flow of the tide. The sun was just sinking down, closing in on the horizon, and she had a date with a man who seemed too good to be true.

And that thought kept wiggling through her mind no matter how many times she told herself to just let it go.

"I'm sorry about that guy out there."

"What? Why are you sorry?"

"I mean I know what he meant, but to say something like that in front of you pissed me off."

"That was pissed off? You were very smooth." He had been, too. It seemed nothing ruffled Owen.

He grinned as he placed his napkin in his lap. "I have a bad temper. It takes me a long time to get there, but I've scared more than one person. Including a few hard ass Marines."

The word hard ass got her thinking. "How are things between you and Harper? It seems better."

"It still gets a little dicey at work. Nate and Jason are very hands off and she pretty much ran the place. I respect Harper tremendously, but this is our business, and I think we need to be making the decisions." He slumped back in his chair and fiddled with his fork. "They understand and are fine with me taking that role, but Harper is pissed."

"You'll win her over."

"I'm not as close to Harper. She keeps her distance from me."

"That's because you challenge her. I get the sense she's gotten used to getting things to go her way." Kim took a sip of water. "By the way, I've been meaning to ask how it's going with your vets."

"Still having issues. It's just not right. I need someone like you to work for me."

Kim raised an eyebrow. It sparked an idea. "I'm happy to help Helen. What if I see if Harper can spare me for a couple of days and I can get Helen some names and numbers?"

"You'd do that?" He physically relaxed and looked so relieved. Kim felt a snap of pride. She loved that she could help him.

"Of course. Whatever you need."

He nodded slowly, taking in what she said. She could see his gears turning as he fiddled again with his fork. "Speaking of vets, we have to start talking about our own experiences.

There are some things you need to know about me before you decide to take this forward."

He was suddenly so formal, and Kim didn't know what was circling around his brain. But whatever it was seemed serious.

It was Kim's turn to reply. But she didn't have anything to say. Her heart was tripping against her ribs wondering what he was going to tell her. He was right. They had to talk. He needed to know all her baggage, everything she brought to the relationship including her trust issues, and she needed to know his. But at that moment, all she saw when she looked at Owen were the possibilities he represented. The intensity of what she was feeling could have overwhelmed her, but instead, Kim decided to put her worries on hold and let the wave take her.

HE WANTED to talk to her about what happened that day in the hospital. She needed to know the truth, if for no other reason than to tell her he thought her fiancé was an idiot. Tom may have been a good Marine, but he didn't deserve her.

Owen didn't think he deserved her either. He thought about taking the leap and telling her he loved her. It wasn't a lie. In fact, it was the truest thing in his life. His worry was that Kim wasn't ready to hear it. Especially when she found out they had a history she didn't remember.

"I want you to know, being asked to get you at Starbucks that day was the best thing that's ever happened to me."

"Owen..."

"No, you don't understand. My last tour was a nightmare. I lost half a dozen men under my command."

She didn't say anything but reached for him across the table. They linked hands and Owen hoped it would give him the strength to tell her everything, knowing he might lose her. "You know how it was. Everything was quiet, boring almost, and then all hell would break loose. There'd be mortars or someone would buy it on an IED. No warning. They'd just be gone.

He was describing what happened to Tom, and whether she realized he was doing it on purpose or not, she teared up.

"I watched too many men die, and saw how it affected their commanders." Kim squeezed his hand. "Knowing you, I can only imagine how hard it was. You don't blame yourself, do you?"

He thought about that. Did he? "Not directly. But I feel responsible for everyone under my command. I'm not suffering from PTSD like a lot of guys. I don't have flashbacks and nightmares, I'm not wired like that, but I think about the guys. About their families. I wonder why some make it, and others don't."

"There's no reason and I think that's what makes it so hard. You're methodical. And you're a man. There's nothing for you to wrap your head around."

"I guess."

"You can't fix it. No matter how hard you try."

"You seemed to have it figured out."

"Me? Hardly. I've just gotten good at faking it."

Owen reached out and tucked a stray lock of hair behind her ear. "You never have to fake it with me. Never."

He sensed by the way she smiled, by the tears pricking at her eyes, she already knew this.

He took her hand and left a gentle kiss on her palm. Her

face flushed to that perfect shade of pink that told him he'd hit the desire switch. It seemed fair. He wanted her so bad it hurt. Pretty much all the time.

Based on the way she was looking at him, she felt the same way.

"Kim? Is that you, honey?"

"Oh, no," she whispered.

He turned in the direction of the voices and approaching them was a round woman and man, both with unnaturally dark hair. Turning back, he saw Kim in a flat stare. Her eyes were locked and focused straight ahead. The color had left her face. There was no movement. Nothing.

He couldn't hear what she muttered when she pinched her eyes shut, but by the time the couple got to their table, she'd managed to compose herself.

"It is you! Oh, darling, it's so good to see you."

Kim stood and allowed the older couple the kiss her cheeks. Owen rose as well and positioned himself right next to her. "Zia Bunny, Zio Marco, good to see you both."

"What are you doing here?" Bunny asked as she looked Owen up and down.

Kim laid her hand on Owen's bicep. "This is Owen Kent. We were having dinner." She glanced up at him, and for a split second he saw terror in her eyes. These two people had his girl seriously spooked. "Owen, may I present Bunny and Marco Albanese."

Marco shook his hand. "Her fiancé's aunt and uncle. We've known Kimmy since she was a teenager."

Aunt Bunny leaned in, her face solemn. "This isn't a date, is it? I mean Tommy hasn't even been dead a year."

Owen let his hand drift up and down over her back, hopefully letting her know he was right there if she needed him. But Kim didn't hesitate. She went all in.

"Yes, it is, actually. Our first." He grinned. Technically, it was their first date. "I met Owen a couple of weeks ago and we hit it off."

Marco leaned in, and Owen didn't like his posture. It was aggressive, hostile, threatening. "You should be ashamed of yourself young lady," the uncle snarled. "Your man died for his country. Show some respect."

Respect? Granted, Albanese didn't deserve to die, but he'd be hard pressed to use the word respect when talking about him, especially inside a relationship. But what was burning his ass was the way these people thought they could talk to her. It was like she was wearing a tag that said "Property of the Albanese Family."

"Have you no heart? Think of what his family is going through. Couldn't you at least wait a year?" Bunny's voice was getting louder and louder, and Kim was shrinking into him. What the hell? Kim had nerves of steel and didn't back away from anything. And as far as having a heart, no one he knew had a bigger or more sensitive one.

They were shaming her for moving on with her life.

Not while Owen was there. Not while she was with him. No one was going to talk to her like that. "That's enough." Owen said quietly. "Sir, I think you and your wife should move along."

"Who are you to tell us to move along? How dare you?" Bunny put on an offended air that only a woman of her age could pull off. Marco on the other hand was meaner, and Owen could see that. The old man was just about to open his mouth again when Owen laid a hand on Marco's shoulder.

"Don't say another word. If you do, if you hurt her any more than you already have, I will make you sorry for it."

Marco, was easily thirty years older than Owen and a full head shorter. Owen probably should have felt guilty threatening him, but when it came to protecting someone he loved, nothing else mattered.

Owen considered himself a mild mannered guy. He was slow to anger, didn't succumb to things like road rage or getting angry at store clerks or food service workers. No, as a rule, he was pretty laid back.

But his reaction wasn't about someone cutting him off on the expressway. This was about Kim and he'd discovered last year, when he held her in that hospital, that he was hard wired to protect this woman.

Bunny and Marco left without another word, and Kim turned into him, resting her head on his shoulder. "I'm sorry about that. If you want to go…"

He pulled her close and pressed his lips against her hair just so she'd know there was nothing to worry about. "Only if you want to."

"I don't want to leave. I just feel bad they spoiled it, and now they're going to go back to Tom's family and tell them everything." She sat down, hoping no one paid attention to the scene.

Following her lead, he sat, but kept hold of her hand. "Jenna's going to have your back. I think she likes me."

"She does, but you don't understand. The Albanese's will swallow you up. They're good people. Very close. Loyal. But being with them is like being sucked into a tornado."

"They have to know you'd move on, Kim. You're young. They can't expect you to mourn their son your whole life."

"Oh, but they do. Bunny and Marco are the worst of the bunch. Both are petty gossips, who have wicked mean streaks. Most of the family barely tolerates them, but they have a story to tell now, so everyone will listen."

All of a sudden it hit Owen. They'd tell the Albanese's the name of the man she was with and that's when it would be on. He'd written a letter to them. Tom's mother had written back. They'd make the connection and then all hell would break loose.

"You probably think I'm a horrible person," she sighed. "I should still be mourning him. I shouldn't be ready to move on."

"Why do you think that? You're ready when you're ready."

"It's just, there were things about Tom no one knew but me. Everyone thinks he's a saint, but he hurt me and while no one should have suffered like he did, and he did suffer…it was awful…I'm not grieving."

She wasn't grieving because the best Owen could figure, Kim knew she'd lost Tom Albanese long before that bomb exploded. The two of them had to talk. She had to know the truth about him and his connection to the whole ordeal last year. He was hoping it would bring them closer, that Kim would see that he understood. That he knew why she hurt so badly.

"I'm sorry," she said. "I was the one who wanted to keep the war out of things."

"I do understand your reasons, but we can't avoid it anymore."

"I know. I'm a little nervous to find out about you. We've gotten so close, so fast and the more I think about it, there's a lot I don't know, isn't there?"

He watched her sip her wine and the need to hold her close washed over him. She did that to him, made him want. Need. "Let's get some dessert and take it back to my house. You're right. There are things we have to talk about."

Her hair was falling across her face, dark and rich, the gold highlights picked up and she tucked it behind her ear, allowing him to see her eyes flash. There was no denying that things between them were about to change. "You have nothing to be afraid of. Nothing. My only concern is you. It always has been."

"Always? What does that mean?" She was hyperaware, picking up on every word, every detail.

"Let's go to my house, we'll get away from all the people and the noise and I'll tell you. Just promise me you'll hear me out right to the end before you say or do anything."

"Is this bad?"

"No, but it's important."

KIM DIDN'T KNOW what was going on, but ever since meeting Bunny and Marco, Owen was wrapped pretty tight. He said what they had to talk about wasn't bad, but *important*. Was he married with a wife tucked away near one of the bases? *No, that would be considered bad.*

She couldn't imagine what he had to say. That was a lie. She could imagine plenty. But at the same time, Kim trusted Owen and she had to hang onto that. As they walked to the valet, he barely said a word and she couldn't for the life of her put her finger on why he was so tense. Just as they pulled out of the parking lot, her cell phone pinged. It was the sound she'd assigned to Jenna's text messages.

Fishing in her bag, Kim really didn't even have to look. She knew Marco and Bunny were already at work, butting into her life and making it a living hell.

The text was predictable. *OMG! Crazy aunt and uncle. I am so sorry you guys had to deal with that.*

How is your mom? Kim didn't really want to know this part, but if she was going to get the information anyway, she might as well control the conversation.

Sobbing in her room. I'm sorry. I shouldn't have told you that. Jenna shouldn't be apologizing, but her batty relatives should feel badly for upsetting her mother.

Please don't apologize – it's not your fault. I don't want her upset. Have you told them you already know about us?

Not yet.

And she probably wouldn't because Jenna was Jenna. For all her free-wheeling, devil-may-care attitude, her family was everything.

Kim turned to look at Owen. "It's gotten to the Albaneses."

"Is that Jenna?"

"Yes."

In truth, Kim shouldn't care. She should be able to do what she wanted with her life when she was ready, but the family had meant something in her life and deep down, Kim had hoped they might be happy for her. But with their own grief, they couldn't be happy for anyone and they weren't ready to let go.

Oh, shit, Kim... The text had a tone, which was unusual in itself, that made her take notice, not that texts or emails could do much of anything with regard to mood or feeling, but Kim had a horrible feeling about this one.

Owen pulled in his driveway, threw the car into gear, and took her phone.

There were times when pure raw instinct took over and this was one of those times. "Hey! Why did you do that?"

"I need to talk to you before the next text comes in."

Kim pressed her back into the seat. She didn't go after the phone. Instead she mentally prepared herself because she knew something awful was about to go down, something that she wasn't prepared for.

"First, I want to tell you something I've never said to anyone. I've been dancing around it, but before this all comes crashing down, I want you to know that I'm falling in love with you. I know it's only been a few weeks, but that's how I feel. This can be amazing between us, Kim. Please believe that."

"Owen," Kim reached for him, but he pulled back. Now she was starting to freak out.

"Honey, this wasn't the way I planned any of this. I don't know how to explain what brought us together. Maybe it was fate, the planets aligning, I don't know. I just know you are in my life and I don't want you to leave. How you got here doesn't matter."

"You're rambling. I don't understand." Another ping hit her phone. Then another. "Are you going to give that back to me?"

"No. No, what's on this phone you need to hear from me."

"You don't know what she's saying. They're upset."

"I get that. I know why." The iPhone was in his lap, only a bit of it visible under his suit jacket.

"It's because I'm dating again. And it could be serious."

"I wish that was it."

"What are you talking about? How can you possibly know?"

"I do know. More than you think."

"What's this all about, Owen?" Her mind was going in too many directions.

"It's about Afghanistan."

"I wish we could just forget about it. Nothing good came from us being there. Nothing."

"We can't just forget." He swallowed hard, and his large hand slid into the hair behind her ear while his thumb softly brushed her cheek. "There's no easy way for me to tell you this, but I knew Tom."

"YOU—EXCUSE ME?" There was nothing subtle about an emotional body slam. He could see her whole world being knocked out of balance. Tears flooded her eyes. "You knew him?"

"I was his commanding officer."

"I don't understand. How is it…"

"I was only in command of the unit for two weeks before he was killed, but I took care of contacting his family and I…" He stopped because this next line was going to kill what had started between them. "I knew about you."

"Me?"

"I went through his personal effects. I saw letters and pictures you'd sent to him. I knew you were stationed at the hospital. I even drove over there at one point to see you." He was leaving out a big part of this story, but he couldn't do it, not the way she was reacting.

"Oh, my God," she whispered. Grief poured off of her. It

was painful to watch, and Owen just wanted to hold her, comfort her. Without warning, she released her seat belt and got out of the car. He watched her as she made her way down the path to the water and stood at the edge of the dock. He didn't go after her immediately, giving her the space she needed, but then it was too much to let her handle it on her own. So he got out of the car to be with her.

Owen's mind was racing. He knew on one hand he should have pushed back on her rule that all talk of the war was off limits and told her immediately that he knew Tom. On the other hand, there'd been something really good about their getting to know each other without his ghost hovering around. For all he knew, if he'd told Kim the truth, she would have slammed the door shut and he'd have had no chance to get in.

No, not being with her wasn't an option. He'd take his hits for not telling her, then he would fix it. He loved her and unless he was reading her all wrong, she felt the same. That had to count for something.

He approached, not knowing what to say. He'd just torn open wounds she'd spent a year healing. She was still at the end of the dock, her arms folded protectively across her middle. She was hurting. Just like the day he met her in Kandahar. The day he held her. He had no idea if she'd let him hold her again, but Owen stepped behind her and wrapped his arms around her, pulling her close. He bent his head close to her ear, "I did not mean to hurt you, please believe that."

"When you met me in Starbucks, you already knew who I was? You read my letters and..." She pulled in a great gulp of air, stepped away and turned. "Has this been fun for you? How much do you know?"

Owen hesitated. "I know everything. I know about Corporal Lynn. I know you were sent home."

Kim was crying, quietly now, much like the day when Tom died. Owen couldn't handle watching her stand there, breaking apart because of him. He needed to hold her, so he gathered her in his arms. She fought him, but barely. "Don't, shhh. Don't push me away."

"I should though. You lied to me."

"No. I would have told you sooner, but you wanted to keep the war out of everything. And in some ways that wasn't a bad thing."

That excuse didn't fly and Kim pushed out of his arms. "So you lying to me, is my fault?"

"No. I didn't mean that. Shit." He scrubbed his hands over his face. "Of course it's not."

It went silent between them, only for a few seconds, but it felt like hours.

"I can't stay here. I…I have to think about all this."

Kim stepped back and now the silence was replaced by a chill. He couldn't let her leave without getting her to understand. "Can I tell you what I think?" he said.

She looked at him, her eyes stormy, like the ocean. "What?"

"I think your fiancé was one lucky bastard. I don't think he knew how good he had it and he took you for granted." Swallowing hard, Owen tugged her hand and she collapsed into him, her face buried in his chest. "And if you can find it in your heart to forgive me for not telling you who I was right away, I promise I will never make the same mistakes."

He cupped her cheek and marveled at the softness of her skin. When she leaned into his hand, Owen felt like there might be hope. "Don't end this before it has a chance to begin," he pleaded. "It's so good between us and it could be better."

"…"

"But nothing." He slipped two fingers beneath her chin and made her look at him. "I know you've been hurt, but promise me you'll a least think about us before you tell me to get lost."

She sniffled then reached out, to stroke his cheek. "I don't want to tell you to get lost."

"No?"

"No, but I'm going to need some time."

"You can have whatever you need."

She nodded and stepped away, and he missed her already.

He watched helplessly as she wiped her eyes.

"Could you take me home now?"

"Kim…"

"Owen, I can't stay here. I feel…manipulated."

"I'm sorry. That's never what I wanted. I just wanted to be with you. From the first moment I saw you."

She nodded and gave his hand a gentle squeeze. "Take me home, please."

As bad relationship scenes went, it could have been much worse. She didn't hate him and that was a big plus, but he died a little when she asked to leave.

"Kim, please stay…

"Take me home, or I'll get my own ride." Her word on it was final.

Owen didn't fight her on it. He'd been such an idiot, had done everything wrong. He should have told her when they first met, before there was anything invested in the relationship. Now, he was no better than Tom Albanese. He'd let her down, and he'd broken her heart.

OWEN HANDED Kim her phone when they got back in the Vanquish. An evening that was supposed to be so romantic, so perfect, had turned into a disaster. He said he was falling in love with her, but he hadn't trusted her with their shared past. That's what Owen didn't seem to get. He thought it wasn't just because he'd hidden the information about Tom. He didn't trust her to know her own mind.

Kim had spent a year fighting against being a victim. Sure, life sucked. She'd been dealt some really bad cards, but she'd taken herself away from everyone who was going to utter *poor Kim*. That included her own family. Part of it was about protecting Tom's memory. The other part was about protecting her own sanity.

So she took care of a little girl, helped manage a busy household, she read, she kept up on the latest critical care techniques with online courses. She relaxed and traveled, but she was not a victim. With one well concealed lie, Owen had turned her into a victim. He didn't even realize it. Sure, he was trying to protect her from the memory, from the hurt, but he didn't trust her to handle it.

If she couldn't handle where they'd been, how could she handle where they were going? If there was going to be a future he had to know she'd be there with him as a partner, not someone who needed to be sheltered. Not someone who needed protecting. Kim thought she might love Owen, but right now she couldn't be with him.

Kim texted Jenna. She texted Joey. She texted Harper.

Simple messages. *Meet me at the cottage. Be there in twenty.* They were her ride or die. She knew they would show up for her.

She leaned into the passenger door, the cool glass soothing her throbbing head. All she wanted was to be happy. That was all. She didn't need billions of dollars or mansions. She just needed someone who would respect her.

She thought Owen had everything she was looking for. She loved his brains, his sense of humor, his inner goodness, but she didn't love that he threw up a screen because he thought something would be too tough for her to handle. If they were going to make it, they would have to handle much worse.

At some point the ride home became a blur, and all Kim wanted was to feel Owen's touch. Feel his kiss. She physically hurt already from missing him. The tears kept coming because when he said he was falling for her, she knew he said it from his heart.

But what did it mean if she couldn't trust him?

When they pulled into the driveway, Owen put the car in park, and neither of them spoke. The tension in the car was palpable. "Kim is there any chance we can talk this out? I don't want to leave you like this."

"I'll be fine, and I won't be alone, okay? I'll tell you when I want to talk."

Kim was out of the car before Owen could even open his door, but she heard his footsteps following her down the walk. Harper intercepted them at the steps to the deck and Kim could make out Joey and Jenna sitting on the cottage's front porch, she stopped and faced him.

"I'm good, Owen."

She took a step and he caught her hand, pulling her back. His hands came to her face, gentle, sweet. The feel of him touched her right to her core. No one ever made her feel like Owen, and no one ever would again. He kissed her forehead, whispered against it. "Please don't let this be over."

Unable to make eye contact, Kim lifted her hands to his chest and gently pushed herself away from him.

"I have to go."

Kim couldn't say anything else. Everything hurt. Absolutely everything.

Joey stepped off the porch, looped her arm around Kim's shoulder and walked her inside.

OWEN WATCHED the love of his life walk away. Just walk away because he'd been an idiot.

He took out his phone to text Nate and Jason about going out on the boat tomorrow, but instead decided he needed the time alone to clear his head.

God knew he still needed to shake out the past year. He definitely wasn't acclimating to being home as easily as he'd done in the past and part of that had to do with Kim. The woman had him twisted up in knots. He thought about her all the time. Wanted to see her, make her part of his life. When he looked at her he saw his future. Everything was laid out right in front of him...her, kids, his friends, his business. It was all there and she was at the center for him. The center of everything he wanted.

He'd always prided himself on keeping his life simple, but getting involved with Kim Torres had mucked up the works good.

What told him he that he would never be the same was that he wouldn't have changed anything, even if he could. He was in love with her. No doubt. No question. She was every-thing and he had to find a way to make her understand that he needed her.

He drove home on auto pilot, put the car in the garage and after taking care of the dog, he went to bed.

But Owen didn't sleep. He lay in his bed thinking about Kim, wondering if he'd she'd give him another chance, wondering what he could do to fix this disaster. He heard his tablet ping and grabbed it from his nightstand. One of Kim's hair scrunchies stuck to the Velcro on the case. It was blue, and when Owen twisted it between his fingers, he visualized her playing with that mess of gold and brown hair in the morning, running her fingers through it and pulling it all into a ponytail. The faintest scent of flowers lingered on the comforter and he felt her against him, curled up, purring softly in sleep.

He'd fucked up so bad. He didn't know if there were words for it.

"Work the problem, Kent. Work it." But there was no easy answer for this, no fix. Kim was calling the shots.

He opened the tablet and checked his email and texts. Nothing from Kim. Instead, he found a message from a buddy of his asking if he was going to accept the voluntary assign-ment to assist with the drawdown. He'd been asked to go back to Kandahar in July and stay for two months. He'd be there during the hell of summer, sweating his balls off and risking his life getting the Marines ready to move out. He was glad for the drawdown, though. They'd been there too long, and too many people had been hurt, too many parents had been pulled away from their kids, and too many people had died.

Owen hit reply and told his friend he was thinking about

it. He still had a few weeks to decide, so he could wait and see what happened with Kim. If they worked things out, he'd try to get the duty switched stateside, but his worry was that if he didn't volunteer, they'd send him anyway. But if things didn't get better, if she couldn't forgive him, he'd accept whatever assignment there was because Owen was going to need to get away from here.

There was no better way to get a woman out of your system than to put a target on your back. *Oo-rah*.

KIM WALKED into her sister's embrace and Jenna closed in around her. Harper stood back shaking her head.

"I obviously have to kill him." Harper was pacing in the living room, fuming. "How could he not tell you that? I mean, come on."

Sitting on the couch, Kim snuggled into the crook of her sister's arm. "He was trying to protect me. It was dumb, but I think deep down that was the whole point."

"At least he didn't tell you he wasn't the commitment type," Harper said.

"I can't believe he was Tom's commanding officer," Joey said. "What are the odds?"

"I've discovered the world is a very small place," Jenna replied.

"What did your parents do?" Kim was still thinking about them. She couldn't help it.

"Well it didn't help that Zia Bunny came in wailing. You would think Tom just died. She told the story and Mom remembered Owen's name. Well, Zia Bunny went off carrying on like Owen was my brother's executioner. It was hard for my mother. You have now been dubbed "that slut." Zio Marco was going all good fellas. He's *got a guy*, by the way."

"Oh, good to know. He wants to off Owen and I'm a slut."

Harper raised an eyebrow. "Holy shit, I thought the redneck family my mama married into was bad."

Jenna shook her head and poured everyone some wine. "The rednecks have nothing on the mob."

"Kimmy, are you alright?" Joey brushed back her hair, and Kim was so thankful they were all there.

"No," she sniffled. "He told me he told me he's falling in love with me." She swallowed and tried to bite back the emotion, but it was too much. Deep sobs racked her, the tears blinding her eyes and choking her voice.

The grief and the sadness went so deep, and it wasn't just about Owen. There was so much loss, and she didn't want to feel anything anymore. She just wanted the hurt to stop.

Jenna sat on her other side and Kim felt the warmth of her oldest friend and the love of her sister. When Harper crouched in front of her and handed her some tissues, Kim felt like she might get through. These women gave her strength. "Mop your face. My goodness, you are an ugly crier. Don't ever try to get Owen to do something for you by crying. You'll just send him running."

Kim let out a watery laugh.

"Now, our boy Owen, he's never said he's in love with anyone before. This is serious stuff."

"I completely believe him, but how could he not tell me about Tom?"

"Like you said," Jenna began, "he was trying to protect you."

How did Kim explain to everyone that she didn't need

protecting? She just needed the truth. There had been so little of it, and not just from Tom, but from her as well. If she dug really deep, she knew they weren't meant to be married. They'd loved each other but theirs was a love born of innocence, a close friendship, and if she was really honest, habit. Granted, good marriages had been built on much less, but neither of them should have had to settle and that's exactly what would have happened.

"What do *you* want?" This was Jenna. Always practical, straight to the point.

She couldn't stop the tears from leaking out of her eyes. "I don't want to lose him, but this is a lot to take in."

Harper had taken a seat in one of the big, overstuffed chairs. "I don't get it. Owen is a freakin' Boy Scout. I can't believe he waited this long to come clean."

Kim shook her head realizing what she'd done. "I told him I didn't want to talk about the war. At all. It's possible I suspected he might know Tom. He was based in Helmand Province, so it was possible. But I told Owen that I wanted to keep Afghanistan out of the relationship."

"That explains a lot," Harper said. "But he should have told you anyway."

"He said he drove to the hospital to see me. That he had letters I wrote and photos, but I'd gone home already."

Kim heard a ping from her phone and rose to get it from her purse. When she looked there was a text from Owen. *I'm so sorry.*

She knew he meant it, but there were other reasons for her to stay away. The biggest reason was to get used to the idea that the relationship had gotten so serious, so fast. She needed to take a breath. His declaration was honest and true, she had no doubt about that, but Kim had been through the wringer and she wanted to make sure Owen got her best in return. She loved him, with all her heart, but she didn't know if she could trust herself to make it work.

Harper held up her cell phone. "Everyone needs to pack a bag, I have just gotten husband-boyfriend clearance for the weekend. We are all going to Caroline and Josh's house on the North Fork for an extended. The daddies will be in charge. Joey, Jenna you are coming as well."

"I don't know Harper. I won't be much fun." Kim didn't know if she was up to a girls' weekend. She was sure she was going to end up a sloppy, crying drunk. Then again, she hadn't had a night like that in a long time and maybe what she really needed was a good cry with her friends.

She kept thinking about Owen's text and how much she wanted to be with him. It would be so easy to climb in her car and go to him, but her brain needed rest.

"You'll have fun and it'll take your mind off the man. It's all good. See you in the morning." Harper left with a wave and a smile and as soon as the door closed behind her Kim shook her head.

"I know Harper means well, but I'm not sure about this weekend. I'm taking Mom out to lunch Monday, and I don't know if I want to figure this out by committee."

"You love him, don't you?" Jenna asked.

"I think I do. But I'm terrified. What if it all goes south?"

Joey hugged her. "If you want it, it won't. You give your whole heart, Kim, it's scary as hell, but it's all you've got."

"I want to talk to him. I have so many questions, but I need to sort through the jumble in my head." She pulled her knees up, and wrapping her arms around her legs dropped her head. "Ugh. I'm so conflicted. In some ways it's surreal. Of all the people in this world, in the military, what aligned in the universe to bring us together."

"Maybe it was meant to be," Joey offered. "What ever you call it…fate, destiny, soulmates…you found each other."

"We just met. Is this real? I knew Tom for years." But did she really know Tom? It seemed she didn't.

"Kimmy, I don't think you can put love on the clock. I mean, Nonna and Poppy married a month after they met— they adored each other" Joey was right. Her grandparents were devoted to each other, more in love after 60 years of marriage than ever before.

"Why don't we go out east tomorrow with Harper?" Jenna suggested. "We'll have some wine, eat, you can sleep if you want and then we'll head back Monday right after breakfast. I'll take a day off."

"That's a good idea," Joey said. "It will give you a little space, but not too much. I think if we kept you away from him for too long you might swim home."

The reality of what she wanted was obvious. She wanted Owen. They had things to work out, no doubt, but she was all in. Kim considered her sister's words. Maybe there wasn't a right way to fall in love, that a relationship didn't require a certain number of months or years to be a thing, but love happened when it was meant to. "I never thought I'd want to be with anyone again, but the thought of not being with him shatters me."

"Then you have your answer," Jenna said. "I'll talk to my parents. You deal with your guy."

14

O WEN SAT IN AN A DIRONDACK CHAIR AT THE END OF his dock, nursing a beer and listening to the dog whimper while he thought about whether or not he was going to take the boat out. What he wanted to do was get in his car, go find Kim and take her someplace where they could be alone and he could make love to her until they didn't know where one of them ended and the other began.

"I don't care how much you cry, dog. You're wearing the life vest."

He had to admit the dog looked stupid in the multi-colored vest, but she was a puppy, and he didn't want to take the chance she didn't know how to swim. One good wave and he could lose her. That would be just his luck.

He took a long pull on the beer and thought about Kim and how she was when she left him last night. He'd texted just to let her know she was on his mind, but she hadn't answered. Every hour that went by without a word killed him a little, but he knew she needed time. He'd dropped a lot on her the night before—the news about knowing Tom and then telling her he was falling for her—she was probably considering running for the hills.

Even though she said she didn't want to end things with him, not that they'd really started, Owen had his doubts. Especially when she didn't answer him. He hadn't been honest with her, and in fact, he'd held more back than he'd told her. It would serve him right.

"Because you're a fucking bonehead," he said to himself. There wasn't a lot he could do about it now, so a sail was definitely in order to clear his head. Dropping the now empty bottle of beer on the dock he heard the glass clink against all the other empty bottles—he forgot how many—and he realized he was too drunk to sail. In fact he was too drunk to do much of anything. God, he was going to feel like shit tomorrow.

Casey turned and a low growl came from her chest. Best case, Nate and Jason were there and they brought more beer. They'd been calling, and texting, because they'd obviously heard he'd been an asshole, but he hadn't answered. Worst case, the zombie apocalypse had begun, and Owen was screwed because not only would there be no more beer, his gun was locked up in the house.

"Which is it girl? Zombies or beer?"

She yapped.

"It's beer. But you don't get anymore because you're already shitfaced." That was Nate. He could tell if someone was drunk from twenty paces. He had drunk ESP.

"What the hell happened? You don't do the beer drunk anymore. You should at least be getting wasted on 21-year-old scotch. " Jason nudged the empties with his foot and Nate crouched down to scratch Casey's ears. "Meg's mom and

Harper's mom are watching the kids because the girls—including yours—all went out to Josh and Caroline's."

Owen scrubbed his hands over his face and looked out at the harbor. "I got bored. So I had a few beers."

"It looks like you had something like eight beers, bro," Jason said.

Nate poked him in the side and Owen swatted at his hand. "Let's get you in the house," Nate said, "And let's get that poor dog out of that thing you have her in."

"It's a doggie life vvvvvest."

"That's fine, if we were going on the boat, but we're not." Nate hauled him up by his arms and Owen leaned into him. "Shit you're heavy. How much do you weigh?"

"Iiiii dunnno. Two-ten?"

His brain wasn't really cooperating at this point and he just followed Jason and Nate into his house. God, he felt like shit. Between everything going on with Kim and now all the beer he just wanted to sleep. His friends helped him into his den and pushed him onto the big leather sofa. There was a pillow under his head. It felt good.

"I fucked up with her."

"We heard," Nate said hoisting his legs on the couch. "Sleep it off, buddy."

That was a really good idea. Sleep. Owen felt something cold and wet against his hand and looked down to see Casey nudging him. "Hey, girl." He glanced at Nate who looked really big standing over him. "Did you grow, dude?"

"Dude?" Jason said. "Did you call him dude?"

"Fuck you. Take care of the dog, okay?" That was the last thing Owen remembered clearly before he passed out.

. . .

DAPPLED LIGHT FILTERED in the big window behind the sofa in his den. He could hear the gulls outside and hoped the feathered bastards weren't crapping all over his boat. He sat up, planted his feet on the floor and gripped his skull. *Fuck.* Owen didn't know if his head hurt because of the beer he'd consumed or because of what went down with Kim. It didn't matter--either way it was Karma and he deserved it. He heard voices and rose to find Jason and Nate, who had probably eaten everything in his fridge. Once he got into the kitchen he sat at the island and dropped his head into his arms.

"You want to tell us what's going on? Last night you and Kim are doing great, you tell us you have reservations at Grill, and now we find you drunk off your ass on your dock."

"I told her I loved her."

"Already?" Nate said.

Owen nodded.

"So what happened?"

"I told her the truth."

Both his friends sat at the island. "Owen, that covers a lot of ground. You want to fill us in?"

"I told her I was her fiancé's commanding officer. That I knew who she was. I told her about writing to Tom's family, about reading her letters and she got kinda freaked out."

"Yeah," Nate said. "That might do it."

"I love her. I really do and not just because of the hospital or anything. She's amazing and I'm a dick."

"What did she say?" Nate wanted details.

"Hold on," Jason stopped Owen before he even started to answer. "The hospital?"

Owen froze, knowing he let the big one drop. *Shit.*

"Owen, what hospital?" Jason asked pointedly,

"You guys have to take this to your grave. If you don't I will send you there early, in fucking pieces. I still have to tell her this, so don't let it slip."

Nate and Jason didn't budge because at that point they knew he was completely unhinged. Owen was fine with that. "There were two victims of the IED attack that killed Tom Albanese. I cut my hand on some stray metal when they were loading them into the helo and used it as an excuse to get myself, our medic and Albanese's girlfriend to the hospital."

"Whoa," Nate said. "Girlfriend?"

"Yes." He went slow making sure not to leave anything out. "Albanese was cheating on Kim. The two Marines expired at the hospital before we got to Kandahar, and when I walked into the trauma unit, I saw this tiny, brunette nurse. She looked like hell, but tried to help me."

"Kim." Nate said.

Owen gave a quick nod and kept going. "Corporal Lynn—his girlfriend— was distraught at the news of Tom's death, but this nurse looked like she was going to lose it. Eventually, she did, collapsing right in my arms. Went down hard. She could barely breathe. I was sitting on the floor with this sobbing woman in my arms and something in me snapped. I knew immediately she was the one. I don't know how, or what it was."

"That's romantic, I guess, but it sounds like bullshit." Nate was still skeptical. Understandable.

"I thought the same. I figured I just felt bad. I mean I don't fall in love like that. I know who I am. I tried to see her again, but she'd been sent home. I tried to forget about her, couldn't. I had a nightmare of a tour, I came home. Slept for about two weeks. I dreamt about her every time I closed my eyes."

He stood and walked to the big picture window. "Then Harper calls me to pick up her nanny on Memorial Day and BOOM. There she was. I'm sorry, but that's some powerful shit right there. I have no intention of messing with it. I may have had this image of her in my mind, but the real Kim is more than I ever dreamed. I want to marry her. Now I don't know if she'll have anything to do with me."

"Because you were a dick," Nate said. "Jesus, Owen," How could you not tell her. No wonder she's not talking to you. If she forgives you, you are officially the luckiest son-of-a-bitch I've ever met."

"Have you heard anything from her," Jason asked.

"Nothing really. She was so upset. I made her cry and I feel like such a shit." He was so restless. He came back to his friends. Sat.

"Did she tell you she doesn't want to pursue anything?" Jason put an open bottle of water in front of him.

"No. She said she needs some space and some time." He sipped from the bottle. The cold water felt good sliding down his throat. "So she can get used to the idea, I guess."

Nate and Jason looked at each other. "I know," Owen said. "It basically means it's over before it really started. Why do you think I got drunk?"

"She's not in great shape either." Jason picked at a bunch of grapes that were in a basket on the counter. "Meg told me she fell apart with Harper, Jenna, and her sister last night. That's when they hatched the plan to go out east to Caroline and Josh's house in Cutchogue."

"Just for the night?" Owen lifted his head up. "Or for longer?"

"You know what," Jason said. "I'm not sure. Meg's gone till tomorrow night."

Nate grinned. "You want to crash the party?"

"Maybe," Owen said. "If only so I can beg her forgiveness."

Laughing out loud, Jason grabbed another beer from the fridge. "I would pay real money to see that."

Owen shook his head. He hated that he hurt her, that he made her cry. God knows she'd probably shed more than enough tears in the past year. But yet he did it to her just like Albanese. He remembered when he wrote the letter to the family. Sat there with pictures around him, with letters from Kim. Things that told him about the man who died because in truth, he got more about him from her letters than he did from the Marine himself.

He spoke to everyone he could. His buddies in the unit, even Corporal Lynn, but nothing got to him like Kim's letters. She knew this man and she shared every part of herself with him.

And in Kim's case, that's what Owen wanted. Every kiss, every touch had him wanting her in fifty different ways. It was more than sex. He could get sex anywhere. He wanted her to let him love her. He wanted to be on the receiving end of all that kindness and heart. He wanted to fall asleep holding her and wake up the same way.

Drunk or not, Owen knew this was it for him. She was it. He might as well turn in his man card because he realized last night when he watched her fall apart in front of him that he would do anything to make her happy. Absolutely anything.

That was why he'd gone on a bender. He didn't know how to fix this. He had to wait for her to let him.

"Jesus Christ, I'm a fucking wreck. Is it supposed to be like this?"

Jason gave him a quick slap upside the head. "How did you think it was going to happen? That's what they do to us. They wreck us. Totally and completely."

Nate leaned back and stretched his arms over his head. "Great. Something to look forward to."

"Even if she forgives me for that, the truth is I might have another deployment and while I don't think it would be for long, she's not going to be able to handle it."

"You're going to leave again?"

"Possibly. I'm going to try to stay stateside, but I don't know. I have to see what's happening." He took another drink. "I was asked to volunteer for a three-month tour, which usually means do it or we'll send you away for longer and you can't do anything about it."

Owen dropped his head again and the room started to spin. He needed a plan. Something that would help her see he was sincere and that she could trust him. Groaning, it didn't seem that was even possible.

CAROLINE ROSSI-CAMPBELL AND HER HUSBAND, Josh, had restored the beautiful, shingled waterfront home on Long Island's North Fork to absolute perfection. With two levels of decks that circled the outside of the house, the back of the house faced the Long Island Sound with views straight to Connecticut. There was a pool, a deck overlooking the water, a beach, and a dock. Kim never knew people who lived this kind of life. Now she was surrounded by them.

There were seven bedrooms, eight bathrooms and every conceivable luxury, yet the place still felt like home with its warm décor and welcoming quiet. Kim didn't know if she would be fit company when they arrived on Sunday, but the group took an excursion to a local vineyard. Picked up fresh produce, seafood, and groceries and then in the most stunning kitchen she had ever seen, she and her new friends, her oldest friend and one of her sisters made a gourmet meal while it stormed outside.

Now, sitting on the second-floor covered deck, staring out at the water, Kim reveled in the cool breeze of the early Monday morning. She'd become an early riser while she was in the Navy and since she'd been out, she kept up the habit. There was something very soothing about the alone time someone could only get in the very early morning. So sitting there in her pajama pants, fuzzy socks and a Navy sweatshirt, Kim let her mind wonder what Owen was doing.

Was he up? Was he on his deck looking at the water? Did he sleep okay? Because he told her just the other day that he slept better with her than he ever had in his life. She didn't like that he kept the information about Tom from her. She felt foolish, in fact, and she was trying to see it from his side, but it wasn't easy. Even so, she missed him. Missed his warmth and his voice. They'd spent almost every night together over the past week and just hearing his voice in the morning was like waking up to music.

She heard the telltale click of a door handle and Meg emerged from her room, stretching as she stepped close to the deck railing. "What a gorgeous morning." She turned and smiled at Kim and pulled the chaise lounge closest to her room right next to Kim. "My sister and that husband of hers outdid themselves with this place. I love it here."

"Don't you have a place on The Cape?" The story of Jason buying Meg a multi-million dollar summer cottage when they were on their honeymoon was becoming family legend.

"The Vineyard. Yes. I love that house, it's right on Vineyard Sound, but it's so far. It takes hours to drive there, so if we opt not to drive we have to fly. It's not great for a quick getaway. It needs some planning."

"It still sounds wonderful." Speaking as someone who spent summers in a crowded bungalow on Lake George in the Adirondack Mountains, a big place with room to breathe, like this one, was pretty appealing.

"You can go there anytime you want. If you want, you can head up tomorrow and hide from Owen. Just say the word. I'll arrange everything."

It was tempting. It would be so easy to hide from him, but at what cost? Her heart, maybe? She wasn't about to do that again. Kim was tired of dishonesty in her relationships. With Tom, they'd both avoided the conversation that their relationship wasn't what good marriages were made of. Neither of them was blissfully happy and the result was him cheating and her being hurt. In the end, with his death, nothing mattered, but they should have been able to talk out what was going on between them.

It was the same with Owen and running away wasn't going to help. "I'm actually going home this morning. I have a lunch date with my mom, and I was thinking I might, I don't know, take a sail later."

Meg smiled, reached out and grabbed Kim's hand. "He's

such a good guy and I can see he's a goner over you. I hope it all works out, I mean he should have told you, but still..."

"He should have told me. He's in deep trouble for that, but I can't walk away from him over it. Does that mean I'm weak?"

"No," said a voice from behind her. It was her sister, Joey holding two mugs of coffee. "You're in love with him, Big Sis. When that happens, I'm told you tend to look at the big picture rather than nitpicking the little things. Which is how I know I don't love anyone." Joey handed Kim one of the mugs. "I nitpick like crazy."

Wrapping both hands around the warm ceramic mug, Kim may have been nursing her wounds, but she was glad she'd made the trip. The energy of all the people around her over the past twenty-four hours had a healing effect. These women were all so accomplished, so strong, and they were all there for her. It was humbling, and it helped. She felt better. Stronger.

She was ready to face Owen.

She was ready to tell him how she felt.

Jenna eventually joined them and then Harper and Caroline. Eventually the group moved to the kitchen to make a big breakfast.

Jenna was turning the bacon in the pan and the whole house smelled of hearty breakfast.

"So," Jenna said. "Are you going back to talk to him? Jump him? Or a little of both?"

Kim was cutting up fruit at the kitchen island that was roughly the size of the state of Rhode Island. The thought of what she had planned made her smile, but she didn't say anything.

Caroline elbowed her gently. "She's not talking. She's jumping him first."

There were peals of laughter to go along with speculation of what she had planned.

Kim expected she'd find Owen on his boat. He loved that damn boat. It seemed fitting that they'd spend some quality time there. But she wasn't going to tell her friends, no matter how much they teased her.

Someone's cell rang and everyone reached for one device or another, and Meg discovered she was the lucky winner. "Hi Honey!"

Obviously her husband.

"No, Kim isn't staying. She, Jenna, and Joey are heading back today. Okay. Of course." Meg walked around the kitchen, a mass of kinetic energy to go along with her mane of blonde curls. She waved her hand at the group of them to quiet down. What was Jason telling her? "Oh, oh really? No, of course I won't tell her."

That was a dirty lie if she ever heard one.

"Right. Oh, poor Owen. No, she's leaving, so he shouldn't sail all the way out here. You should stop him."

Meg gave her a huge smile and a thumbs up. "I miss you too, baby. I'll see you tonight."

She pressed the screen of her phone and tossed it on the kitchen table. Meg stood quiet for a second and then burst into a squealing mass of bouncing blonde hair. She was jumping around like a lunatic. "Owen is toast. He is so miserable, he almost sailed out here last night. He figured he could have been at the dock in the back before daybreak and surprised you. Then he planned on begging. God, this is so great."

"He was going to sail all the way here?" Kim could hardly believe her ears.

"Jason and Nate found him on his dock yesterday," Meg continued. "He was sitting in a lawn chair, drunk off his ass. He has it so bad it's not funny. He's all yours if you want him. Tell me you still want him?"

Kim kept her head down, focusing on cutting a very ripe mango. Her eyes were burning and then she felt the first tear slip. She had to stop crying, especially when the news was so good. The big dope really loved her.

"I still want him," she whispered.

Joey walked behind her bringing a pitcher of OJ to gigantic farmhouse table. Her sister leaned in and kissed her cheek. Between all the love in the room, and all the love she felt for Owen, this was shaping up to be a really good day.

15

KIM WAS NERVOUS. HOW SAD WAS IT THAT SHE WAS nervous for a lunch date with her own mother?

It was her own damn fault if she was. Things had been better recently, but since seeing her mother on Saturday, a lot had changed. Again. Her mother had been great at the cottage, but she hadn't asked Kim a lot of questions. Now with all the gossip about her and Tom and Owen floating around their neighborhood—thanks to Zia Bunny and Zio Marco—Kim owed her mother the full story.

The day out east gave Kim time to process everything that had happened. Thinking back, she realized there were times Owen tried to tell her. He wanted to talk, and she'd pushed the conversation away. Not that it was an excuse, he'd still lied, but she had to acknowledge that he did make the attempt.

She was so torn. Her emotions were a jumbled hot mess, with two sides of herself warring with each other. The practical side said this whole thing with Owen was doomed to fail. There were trust issues and they had too much common baggage. But part of her held out hope. Hope that somehow they might find a way forward, and that by sharing the load, they could both move on. Together.

She always thought of herself as such a badass. She'd been to war. Had worked in a trauma center. It was impressive work, good work, but it was all about a rush, pressure, it was never about her heart. About a risk that really mattered. In reality, that meant she was a big wimp. And she expected her mother was going to tell her the exact same thing.

Kim was counting on it.

Her mom had suggested their favorite Chinese restaurant. It was a place Kim always picked for birthdays or special occasions because the ornate interior and the fussy wait staff made her feel extra special.

The place had been in business forever and the owners, Mr. and Mrs. Lee, knew all their regular customers. Kim was looking forward to going. Even the prospect of a tongue lashing couldn't dim the excitement of revisiting this particular part of her childhood.

Walking into the restaurant, Kim could see not much had changed. Ornate, dragon painted screens divided the dining areas and paper lanterns decorated the walls. She could see her mother was already seated, and waved to her before walking over.

Whatever worry Kim felt, it dissolved when she got close enough to see the tears in her mother's eyes. Feeling the burn in her own, she covered the last few steps in record time and when her mother jumped from the booth the two embraced. Kim relaxed at her mother's touch, hearing her mother's voice.

"Whatever it is, baby, it's going to be okay. It's going to be okay."

"Oh, Mom."

They held on for an extraordinarily long time and finally when they sat, she relaxed, believing her mother that everything would indeed be okay.

"You couldn't have picked a more perfect spot," Kim said.

Mom smiled. "I wanted you to be comfortable. I know how much you always loved it here."

"I bet they still have the best egg rolls."

"And wonton soup."

They held hands across the table, her mother's thumb gently rubbing hers. It was the same thing she would do when Kim was little and had a bad dream.

"How are you?" Mom finally asked.

"Oh, you know...not great."

"Yeah. I kind of figured. Joey told me a little but I really want to hear it from you."

Lucia Torres never had a lot of tolerance for nonsense. That's what made her life as a school administrator and mother of six bearable. She loved fiercely, disciplined fairly, and listened to anyone who needed an ear. She'd give advice if asked, but often it wasn't what the person wanted to hear. Kim was counting on that part. She didn't need to be placated anymore. She didn't need people walking on eggshells around her. She needed to stop playing games and face...well, she had to face pretty much everything.

Maybe she was right to be upset about what Owen told her. To a point. But then again, maybe she just heard something that deep down, she already knew.

"Tell me anything. There's no judgement."

"Thanks," Kim nodded. "But don't hold back. I'm counting on you Mama."

Just as she screwed up her courage and prepared to tell her mother the whole story, the waiter came over and they ordered. They actually ordered three lunches but everything looked good and her mother's excuse was she could send the leftovers home with Kim.

"Okay," Mom said. "We have drinks. We've ordered, now tell me. What happened?"

Kim drew a deep breath. "I love him."

Her mother sat back, smug. "I guess I should be surprised, but I'm not. The way you two looked at each other was pretty telling."

"It shows, huh?"

"Yes, but you could do much worse. He's smart, charming, handsome and he's rich. My question though is does he make you happy?"

"He could."

"That's not what I asked. Something happened that sent you running, Kimberly. What was it? Did he say something? Do something? What?"

"You haven't heard anything? Mrs. Albanese..."

"Tess hasn't said anything. She's been at her sister's. Joey told me bits and pieces. The only thing I'm getting is that you were disloyal to Tom's memory. What's going on? I get that Owen is a Marine. Is there some problem with that?"

"Yeah." Kim took a deep breath. "We were at dinner when Bunny and Marco saw us."

"They are the absolute worst. The truly enjoy making other people unhappy." Her mom sniffed her disapproval.

"They ran right back to Tom's family, blurted everything

out about me dating, but that wasn't what sent me running. You see, Owen had held back some important information."

"What did he tell you? This sounds pretty bad."

Kim took a deep breath because she knew what she was going to say would knock her mother's socks off.

"He told me that he was Tom's commanding officer."

"What?" To say her mother was shocked was an under-statement.

"I know."

"Honey, that's...wow." Her mother was rarely at a loss for words. Kim felt her own lip tremble as she thought about how everything had unfolded over the past few days. She thought about Owen, how he made her feel. There was magic there.

"Pressing her fingers to her temples, Mom squeezed her eyes shut. "Of all the coincidences. I cannot believe it."

"He knew who I was when he first met me because he wrote to Tom's family. He had letters I'd—" It was getting tough to think about. Owen knew some of her most intimate thoughts, her deepest feelings. Things she'd shared with the man she thought she was going to marry. Another breath. And another. "He'd read letters I'd written."

"Personal stuff?"

"I tended to keep it light, but sometimes, I wrote about how I was feeling about our relationship. About the engagement."

Again she had to fight back the tears, because she was getting to the point of having to tell her mother the truth about Tom and how things were going between them.

Kim's hands were tearing furiously at a paper napkin, leaving little pieces all over the table. She stopped when her mother's hands covered her own.

"Sweetie, what is it?"

There was no easy way to tell her mother that the boy she'd known all those years, the one she'd trusted with her daughter's heart hadn't been worthy of it. "Tom was cheating on me."

With wide eyed disbelief, her mother drew a breath. "Kim, no. He wasn't."

"He was. I found out the day he died. His girlfriend came in from their base. She was devastated."

There were no words to fully express the way her heart hurt, but the gentle squeeze from her mother's hands let Kim know she understood. And she understood in a way that no one else could. From her first crush on the boy next door, to their first kiss behind the garage, there was a lot of history and Kim found telling her mother about his betrayal, someone so close to both of them, made the pain that much more acute. Suddenly, she missed him. The grief she'd been holding onto for a whole year drifted to the surface.

"I hate what he did," she sniffled.

"Me too." Mom was still holding her hands. "I hate that he put you through that and that you've been dealing with it alone. I wish you'd told me."

"I didn't know what to say. I was so shell shocked, you know? I think today is the first day it's really hit me. I mean, I've been angry for a whole year, but this is the first time I really feel sad."

"Why are you sad?"

Kim had to think about that. She was sad because Tom had died. No one should die at thirty. She was sad he suffered, and he had suffered horribly. But more than anything, she was sad for herself because even if things hadn't been perfect, Tom was one of her best friends and for the first time since she'd left Afghanistan, she was able to admit it.

It dawned on her that coming to grips with her feelings for Owen made her able to face what she was feeling for Tom. There were so many emotions, and they ran the gamut.

"I miss him. I know he cheated on me, but I've known him my whole life and I miss the asshole."

"Oh, baby."

"Very few people know about the other woman." She paused. "God that's such a cliché. I've been hesitant to say anything because it's, well, humiliating."

Her mother came around, and slid into the booth next to her looping her arm around her shoulder. "You have nothing to be humiliated about. Nothing. Is this why you cut off his family?"

"I've explained things to Jenna, but the rest of her family is so hurt. I just want them to understand. I don't mean to be disrespectful. I want my life back. I want Owen."

"Owen?"

"I know. I never expected it. He's everything. Charming, smart, so sweet. And he loves me. He's hurting, but he does."

"Then make yourself happy, baby. You're the only one who can.

OWEN WALKED around the deck of his boat aimlessly, putting away line and different pieces of equipment he'd picked up since coming home, and cleaning up from the short sail he'd taken that afternoon. The sun was setting and he had to admit, even in his foul mood, it was beautiful.

He'd been thinking about taking the boat out in the Long Island Sound and heading straight for Cutchogue. Josh and Caroline's house where all the girls had supposedly gone had a nice deep-water dock and if he could get her to see him, Owen could beg for Kim's forgiveness in front of witnesses.

He startled when the dog popped up from where she was curled asleep and let out a few short yaps, scrambled to the cockpit and stared down the dock. Her tail wagged a mile a minute and Owen, who wondered if she saw some shore bird for the first time, felt his heart stop when he looked in the same direction.

Walking towards him, was Kim. She looked absolutely divine, wearing a long, pale-yellow dress made of some filmy material. When the setting sun hit her in just the right way, he could see the outline of her entire body. Her hair was loose and falling in chestnut-colored waves almost to her waist and he could see the only thing in her hand was a set of car keys, which meant she was probably saying her piece and going home.

She came right to the end of the dock and locked eyes with him. She was beautiful. A sweet, sexy vision. Owen didn't know how he was supposed to react. So, he waited. Casey propped her front feet up so Kim could pet her but neither he nor Kim spoke.

"Hey there, Marine," she whispered. He noticed then that her eyes were glistening. "You come here often?"

BAM. Just like that he was out of the boat, on the dock and hauling her close. That silly line told him everything he needed to know. She forgave him. Nothing else had to be said, as her arms slipped around Owen's waist and held tight. Every bit of tension and worry slipped from him.

"I almost sailed all the way to Cutchogue to find you and apologize. I'm glad I didn't."

"I heard. It would have been a wasted trip since I planned on finding you."

"I was out of my mind. I'm so glad you're here."

"It was nice of them to want to include me, but one day was enough. I wanted to see my mom and I was hoping I would get up my nerve to see you."

Owen dropped his head and kissed her. Her response was as gentle and perfect as what he felt for her and Owen was not a gentle or perfect man. "I should have told you right away, I'm sorry. I…"

"Stop." Kim shook her head. "I didn't let you tell me. I insisted you keep the war to yourself and look where it got us? The truth of it, Owen, is that the war shaped us, it defined who we are. I should have listened, not avoided it."

Pressing a kiss to her temple, he breathed in her scent. "I love you. There's no maybe about it. I'm a total goner."

"I believe you. From now on no more secrets okay?"

Owen knew there was one more thing he had to tell her, but that could wait. He extended his hand and together they stepped onto his boat. As soon as she was on the deck, Owen pulled her in for another kiss. This one wasn't so sweet.

His lips moved over hers and she responded with a mind-blowing friction that set him off like a rocket. One sleeve of the dress dropped off her shoulder and he could see she wasn't wearing a bra. The globe of her almost exposed breast glowed in the fading light of the day, and Owen took advantage of the design to tug it down and set his mouth to work on her beautiful pink nipple.

Owen turned her around and backed her into the big

wheel, keeping hold of her hips, and pressing himself against her. He was hard as a rock and he intended to make good use of the time they had together. The way she pressed into him, leaned into his touch told him she wanted the same. He tugged down the other side of her dress, now exposing both breasts and she held his head as he nipped and sucked. She squirmed and moaned, driving him crazy with each sexy sound.

"Do you have anything on under this dress?"

He wished it was midday just so he could see her body bathed in sunlight. He was going to have to take her on vacation somewhere. Someplace where she could lay out naked all day long.

"Not a thing."

"No?"

"No." She inched closer, rubbing her hands over his shoulders and down his back. His erection was straining his pants and she was telling him she had nothing on except a dress he could have pulled off with one tug.

Instead he ran his hand up her leg, gathering the light, crinkly fabric as he went, and eventually felt the soft skin of her thighs and the curve of her ass. Allowing his fingers to travel, he drifted between her legs, stroking the wetness there. "Mmmm…" she said.

"You are very wet,"

"I know. For you."

"I can't believe you want me after what happened."

"I wanted to come back here last night. It was all I could do to keep my head on straight and come today."

He was still moving his hands over her, growing ever more thankful that his woman had found her way into his life.

Beautiful, strong, sexy, he would spend his entire life making her happy.

He slipped one finger inside her and Kim arched her back, straining against him and when he slipped another inside, moving with her own rhythm, he could see she was going to come for him very soon. He went back to her breasts, pulling harder on the nipples, while his hand brought her along. She'd been ready for him. She came, dropping her head back and crying out a little, while Owen felt the moisture on his hands and knew he'd never find anyone so bold, so brave, so perfect for him. She was his match. His mate. His everything.

"Oh, that was not exactly what I had planned, but it was amazing."

"What did you have planned?" Owen couldn't wait to hear this.

Kim pulled him to his feet, her dress was still pulled down, her breasts exposed. The cool night air puckered her nipples in such a way that made him want to taste them again. "Take me below and I'll show you."

"Below?"

"You do have a bed down there, right."

"It's called a berth."

"Seriously?"

"You were in the navy. Shouldn't you know that?" He grinned and kissed her. "I love you."

She stroked his face, loving the strength she found in him. "I love you, too, Owen. I don't know what power brought you to me, but I'm so thankful."

"I'll do everything in my power to make you happy," he promised.

"I'm counting on it. Now, take me to *your berth*."

"Yes, ma'am."

WAKING up in Owen's bed was one of her favorite things in the world. Of course she liked it much better when he was there and waking up meant slow, languid morning sex. But they'd had plenty of wonderful sex the night before and Kim was a little worried about walking today.

He'd done as she asked and taken her to his berth on the boat. Then he'd taken her not too gently. It was amazing, thrilling to be possessed so completely by a man. Kim was getting worked up just thinking about it—thinking about him.

She heard Owen's voice, deep and full. He sounded like he was on the phone. Kim thought about getting up and going to him, but she decided to spend a few more minutes in the big bed and think about her gorgeous man.

"No, anything that needs to be done can wait." She wondered who he was talking to. "It's not that important....I'm staying home today. Yeah. If you need me you have my cell, but...right. Okay. I'll see you tomorrow."

He said the final words as he walked into his room, wearing just a pair of very worn Levi's, with the button at the waistband popped open. He looked amazing. "Oh, wow."

His words came out on a ragged breath and that when Kim realized she was giving him quite a show. She didn't have any clothes on and when she'd sat up, the bedclothes pooled at her waist exposing her from the waist up. "God, you're beautiful, Kim."

"I'm sure I'm a mess."

"You're hot. Sexy. You look like a goddess who's been ravished."

She smiled and reached for him. "Well, that is the truth."

He laughed as he sat on the bed, and ran his hand over one side of her body, then the other. Just being near him had the desire pooling in her belly, the heat gathering between her legs. "I don't want to hurt you. We were pretty busy last night."

"I'm fine."

"Yeah?" Owen held her shoulders and eased her onto the mattress, pulling the sheets down so he could see everything. His eyes traveled over her hungrily, as he drew a roughened finger from her throat down her belly and stopping right above he girly bits. "This is the best way to start the day."

Kim laughed at the comment as he shucked off his jeans and revealed his erection. He leaned over her and she nudged him back. "Lay on your back," she said.

"Oh, really?"

He didn't hesitate for a second and laid back. Kim straddled his legs and let her hands run over his chest, his arms, his big powerful thighs. Then she drew a finger down his body, just as he did to her. This was all new to Kim. She'd never taken the lead with sex before and it was a little intimidating, but it was also empowering. It felt like a reclamation. Looking at Owen, the possibilities seemed endless.

She raised herself up and left a trail of kisses around his neck and collarbone, down his chest and she kept going down, across the flat plane of his belly. When she reached his hard shaft, she licked her lips and looked up at him. His mouth was slightly open, in surprise and in encouragement. He knew what she was thinking about doing and Owen wasn't going to stop her.

She swirled her tongue around the salty tip of his penis

and smiled up at him. Enjoying the look of total surrender. Grasping her own hair and throwing it over her shoulder, she locked eyes with him, smiled and then took him in her mouth. He sucked in a breath and took hold of her hair.

"Oh, God, Kim..."

He didn't pull but he held on as he watched her. She stayed right where she was licking and sucking and watching him completely unravel. She felt everything start to tighten and that was when Owen pulled her up and moved her so she was straddling his hips.

"I want to come inside you."

Kim kissed his neck and chin. Then, going up on her knees, Kim lowered herself onto him, and realizing only after he had fully penetrated her that there was nothing between them. No condom and it felt amazing. "I just thought I should tell you, I'm on the pill."

He thrust up inside her, this new position triggering over-whelming sensations. "No diseases for me."

That was good, he moved again and it was her turn to hiss out a breath. "So good, Owen."

They settled into a rhythm, a steady give and take of bodies—hot, magical and Kim loved how he felt in her and against her. But mostly it was her heart and mind that filled. Owen had changed her, had taken her to a place where she could feel so comfortable and bold not only with her own body, but with him.

There was no hesitancy when he pushed inside her, claiming her with every thrust . "I love you, Kim."

"I love you, too."

He'd given her that, the chance to be in love when she never thought she would be again, Kim thought her heart, her ability to feel, had died with Tom. But Owen had given it back to her. He'd given her everything.

Watching his face consumed with the power of their love-making, Kim leaned in and kissed his lips. It was gentle, soft, a reminder to him to look at her as they finished.

Owen opened his eyes and their gazes met, beat for beat, movement for movement, breath for breath, as they sailed over the edge together, holding on, protecting each other, and laying claim to the other's soul.

16

Kim knew her work at Reliance was only temporary. She sat in the makeshift office she'd been using the past couple of days and thought about all the people she'd been helping, and it dawned on her that she liked talking to adults and solving problems. There was no doubt that she missed Anna while she was doing this project for Owen and Harper, but helping their social worker develop a set of contacts at the VA was proving to be an incredibly rewarding challenge. She was making a difference and Kim felt more like herself than she had in a year. She had Owen to thank for that.

She should have been thinking about the conference call she'd just had with the patient advocate at the VA hospital, but instead she couldn't get that sexy CIO who was in a sales meeting a few doors down off her mind. He'd become everything to her so quickly if was a little mind boggling. But Kim couldn't deny she was happy. She'd never been happier.

Casey had been wandering from office to office because the Japanese banking executive they were talking to about the newest version of the software wasn't fond of dogs.

Kim reached out and petted the dog who was sitting next to her chair. "What am I going to do about him Case?"

The dog didn't answer.

She and Owen had settled into a comfortable routine. It had been almost two weeks since they'd committed to each other and the past few days she'd been helping Helen establish a network for the returning vets. It was going really well and pretty soon Reliance would have a model program for not only veterans, but their families.

Thinking about veterans, her mind drifted back to her own Marine. At night she either slept at Owen's or he was at the cottage for which he took a lot of shit from Harper. She was of the mind that everything was going too fast, and even though Kim was wrapped up in the whirlwind, she sometimes felt that way herself.

It had been two weeks since he told her he loved her. They'd had dinners out, breakfasts in and time on the boat. Everything about them was right. Everything. Except Kim's worry that something was going to go terribly wrong. She didn't know why she felt this way and she spent more time than she should tamping down her doubts.

Helen walked into her office and the old lady, who was as sweet as could be, shuffled to a stop and cocked her head. "You're tinking again."

"Occupational hazard."

Helen walked to the chair on the opposite side of her desk and sat. "I tink you should just tell him something is worrying you."

"I'm a big chicken, Helen. We've established that."

"Well, you have to get over it."

"Get over it. That's your sage advice."

"Yup."

"Nothing I should reflect on?"

"Nope."

"What kind of therapist are you anyway?"

Helen laughed. "A realistic one who isn't going to lie to you. Talk to him. If you don't then something *will* go wrong."

"You're right, of course."

"Yes, I am. You have all the power and you have someone who really cares about you. Be brave, Kim. He's not the other man who hurt you, stop acting like he is."

Whoa. That was a low blow and Kim didn't know what to say. She was hurt. She'd had her heart ripped out. What stung was that Helen could see she still had scars.

"It was a year ago. It's time to let it go and move on. You can't blame the man you once knew for your unhappiness now."

"I'm not unhappy, but I just don't know how I can forget it."

"Until you do, you'll never be able to give everything you have to Owen. And doesn't he deserve that?"

He did. He deserved everything from her and she hadn't given him the most important thing: her whole heart. Kim had held back a little piece, the very one that was warning her something wasn't quite right.

Casey, who'd laid down on her pillow under the window popped up and scurried toward the door. She stopped, listened, and then took off down the hallway. The meeting must be over because somewhere in the building, Owen had whistled for his dog. And that was Kim's cue.

Kim stood, straightened her dress, and took a breath. Helen, likewise, stood. "You're braver than you think, Kim."

"Helen, why is it you're the only one who's leveled with me?"

She shrugged and raised her hands as if she was making an offering. "I'm an old lady. I can get away with it. Not everyone can."

Helen left Kim to think about what she was going to do. Either she got rid of the doubt or she let it nag at her. Hearing a ping on her phone, she saw a text from her sister. Something about her prom, which was that night. It was a busy weekend for Olivia. But it gave Kim an idea. An idea that would show Owen she was ready to let him in, and she was ready to face down the ghosts of the past year.

She was going to bring him home. Sure, he'd met her mother and sisters. Since the weekend in Cutchogue, Joey had been around more and Owen had gotten to know her better than any of the other members of the family. But to have him there beside her in front of all of the family and friends? That would mean something to him.

First, she was going to talk to Owen. His office was on the other side of the building, so that would give her plenty of time to think of what she was going to say. He said his door was always open, that it wasn't a problem if they talked at the office.

The walk was longer than she thought. Maybe she was just more aware. People nodded or said hello as she passed, and it made her think. What would people make of her just waltzing into his office like she was important to him or something. She was crossing through the lobby, and Carol smiled and waved.

"Hi, Kim! Taking a stroll?"

"Yeah, you could say that."

"Meeting's over, in case you wanted to know."

"Thanks." God, she hated this. She was the boss's girlfriend.

It wasn't much longer and she was in the common area of the executive suite at Reliance.

There were six desks, occupied by the very busy assistants and for a second, she thought she could leave without being noticed. What she had to say wasn't all that important and she could wait.

"Can I help you, Ms. Torres?"

She turned back and saw Owen's assistant, Marla, looking right at her. "Do you want me to see if he's free?"

"Uh, um..." Kim glanced at Owen's door and saw it was closed. "I don't want to bother him."

Marla crooked a finger and indicated Kim should come closer. The assistant had a grin on her face that was positively conspiratorial. "He told me that if you came down here, I was to interrupt him."

"He did?"

"He did." Marla stood, smiled. "You don't want to get me in trouble now, do you?"

Kim didn't even have a chance to answer. Marla was knocking on Owen's door before she could even nod. She watched as Marla poked her head in the room and then stepped back as Nate and Jason came out. Each of them smiled at her as they walked by. Why did this have to be so embarrassing?

"You can go in, Kim."

It felt like all the assistants were watching her and taking a quick look around she saw that they were. And they were grinning.

Straightening her back, Kim walked right in and then jumped when she heard the office door click shut. It only took a second for her to realize two things. One, she was totally overwhelmed by this space. No matter how many times she saw it, it never failed to impress her. It was big, beautiful, and meant to intimidate if necessary. Second, Owen wasn't in the room. So here she was, nervous, embarrassed, and alone.

"Hey beautiful, you come here often?"

"Oh!" Kim turned, startled by Owen's voice floating in from behind her. But her heart totally stopped when she saw him. He leaned into the door jamb of the adjoining conference room, looking every bit the confident executive. His dark suit was perfectly tailored over a white shirt and his blue tie set off the blue of his eyes. He'd shaved today - she knew that because she'd watched him - but a shadow was already appearing on his jaw. "How was your meeting?"

"Great. We got the account. He was very impressed."

"Well, how could he not be impressed? Congratulations."

He left the doorway and approached her. It was times like this that Kim was so aware of his size, how she melted from the heat that came off his body. How she craved his touch.

"So," he said while slipping a hand around her waist. "What brings you here?"

"Um. I wanted to ask you something."

At this point she was dying because he'd pressed his hips against her and she felt his erection hard against her belly. It was so wrong, but Kim was completely thrilled that he couldn't see her without wanting her. At least her feelings were reciprocated. God knew, she wanted him. Badly.

His lips brushed her cheek. "What did you want to ask? I'm going to say yes. But ask anyway."

Kim smiled. "You don't even know what I want."

His warm laugh filled her. "I'm hoping you want me."

"Oh, for Pete's sake," she said. "We are at work."

"So? There are locks on the doors. Give me something more to think about than working."

This was too much. Pushing away from him, Kim took up position behind a big leather chair. At least now there was some distance between them and if he came for her again, she'd have a chance to outmaneuver him. "Stay there," she said.

"Why?"

"Because we have to talk."

"You can't talk when I touch you?"

"Not coherently. No."

He laughed and she was so annoyed with herself. The man drove her to distraction.

It was too bad she was set on behaving because letting him take her bent over that big desk totally turned her on. Everything about him got her motor running. But that wasn't why she was here. If only it was that easy.

"Okay," he ground out, clearly frustrated. "What's on your mind?"

"Tonight is my sister Olivia's prom. And they're taking pictures at my parent's house."

He came toward her but kept the chair between them. "Okay. And?"

""I'd like to know if," she paused. "If you would like to come with me and meet the male half of my family? My mother also wants to see you again. For an interrogation, I'm sure."

Nothing.

He stood there, stunned, and not uttering a word. Okay. She guessed that was a no.

"It's fine. You don't have to. It's too much and it's too soon. You shouldn't have to deal with..."

Yeah, the chair did her no good at all. When Owen decided he wanted her, he moved like a big cat, grabbing Kim's hand and pulling around and down onto his lap as he sank into the chair.

"You want me to meet your dad and your brothers?"

She nodded.

"And you didn't think I'd want to go?"

"No," she squeaked out. "I mean. I wasn't sure. It's still new between us and I would understand..."

He put a finger over her lips and Kim stopped talking. Owen's crystal blue eyes were locked on hers and she fell right into them as she always did. "If it's important to you, I want to go. I can handle any interrogation. No question about it. Just tell me what to expect. Give me a family recap."

"Alright. My dad is a very nice man, but he works too hard and he's very protective. Even of me and I've proven I can take care of myself."

"That sounds perfectly reasonable to me. Your dad's a math teacher?"

"Yes. Over thirty years doing that and he directs the stage crew. He was going to retire this year, but Livy is going to Yale, so a few more years for him."

"He should let me pay for Yale. Then he could retire if he wanted."

They'd actually had a bit of an argument one night when he overheard her talking to her sister about student loans. Owen thought it was ridiculous that Kim or her family should stress about money when he has so much he didn't know what to do with it.

"Okay, here's a dad tip, don't bring that up. He has his pride and as well-meaning as you are Owen, it would embarrass him.

"It's only money, but I understand. It sounds like he's got his priorities straight. What about your brothers?"

"Jimmy is a city fireman. He just got engaged. He's the shortest of my brothers. About your height." She'd warned Owen that her family ran tall. Her dad was six-two. Her brothers and her one sister were tall, but there was definitely a short gene running around the DNA. "Jeff is an accountant, he works for one of the banks in the city. He'll get there, but it will be late. And Mike is in college. He's starting his last year in September."

"Is he going to be there too, or is he still away?"

"He'll be there. Everyone will be there. My grandmother, my grandpa. Aunts, uncles. It's an event."

Owen leaned in and kissed her soundly. "Sounds like fun."

Kim was relieved, but still there was so much to worry about. She rested her head on his shoulder absorbing a little of his strength so she could tell him the rest.

"What's wrong, Babe? Tell me."

"There's a chance Tom's family will be there. They live next door and since it's not just our family, but all the kids in her prom group and their families, everyone will be milling around for pictures and stuff. They could be extremely difficult.

He held her close, and she could almost hear him thinking. "I suppose we could say we're just friends. That could ease some tension, right?"

It could but the thought of it made her more upset. "No. No. I don't want to hide you or how I feel about you. I mean..."

Kim reached up and stroked his face, feeling so blessed at the warmth and kindness she saw there, knowing that it was all for her. "Do you honestly think I could hide, for even one second, how I feel about you?" She kissed him. "Not a chance. No one would believe me."

He kissed her this time. "Thank you for that.

"Thank you for being patient with me."

He reached for her hands and held them. "It's going to be okay." He kissed her. "We'll figure it all out."

"I'm so worried Mr. or Mrs. Albanese is going to off on you, or me for that matter. One of his sisters could, too. It depends on who's there. I don't want anyone to ruin Livy's day. Jenna will try to run interference, but you just never know."

"Then why ask me?"

"I want you to meet my family, Owen. You're important to me and I don't want there to be any doubt about that."

Cradled safe on his lap, Kim rested her head. It was the one place she felt completely safe, and she wanted to enjoy it before all hell broke loose later on.

OWEN HATED that he was keeping the news from her. But he'd just gotten final word that he'd be going back to Afghanistan in three weeks for two months to work on getting more troops out. The drawdown was requiring administrative manpower and as much as Owen didn't want to go back, if it meant more Marines would come home sooner, he couldn't say no.

He'd let Jason and Nate know and he was planning on telling Kim over dinner. Now he'd wait until after they'd left her parents' house and were back at his house for the night.

He also had to pick up the ring he was going to give her before he left. There was no way he was going anywhere without proposing.

In a little over a month's time, Owen had gone from confirmed bachelor to total goner. He loved her so much it hurt.

The ride to her parents' house was uneventful as was meeting her brothers. They respected their big sister, her choices, and he had a feeling Joey, Livy and their mom helped pave the way. Jenna sneaked in the back door and found Owen nursing a beer with Kim's dad, a nice man whose acceptance was tempered with warning. He didn't care who Owen was, he didn't care about anything except his family. Money and zip code meant very little to this man. Where her father was concerned, only Kim's happiness mattered.

"Hey, Mr. T." She kissed him on the cheek and patted Owen's shoulder. "Hey there, big guy, you've been keeping my buddy all to yourself."

"Sorry." He really wasn't. "How are you, Jenna? Should I expect incoming?"

"Possibly. My parents have a friend of my brother's stopping by. Dave Ryan. Do you know him?"

He did know Ryan. Good Marine, kind of an asshole. "Yup. Okay. I'll be prepared."

Joe Torres looked up. "You'd think for all the love your parents claim to have for Kim, they would let her have a happy life."

Jenna agreed, nodding. "I don't know what to say."

Olivia walked into the kitchen and her father smiled. "Look at my baby princess."

Owen couldn't believe how much the three sisters looked alike. They favored their mother...dark hair and eyes, wide smiles and serious brains that were evident the minute one of them spoke. Olivia's dress was long and blue with more sparkles than he'd ever seen on one garment in his life. She looked beautiful, classy, and her date should feel like a very lucky kid.

The party got going outside on the patio of the modest home. Kim hadn't exaggerated when she said the house was small, but it was warm and comfortable. He could see a happy family lived here.

While pictures were being taken, Owen pulled back and stayed inside looking at all the photos in the living room. The place was overrun with small and large frames, and he felt like he was looking at a family history. He first looked for all the pictures of Kim. She was a peanut of a kid. Skinny with knobby knees, but in all the pictures he could see she was feisty. A little powerhouse who dominated everything she did with the sheer force of her will and her enthusiasm. She was always smiling. A wide bright smile that took over her face, sparkled in her eyes.

He recognized people he'd gotten to know over the past couple of weeks...Joey, and Livvy. Jenna was in many of the photos and there were several pictures of Kim with Tom Albanese. One looked like an engagement photo.

"My mom would have taken those down if she realized you'd be looking."

Owen turned and faced Kim's brother, Jeff. He'd arrived a little late, as she said he would, but of the three brothers the posture he conveyed was the most relaxed. Kim wasn't kidding when she said her brothers were big. Jeff had to be six-four.

"It's fine. It's part of her. It's not like it's a surprise or anything."

"She's happy," Jeff said. "That's all we want for her. She's been through a lot."

Didn't he know it? "I'm going to ask her to marry me sometime this summer. I'll talk to your parents before I propose, but if you could give them a head's up, I'd appreciate it."

Jeff grinned and shook his hand. "Just take good care of her. That's all we ask."

"I will. She'll never want for anything with me."

He and Jeff made their way outside where young women in expensive gowns and their dates posed for pictures. The girls were trying to pull off sophisticated looks, but the guys looked awkward. Owen wanted to let them know they might always feel awkward or tongue tied or nervous around women.

There was no way to stop it. Catching Kim's eye, all he could think was that he wanted to do right by her, and Owen worried about all the ways he could still screw this up. He was taking her back to his house after the party was over and telling her about his deployment. He was leaving in a few weeks for a quick two-month assignment. He should be home before she knew it, but Owen had no doubt Kim was going to be upset.

The backyard was fairly large for the area and was bordered by shrubs and trees. There were lots of places to take pictures and once that was done, the couples filled up a giant, white stretch SUV and departed for their prom. That left the parents and relatives in the front yard waving goodbye. Everyone was milling around and talking and Owen wished he could just get out of eyeshot of the house next door. The potential for disaster was huge.

Owen stuck close to Kim, making conversation, until he saw an older man and woman come out of the house across the street with a younger man he knew to be Dave Ryan. Ryan glanced at the crowd and by some sick twist of fate, spotted him immediately. He waved, and said something to Tom Albanese's parents who, once they made eye-contact, made a beeline for the Torres' yard.

"*Shit.*"

Jenna, who was standing near Kim looked up. "What?"

"Your parents."

"You have a lot of nerve coming here." Mrs. Albanese yelled. "First you send my son to his death and then you steal his fiancée?"

"Ma'am," Owen said, calmly. "This is not the place. If you want to talk to me about your son, I will happily do that, but these other families don't need their event ruined."

"What, don't want them to know what you did?" Turning to Kim, she cut loose. "And you, Kimmy. How could you? My son loved you. He honored you with his ring. And you whore yourself to this man?"

"Mom!" Jenna screamed. "You sound like some crazy woman from the old country, shut up!"

"Whore myself?" Kim looked at her father who was about ready to explode.

Owen took her by the shoulders and stepped in front of her, his back stiff with tension. Part of him wanted to react, to protect Kim, but he also knew he was dealing with a grieving mother and nothing was going to change that. He had to think of a way to handle this, and attacking this woman wasn't the answer.

"My Tommy was a hero. A good man. He loved you and would have done anything for you. He wanted to make a life with you."

Owen and Ryan exchanged glances. Ryan knew everything. He knew about Tom's extracurricular activities, all of it. The man looked uneasy, and Owen knew he wasn't going to get involved.

The front yard hastily cleared, and Owen could hear the murmuring of the crowd in the backyard. The Albanese's and the Torres' were left facing off on the front lawn.

Quietly, Kim slipped out from behind him and walked to the car calm and composed. He couldn't imagine she'd just get in and expect to leave, but then Owen remembered that she'd put something in the back seat of the Rover before they'd left the cottage. When Kim came back, he saw what it was. A black wooden case that held an honor guard flag. Wow. He knew exactly what she planned to do and by his estimation, it could be a touching gesture or a slap in the face. But he had to give her credit for her nerves of steel.

Kim held out the flag to Mrs. Albanese.

"What is this?" The woman swallowed her tears. Shocked.

"It's Tom's flag."

Jenna uttered a simple cry, and one of Kim's brothers took her in his arms to console her.

Kim swallowed. "You should have this, Mrs. Albanese."

Owen would never get over the mettle of this woman.

"What? Are you trying to purge yourself of guilt by giving away everything of his? He loved you—"

"NO!" Kim's lip trembled and he stepped next to her putting a hand on her back, just so she would know he was there. That was all Owen could do—offer support. There was no way for him to dull the pain any of these people felt. "No, he didn't. He loved someone else."

"How could you say such a thing? Tommy was devoted to you."

Kim was hurting now. He could see the toll this was taking on her, but still she pressed on. "No, he may have loved me as a good friend, but both of us should have seen it for what it was. Tom had someone else. Someone who grieved for him, and while I will miss him, it wasn't that way between us anymore. I think we wanted it to be, but it wasn't. You should take the flag. He would have wanted you to have it."

If there was a moment of clarity between Kim and Tom's mother, this was it. Mrs. Albanese's fists were clenched, and she couldn't bring herself to make eye contact with Kim.. When she did, when they locked gazes, the older woman broke down. Her husband went to her, while family and neighbors all remembered the life that was lost. So much time had been wasted fighting over something so pointless. Everyone had been hurt when Tom Albanese died. Did the man make mistakes? Of course he did. All men do, but he wasn't a villain, and it was time for everyone to understand that no matter what happened he could be remembered by everyone with love.

Still, she wouldn't take the flag. It was almost as if the flag represented a finality Mrs. Albanese didn't want to face. She was leaning into her husband, crying. Her daughter was hugging her from the other side and Kim's family surrounded them. Only Kim stood apart. She stood with Owen, holding her Tom's flag, hoping to give his mother some closure. She was hurting.

Owen knew what he had to do, and stepped forward.

He was still in his suit, his tie loose, but he was still a Marine and Semper Fi meant something to him. Owen reached out, and Kim handed him the flag as if she'd planned this all along. He didn't have authorization to do conduct a ceremony, but what were they going to do to him? Court Martial him for helping a grieving mother? Let 'em try.

He stepped toward the Albanese family and leaned in. His words were spoken quietly, so only those close to them would have been able to hear. "On behalf of the President of the United States, the United States Marine Corps, and a grateful nation, please accept this flag as a symbol of appreciation for your loved one's honored and faithful service."

He handed the flag to Tom Albanese's now sobbing mother, her tears so real, so full of everything she lost. Her husband held her and his eyes, also filled with tears, locked with Owen's. All he said was, "Thank you," before leading his wife back into the house.

Once they'd all gone, Kim reached for him and hugged him tight. "Thank you for that. It was perfect."

"I hope it helped."

"Major Kent?"

"Sergeant Ryan." The two men shook hands, but he didn't really pay attention too much to their small talk because his mind was on Kim. That was until he heard the word Kandahar.

"I was surprised they called you back so soon."

"What?" Kim's face had gone pale. "You're going back? When?"

Ryan would not shut up. "The drawdown is really accelerating. It will be good to have your skills there. See you soon."

The men shook hands again, and then he had to face Kim. Why was it that no matter how hard he tried, he couldn't get this right with her. "You're going *back*?

"I was going to tell you later tonight. I have to. It's just for two months. I'll be back in September."

"You can't go back. You can't! You've barely been home."

"Kim, calm down. I knew it was a possibility when I got home that I might have to do a short stint. Nothing is normal with the troops pulling out. I have to help."

She picked up on what he said, immediately. "Wait. Did you volunteer?"

"Not exactly. They asked. I said yes."

"What about us Owen, what about what we've started here?"

"I'll be back in two months." Two of the longest months of his life. He was going to be miserable without her.

"And what if you're not? I can't go through this again." Kim turned and walked into her parent's house. Owen followed, catching her hand when they were finally alone in the kitchen.

"You have to know I'll be thinking of you all the time. I'll be okay. The last they told me it's mostly administrative. I'll be doing a lot of paperwork.

"Then why can't you do the work here? I'm going to be sick wondering if every time you walk outside you're going to be blown to bits."

"Kim, please."

"No. How could you do this without talking to me first? I

get the whole duty thing, but what about your duty to us Owen? You said you loved me."

"I do!" Owen pressed the heels of his hands against his eyes. Then he looked at her. "I love you with all my heart. But if I didn't say yes, they would have ordered me back and then it could have been for longer."

"How can you say that?" she yelled. "How can you say you love me when you don't tell me anything?"

"For God's sake!" he snapped back. "I think I've loved you since I held you in that fucking hospital."

Oh. No.

"What did you say? When you held me in the hospital?" Her jaw trembled as she processed what he said. Her eyes closed, squeezed shut like she was reaching back in her mind for the memory. A memory she'd crushed because it was too much to handle.

"Kim…" he reached out and she stepped away.

"It was you. You were the one. You were there." She grabbed his left hand and found what she was looking for. The scar. "Is there anything else? I don't know what other secrets you could keep from me, but I guess I should ask."

"Kim. Please don't do this."

He had no idea if his words landed. Kim had focused her eyes out the kitchen window and she had gone completely still.

"You need to leave, Owen." She was calmer now, resigned and that scared him more. He could console her if she was upset, but when she froze him out like this, that's when he knew she was done talking.

"I understand why you're upset. I'm sorry. Let's talk this out at home."

"I can't." She shook her head. Her breathing was unsteady, but her eyes had cleared. She stepped away from him. "You should have told me everything."

"Kim... don't do this,"

"Goodbye, Owen. I love you. I love you so much and I'll be thinking of you every day, but I can't do this. I can't go through this again."

Stunned, he watched the woman he loved, the woman who brought everything good into his life walk out of the room.

He was alone. Alone in every way possible.

17

Dear Owen,

I love you.

There. If you got that far, maybe you'll keep reading, and I can beg you to forgive me for being so horrible before you left.

I don't know if I have an excuse that will give you enough reason to forgive me. I was scared. So scared. I still am. I'm afraid of what's going to happen to you over there, what I'm feeling for you and while I'm terrified that you could die, all I know is that I'd rather be scared with you, than without you. You're worth the risk, Owen. There were so many things I had to work through, but you shouldn't have been one of them. You were the one who helped me get past the darkness inside me, who helped me feel whole again.

It's been a tough month since you've been gone, and I've made some decisions. The first thing I did was come clean with Tom's family and told them everything about the day he died. I called Mrs. Albanese and went to dinner at the house with her, Mr. A, all the girls, and about twelve thousand relatives, including Zia Bunny and Zio Marco. You know what? Tom's girlfriend wasn't a secret. Corporal Lynn paid a visit to Mrs. A. a few months ago, and she never told anyone. I decided to let it go. She lost her baby, her son. I can't even imagine her pain.

Once all the information was out in the open, we had a good cry and called him an asshole, but there's no denying we all miss him.

Also, I read the letter you wrote to Tom's parents. It was beautiful, Owen. Eloquent, simple, and so very kind. Tom's mother told me it was a great comfort to her and she reads it over and over. You touched her with your words, and presenting her with his flag meant the world to her, and me. She told me that we were lucky to find each other and she hoped we'd be very happy.

She meant it. Of course, that's when I started crying and told everyone what had happened. I've been so miserable without you, Owen. I miss you so much and I'm so worried something's going to happen to you. But I can't let that keep us apart. When you get home, I hope we can talk and I hope you can forgive me for not having faith in us.

I don't deserve you. You're so good, so kind. I had no idea how empty I would feel without you here. Or maybe I did. Maybe I knew and I thought if I pushed you away it wouldn't hurt. The thing is I hurt more.

I love you so much. I hate that you're back there, that we're not together. Your sister left the dog with me for a week. Casey thinks I'm crazy. I let her sleep in my bed, and I hold her and cry. I don't want you to think you aren't missed. You are. You are also loved beyond measure.

I think I've slobbered enough for one email, but if you'd like me to do it again, just say so.

Oh, I'm going on a job interview tomorrow. There's a position at a local hospital for an emergency room nurse. I told Harper it was time for her mom to take over for me. Even if I don't get this position, it's time for me to get back to work. Diana is going to move into the cottage and I'm going to move home. With Livvy going to school, my parents

are a little lost. They've missed me, so I'm going to go there until I get
my bearings. I guess that's what I should have done before.

Okay, now I'm done. God, I miss talking to you. I miss listening to
you snore. I miss how you warm up the bed and how you hold me. I love
you. I miss you.

Always,

Kim

LOOKING over the email for the tenth time, Kim hoped it
wasn't too late. Maybe she should keep it simple. Just telling
him she loved him would be the make or break. Either he'd
forgive her or he wouldn't. If he forgave her, she wanted to
spend every day of the rest of her life with him. If he didn't,
she'd go on knowing she'd ruined the best thing that had ever
happened to her.

Kim took a breath. She'd never poured out her heart like
that, never opened herself to so much hurt. But Owen
deserved that and more. She knew how he was living, knew
the conditions were horrible. He was in danger. He deserved
to know not only that she loved him, but how much.

"God, Owen. I miss you." She grabbed a tissue from the
box that seemed to be with her wherever she went. She cried
just thinking about him. Jenna had been watching TV while
Kim finished the email, but friend that she was, at the first
tear, she was pulling Kim into a hug.

"It's going to be okay, Kimmy. I promise."

"You can't promise that."

"Maybe not, but Tommy won't let you be alone again.
Owen's coming home."

Just the thought of anything happening to Owen was too

much. "Oh, Jen. I was so horrible to him." Kim held back as much as she could, but there was no way to stem the flow of pain once it started. After he told her he'd been the one in the hospital who'd held her when she collapsed, the rest of her memory gaps filled in. She remembered him walking in. His hand was bandaged. His bright blue eyes locked on hers. He'd seemed to know immediately that there was something wrong.

She called her old commanding officer and found out that Owen had made the dangerous drive from his post to check on her two weeks after Tom's death. By that time she was already on her way back to the States. But her C. O. said he sensed that something had transpired between the two of them during those moments he consoled her and no truer words had ever been spoken.

Kim remembered the warmth of the man who held her that day. His soft words, his strong arms. He didn't flinch when she collapsed. He just made sure she was protected. It was Owen to the ground.

Looking at the email one more time, she pressed send and hoped for the best. He had to read the first line. That was all. As long as he knew she loved him, she could live with herself. He deserved that much.

Kandahar Province, Afghanistan
July

THE HEAT WAS ALWAYS the killer. But Owen was so numb inside, he didn't really care. He kept his mind on the work and his Marines and he tried not to think about Kim who was thousands of miles away.

The area was more active than he was led to believe. It kept him up nights, and out in the field which meant his admin work sat on his desk for days. He didn't remember how long it had been since he checked his email, but when he found the letter from her that started with "I love you," the day was pretty much perfect. He was going to answer her as soon as he got back from patrol.

He wondered if she knew he was thinking about her—if she could feel him. He hoped she'd forgiven him for not telling her about this quick tour. But he couldn't be sorry that he was helping and that more men and women would be getting home as a result.

There had been an uptick in small firefights and that always meant that the Taliban was gunning for them and it could mean trouble anywhere. So being out with a patrol was not something Owen took lightly. Even though the village had always been friendly, even though they didn't think there was a threat, there always could be.

He got out of the MRAP and he might as well have been walking in a furnace. It was one hundred and five degrees, there had been a sandstorm the day before and everything was mired in moondust. A few kids were playing outside a small house and they smiled and waved.

That was the last thing he remembered before the rocket hit.

Two of his Marines went down and he didn't know if he could do anything. People were running for cover, but Owen could only think about the kids he'd seen.

He didn't know if their parents were close by, if there was

a place for them to go, but from what he could see, he was on his own and he wasn't going to let three little kids die. Gunfire erupted and Owen dodged and weaved through the hot and dusty street back to where he'd last seen them.

They were huddled against a wall, scared, crying. They couldn't have been older than seven or eight. Three little boys.

He ran to them and tucked them behind his body. His brain was fried and he didn't know what he was going to do next when he saw two Afghani men yelling at him. The boys screamed the word for father and he watched them run. The two adults waved thanks and hurried their children inside, leaving Owen alone on the deserted streets.

He heard American voices which meant more of his guys had arrived, but they were distant. He had to get out and find the group. The whole place had gone still. The quiet was eerie.

Owen took two steps away from the wall when there was a flash and he was hit with searing, burning pain. He went into the dust. Looking down, he found his left foot twisted at an odd angle, the boot torn off. His ankle and lower leg were ripped open, the bone exposed. *Shit. Shit.*

There was blood everywhere and the pain hit with such blinding force he screamed.

"Corpsman!" he heard. "Major is down. Get over here. I need cover!"

"Don't worry, sir." One of his men was at his side immediately, but Owen's vision was clouding and he turned, wretched, and threw up.

The voices were becoming distant, faint. He could hear them talking about him, though.

He's getting shocky. Shit, his foot is mangled. Cover us we're going to have to get him to trauma ASAP.

The voices were getting farther away, sounding like they were underwater. It was getting harder and harder to stay awake.

He felt cold. How could he be cold when it was so hot?

His head hurt and then, without any energy left, Owen went to sleep.

WALKING through the corridor of the Landstuhl Medical Center in Germany, Kim worried about what she would find when she could finally see Owen. At least now she knew why he wasn't answering her emails. Three weeks ago, on the same day of the attack that cost him his lower left leg, Kim had opened the door to their relationship, but there had been no response.

She told him she loved him, and that she'd be there when he got home. When she didn't hear from him, she got worried, but it wasn't until Harper came to the cottage a few days ago that she found out what had happened. Mortar attack.

Harper, Jason, and Nate flew her in the Reliance jet, and now a nurse walked her to the physical therapy gym where Owen was doing his exercises. Wondering what she was going to find, what kind of shape he was in, was eating at her, but she had to have faith. He was alive and people came back from injuries far worse than this. And this time she'd be there. She'd be with him every step of the way.

But thinking about what he'd gone through, about the pain and fear, killed her. She'd treated men who'd been brought in injured and who had awakened from surgery missing limbs.

Their grief was palpable, and based on what she'd heard, Owen wasn't having an easy time.

"He's made good progress. Since he was in such good shape, a lot of the basic tasks, like transfers, you know getting from bed to chair, were easy for him."

"That's good. There are no training prosthetics yet are there?"

"Not yet. The stump is still pretty raw. It will be a while."

The gym was an open space, clean and white with tall windows. She found Owen immediately. His strong back was unmistakable. In a t-shirt and shorts, he held himself between the parallel bars, his good leg extended and on the floor, while the stump of the residual limb was in a compression sleeve.

He hopped. A balance exercise.

He hopped again.

Turned around, and saw her.

Kim felt the tears well in her own eyes and saw them mirrored in his. He took a shaky breath and forced down the emotion. Her guy was still trying to be the big tough Marine.

"Hey, Marine," she choked out, the emotions making the words a challenge. "You come here often?"

A hot tear tracked over her cheek as he took three quick hops toward her.

Then three more.

"That's a lousy line," he said.

"I got a million of them."

The physical therapist who stood nearby brought his wheelchair and Owen sat, extending his leg straight. The wound was still healing, but based on the condition and location, he would be okay.

He had to be okay.

Kim was trying to stay composed, but she was failing.

"Thank God you're alright."

"I hardly call this alright. I'm damaged."

"Yeah," she said. "I hear all the best people are."

Dropping his head, she could see the sadness in his bearing. "I wanted to come back to you in one piece."

"Owen," she said softly. "You're alive. You think I care about a stump?" Kneeling before him, she took his face in her hands. "I love you. I love you and I need you to get better. I need you, period."

"Kim, I…you were right. Look what happened to me." His voice hitched and her heart broke for him. This was a blow, to be sure, but they would get through it together.

"I know. But you're still here and I want you to get better so you can marry me and give me babies."

"You want to…really?"

"What do you say? Will you marry me, Owen?"

He reached for her and held her so tightly she thought she might break. "Oh, I missed you. How many babies do you want?" And there it was. She saw that grin, his spirit, everything she loved about him was right there, just for her.

"Not sure yet, but you better work hard because I want my tall, handsome Marine standing at the end of the aisle when I put on that white dress."

"I love you."

"I know. Now get up. You have work to do."

"Slave driver." He growled, and Kim felt her heart soar.

She leaned in to kiss him again. "You have no idea."

Epilogue
Veterans Day

Kim stood with the Albanese family once again, but this time it was at a simple prayer service at the cemetery. Her parents and siblings stood behind her while a priest from a local parish said a few words about Tom, and Tom's sister Tina gave a heartfelt talk about her brother. The biggest difference between today and Tom's funeral just a year and a half ago was the man standing next to her. Owen was with her this time, in his full-dress uniform, looking very impressive even though he was still going to be using a cane for another month, at least. He was improving far more rapidly than anyone anticipated, but Kim figured that was because the man was set on proving the orthopedist and the physical therapists wrong.

The most surprising part of the morning was that when they arrived, Owen told her that Tom's parents had asked him, as Tom's commanding officer, to speak on the family's behalf.

Mr. and Mrs. Albanese had come to grips with the changes in Kim's life and they understood those changes didn't necessarily mean she was disloyal to their son. They had also started to let go of their grief. No easy task, as Kim well understood.

Owen caught Kim staring at her engagement ring and he smiled. He'd given it to her as soon as he'd arrived back in the States, and she couldn't be more excited about the life they were going to have together. But she was reflective, too. A year ago she never imagined she'd be happy again, forget planning a wedding. And it wasn't that she felt guilty. She didn't. She was just aware of how much she had to be thankful for. It was humbling.

"You okay?" he asked.

"Actually, I'm fine. I feel better than I have in a long time."

"Okay." He squeezed her hand. "I'm up."

"Good luck," she said quietly.

Easing his way forward on the blanket of fresh cut grass, he turned, and his full military bearing took Kim's breath away.

"I was asked to speak by Mr. and Mrs. Albanese for Tom. I was his commanding officer, albeit for only two weeks, so I'm very honored to be included. Tom Albanese was a model Marine, a model friend and a model son and brother. He was a leader, and he lived and breathed the Corps."

Kim watched the man she loved deliver the most eloquent of speeches, honoring the boy she'd also loved once upon a time. And that was the difference. Tom was her boyfriend, and Owen had transcended that label from the start.

They'd been through hell and back starting in Afghanistan over a year ago and ending with her going to him in Germany.

It was where she saw the challenges they were facing. Where she cried because she loved him so much, and where she asked him to marry her.

Now she was planning a wedding and the women in the Albanese family were actually ordering dresses. Owen managed to charm every one of them.

Okay. Maybe not all. Zia Bunny wasn't going to be invited, and Tom's grandma still wasn't so sure. Nonna sat in the row just in front of her, and she leaned back and shook her rosary at Kim. "He's too handsome, that one. You be careful."

But Jenna was happy for her and she squeezed Kim's hand. So was Harper, who was losing a nanny, but gaining a live-in relative, since her mother would be taking Kim's place.

For her, Kim had accepted a job as a nurse in a mid-sized hospital emergency room, not too far from where she and Owen would be living. She would see car accidents, heart attacks, and backyard injuries rather than blown-off limbs, but that was fine with her. She was content to do good work with people who needed her. At the end of the day when she walked in the door, she'd be coming home to her guy. That was all the rush she needed in her life.

Owen finished by placing a wreath on Tom's grave. He uttered something, quietly, when he stood at the headstone.

The service broke up and on this fall day, there was no running, no drama, just memories of the man they lost.

While they walked to the car, Kim hooked her arm through Owen's, partially to give him a little extra support and partially to be closer to him. "What did you say at the grave when you placed the wreath?"

Owen stared ahead, not talking, and doing his best to keep his gait steady. Every step was becoming an effort and Kim nudged him toward one of the benches to take a rest. He didn't fight her. "You have to stop overdoing it. Healing takes time."

"It's easy to say when it's not your leg."

"Watch the attitude, buddy."

They sat for a few minutes in silence when without warning, a boy in a Cub Scout uniform walked up to Owen. Around seven years old, he stood ramrod straight and extended his small hand. "Thank you for your service, sir."

Kim was so taken by the boy, she teared up a little. Owen shook his hand and smiled. "Thank you for your support."

"Are you a hero?" the boy asked, pointing at his cane. Owen had told her he hated that his last mission had people calling him a hero. He'd saved a lot of lives and had risked his own. Kim always saw him as a hero. Every single day he tried to help someone. She was damn sure he'd saved her.

"No, I just did my job." He took Kim's hand. "You see this lady here, son? She worked in a hospital in a war zone. She saved soldiers and Marines lives when they were hurt. People like me. She's a hero."

"No, I..." Kim didn't expect accolades.

"Really?" The boy said. "You really did that?"

The conversation continued a few more minutes until the boy's father came over and again, the dad thanked Owen, and the pair left.

"I really hate that people don't know everything you've done. You're the hero."

"I wasn't in it for pats on the back. And I know you aren't either. And me? A hero? I did my job Owen, just like you said."

"You saved people. Gave them a second chance at life."

"Really? I kind of feel like that's what you've done for me. You're my second chance."

They were quiet again, several minutes passed and Kim

realized he'd never answered her question. "You never told me what you said at the headstone."

Owen drew a deep breath and kissed the top of her head. "I told him I'd take good care of you. That I'd wake up every day with the goal of making you happy."

"Oh." Her heart didn't know how it held all the love she had for this man. He was so good. So unbelievably good.

"He loved you, Kim. He screwed up. But he loved you."

And for the first time in a long time, she felt it. And she knew how lucky she was to have been loved by two really wonderful men. "I know."

"I just thought I should say something."

"I'm sure you got a cosmic *oo-rah*!"

Owen laughed and pulled her close. Her face pressed against the clutch of ribbons on his chest, reminders of the trials he'd seen. Of his accomplishments. Of the man he was. And after they'd sat there for a while, just holding each other, he stood. "That *oo-rah* is an awesome thought," he said, taking her hand.

Standing and stepping close to him, she smiled. "I'm sure we have his blessing. Let's go home."

When Owen kissed her, Kim felt one of the small cracks that the past few years had left in her heart, mend. It was like a tiny miracle. Every time he touched her or kissed her or did something kind, her world was better. Safer. More complete.

There were so many things Kim could say to him right now, but silence seemed most appropriate. She thought about Tom and his family. About her family. About Harper and Kevin and Anna and everyone at Reliance. About the crazy string of events that brought her and Owen together.

In some ways, she was still trying to wrap her head around

the last six months. For Kim, love was something you did. You dated someone, the relationship grew and that was that. It was never something that happened, that found you. But in this case, it did. Owen found her. Love happened and it happened big.

She couldn't imagine her life without him.

Owen was her hero. Now. Always. Forever.

THE END

Coming Next

The Boyfriend List
A Forever Love Story
Book 5
May 23, 2023

Jenna Albanese planned it all out at thirteen when she listed the qualities she wanted in her perfect man and years later, she thought she'd found him. When all she got was a load of trouble and a broken heart, Jenna tucked away the boyfriend list along with her belief in a happy ever after.

Nate Bayard has a life most people only dream of—he's a handsome high-caliber polo player and partner in a multibillion-dollar business. But as intelligent and confident as he is on the field and in the boardroom, he's hopeless with women—until he meets the sweet and funny Jenna. She's just about perfect, and Nate's determined to make her his. There's just one little problem. Jenna's unwelcome past is about to make a comeback.

For Jenna, overcoming her mistrust in men—*particularly rich ones*—isn't going to be easy. Then she comes across that old boyfriend list and realizes that maybe it's time for another look, and a few changes, to bring a brand new beat to her romantic heart.

Available for Kindle and Kindle Unlimited and in paperback.
Go to jeanniemoon.com for details.

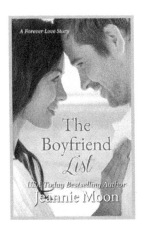

Also by Jeannie Moon

Emotional. Sexy. Romance

The Forever Love Stories

The Temporary Wife

Unexpectedly Yours

The Wedding Secret

The Second Chance Hero

The Boyfriend List (5/23)

Happily Ever After (6/23)

Compass Cove Series

Then Came You

You Send Me

All of Me

My Christmas Wish

Until You

Find all Jeannie's titles on her website

JeannieMoon.com

About the Author

USA Today bestselling author Jeannie Moon has always been a romantic. When she's not spinning tales of her own, Jeannie works as a school librarian, thankful she has a job that allows her to immerse herself in books and call it work. The author of contemporary romance and romantic women's fiction, Jeannie is married to her high school sweetheart, has three grown kids, three lovable dogs, and is a lifelong resident of Long Island. If she's more than ten miles away from salt water for any longer than a week, she gets twitchy.

Connect with Jeannie on social media,
or through her website
JeannieMoon.com